I've travelled the world twice over,
Met the famous: saints and sinners,
Poets and artists, kings and queens,
Old stars and hopeful beginners,
I've been where no-one's been before,
Learned secrets from writers and cooks
All with one library ticket
To the wonderful world of books.

© JANICE JAMES.

ISLAND OF GLASS

Through the eyes of Victoria Lacey, a sensitive, reserved seventeen year old, we are caught up in the joys and tragedies of six cousins. They find themselves having to face the responsibilities of adulthood as they strive to achieve that compromise between duty and the fulfilment of personal identity. Self-possessed Jill, deeply in love with a childhood friend; Stephen and Bob, one uncompromising the other easygoing; Helen, who resorts to shock tactics for her mother's attention. The adults too, are still fighting their own private battles, or living with the consequences of those won or lost years before.

ISLAND OF GLASS

Through the eyes of Victoria Lacey, a sensitive, reserved seventeen year old, we are caught up in the joys and tragedies of six cousins. They find themselves having to face the responsibilities of adulthood as they strive to achieve that compromise between duty and the fulfilment of personal identity. Self-possessed Jill, deeply in love with a childhood friend; Stephen and Bob, one uncompromising, the other easygoing; Helen, who resorts to shock tactics for her mother's attention. The adults too are still fighting their own private battles, or living with the consequences of those won or lost years before.

BARBARA MASTERTON

ISLAND OF GLASS

Complete and Unabridged

ULVERSCROFT
Leicester

First published in Great Britain in 1986 by
Souvenir Press Ltd.,
London

First Large Print Edition
published June 1987
by arrangement with
Souvenir Press Ltd.,
London

British Library CIP Data

Masterton, Barbara
Island of glass.—Large print ed.—
Ulverscroft large print series: general fiction
I. Title
823′.914[F] PR6063.A8/

ISBN 0-7089-1644-9

Published by
F. A. Thorpe (Publishing) Ltd.
Anstey, Leicestershire
Set by Rowland Phototypesetting Ltd.
Bury St. Edmunds, Suffolk
Printed and bound in Great Britain by
T. J. Press (Padstow) Ltd., Padstow, Cornwall

1

IT was the beginning of the last long summer of her life. The last long summer and she lay dreaming it away.

It was mid-morning on the very first day of the summer holiday. Before her stretched six weeks of lazing in the sun or reading in her bedroom, as weather dictated, as moods prompted or as her mother and cousins allowed; the last of these three conditions being the most crucial. Still, at the moment, she was doing as she wished: nothing; just lying on her stomach beneath a high beach wall of grey stone, soaking up the sun, languidly aware of the murmuring beach sounds around her, utterly isolated in her own thoughts, and contented. She groped for a large pink straw hat and placed it on the back of her head to protect the nape of her neck from the intense rays, wriggling into a more comfortable position on the hot, unyielding pebbles. Go away, everyone and everything, she thought drowsily. It was lovely to be alone, shut tightly and safely within her own small world. Soon her cousins would be back, dripping wet and noisy, demanding that she share their fun. They had been taught from an early age, by her mother and aunts, that she could not possibly enjoy being the way she was, but must be wishing continually to be "taken out of herself". How she loathed that phrase! "Darling, let Vicky join in, she needs to be taken out of herself. She's been moping there on her own for ages, poor child."

She was a passive observer of life, doomed forever to be surrounded by active participants, organisers of other people's leisure, marshallers of other people's thoughts. Sporting enthusiasts, who thought you were unwell if you did not feel like a game of tennis; people who were conditioned from birth to consider idleness a self-indulgence.

She could hear them now, those eager, active people, their shouts of pleasure drifting spasmodically across the water from the far end of the rock mass jutting into the sea. They were taking it in turns to dive into the one deep, narrow channel, which experience had taught them was entirely free from submerged rocks. Occasionally her own name was shouted imperatively, rather crossly, for of course they were feeling guilty that they were enjoying themselves and she was not. They really should have insisted that Victoria swam too!

The beach was practically deserted, because it was not popular. It was small and uninteresting; too near the harbour and a main road, which ran parallel to it beyond a narrow grass verge and from which came a constant hum of traffic. They liked it, because it was convenient and familiar; it was the beach upon which they had played as toddlers, watched over by their mothers—the three Le Feuvre sisters, as they had been before marriage—all three dark complexioned, with black hair and fine brown eyes, sitting gossiping and knitting in simple cotton print dresses, while their six children played together with that serious, contented absorption which young children often display on the beach, until they become over-heated and tired. Sandra and Helen, the two youngest, when they were still at the bucket and spade stage—poor Helen already fated to remain at whatever stage of development her younger sister had attained—both continually demanding more water for their sand pies and canals. They were not allowed to venture to the water's edge alone, so when Bob grew fed up with trailing endlessly backwards and forwards with the red plastic buckets, Victoria would take them by the hand and lead them gently over the hard pebbles to the cool strip of wet sand left by the receding tide, where they enjoyed the bliss of dabbling their toes in the warm pools. They never had canvas beach shoes. Their mothers had never worn them and boasted how nimbly they could still walk over the pebbles on their calloused, corn-ridden feet.

As Victoria played half-heartedly with the two little ones, Bob would take the opportunity to slip off after Stephen and Jill who, being older, were allowed to be adventurous and swim or rock climb at will, searching in small pools for darting fish and liver-like anemones, in which to squidge a finger. The unpacking of the lunch baskets would mysteriously bring them back, appearing like a mirage across the beach, trailing seaweed, small crabs hidden in their hands with which to torment the little ones.

As soon as Helen and Sandra were old enough to wander independently into the shallow sea, Bob and Victoria were free to explore as well and the former took full advantage of that freedom. Victoria did not. She went just far enough to be invisible to the adults, where she read, sketched or daydreamed until, inevitably, one of the women would raise her voice and call to an offspring, "Darling, do take Victoria along. I am sure she would rather go than stay mooching about all by herself. You'll find her over there somewhere." It was no good protesting; even one of the other children, more accomplished than Victoria at getting his or her own way, would have given in eventually. After all, what argument prevails when one is exhorted to act for one's own benefit! Feeling aggrieved, but with an outward good grace, she would join in the exploits of her cousins and, truth to tell, quietly enjoyed herself; yet when offered the choice she still persisted, perversely, in preferring her own company.

It was fortunate that she had so many cousins, it meant she did not have to make friends. They had friends, very many, as active and talkative as they were, full of plans for themselves that for fruition needed other people. Victoria fitted into their schemes rather well: shy and docile, ready to please because it was less demanding than complaining; ready to agree, because it was easier than arguing; ready to disappear at the first opportunity and do her own thing, which her cousins were the first to admit was not a lot and could give her little pleasure. She wondered vaguely why they concerned themselves about her, now that they were too old for constant hectoring. This was to be the last summer that they would all be together. Jill was going into her father's office in a few weeks' time and Stephen was going to university in Bristol in the autumn. It would be strange returning to school without them, but Bob would still be there, in his last year, as she would be, and there were Helen and Sandra, of course.

She shifted restlessly, dislodging a large pebble from beneath her hip-bone. She did not like change. She had seen very little of it and sensed in her pessimistic way that it would only be for the worst. It seemed that the voices were getting louder. She sat up quickly, squinting against the sun towards the rocks. Sure enough, her cousins were scrambling off them onto the beach. She remembered guiltily that she had been instructed to place the lunch baskets in the narrow strip of shade immediately beneath the wall. Hastily she collected them and did so, flinging towels and articles of clothing on top to provide extra, if belated, protection. Then she lay back on her towel, placed the hat over her face, watching them covertly from beneath its wide brim as they came crashing up the beach, calling her lazy and pitying her for missing the fun.

Stephen and Bob were the first to reach her, picking up the first towels that came to hand and rubbing vigorously at their hair, sending cold droplets showering over her sun-drenched body.

"I'm famished," said Stephen. "When do we eat?"

"Not for another half-hour," Jill told him as she joined them, closely followed by her two sisters, "I suggest you throw the ball around." Obviously she had no intention of following her own advice. She located her towel, wresting it from Bob's grasp with a sarcastic, "Do you mind?" and laying it alongside Victoria she settled her shapely body upon it with a small sigh of satisfaction.

Bob threw himself down on the other side of Victoria.

"I thought you liked swimming," he said.

"I'll go in after lunch," she promised.

"Good. I'll teach you how to dive properly. Six weeks should be enough, even for you. By the end of the holiday you'll be diving perfectly."

Silence, then,

"Don't you want to learn? You can't go on belly-flopping all your life."

Still no reply. He whipped the hat from her face.

"Why are you laughing?" he demanded.

"I'm not laughing."

"Well, smiling then?"

"Just my thoughts." She smiled more

broadly, turning onto her stomach. She knew he only wanted to teach her so that he could show off his own diving ability to someone who was not going to make every effort to out-do him. People who lack the competitive spirit have their uses as appreciative spectators.

After a few more minutes of silence, Bob rose in exasperation to join Stephen, Helen and Sandra in an energetic game of ball-passing which, on his arrival, resolved itself into boys against girls instead of every man for himself. Immediately shouts of "That's not fair!" came from the panting girls who resented the fact that their opponents, taller, heavier and more aggressive, never remembered that netball, or an approximation of it, was not a contact sport.

"I'm glad this beach isn't popular with the visitors," Jill said, as she leaned on one elbow, languidly watching the others play. "The Bideaus are joining us later and Raoul promised he would come."

Victoria sighed inwardly.

"I shall have to go home for tea," she said, although she had enough food for a siege in her basket.

"Suit yourself," Jill answered, unconcernedly, lying down to snooze.

"Come on, you two!" It was Stephen's voice, urging them to join the game. They pretended not to hear. There were the unmistakable sounds of the slow, purposeful approach of two sets of feet over the pebbles. Jill and Victoria leapt to their feet as one, just in time to avoid being hauled upright by the boys. As Jill caught the ball, thrown hard by a grinning Helen, Victoria made ready to receive it from her, running and dodging to shake off her opponent, Bob. However, Jill did not pass it. She clutched it close to her chest and glared accusingly at Stephen.

"I resent being bullied into playing childish games," she told him angrily, throwing the ball petulantly at his feet. The other five stood still in astonishment, digesting this unaccountable reaction. Then, to the amazement of four of them, Stephen, whose expression had subtly changed to one of chagrin, actually apologised, whereupon Jill blushed, shrugged her shoulders as if acknowledging the irrationality of her behaviour and sat down again on her towel.

Stephen picked up the ball, started across to her, changed his mind, passed the ball to Bob and the game started again, rather subdued. Victoria saw him cast speculative glances in Jill's direction from time to time and she guessed that he had suddenly been made aware of something that she had sensed for many months. Jill the woman was emerging and beginning to demand some recognition.

They felt slightly uneasy at this new isolationist policy of one of their fraternity, who was sitting observing them in a critical, rather than a loving manner; it was with relief that eventually they heard her call them to eat.

Cheese sandwiches, tomatoes, lumps of cucumber, potato crisps, followed by fruit and warm, fizzy drinks, constituted the usual beach fare. If one of the mothers provided something different, she made sure that there was enough for six and it was most often the mother of the boys who gave them a treat, something left over from the tables of her summer boarders. Today it was apple pie.

"Good old Aunty Merle," said skinny Helen, who loved her food. Replete, they lay flat out in a row, dozing, waiting for a decent interval to pass before swimming: an hour was the limit imposed by their mothers, otherwise one got cramp and sank like a stone. It never ceased to surprise them that this disaster never overtook other people's children, who appeared to eat and swim with abandon in blissful ignorance of the possible ghastly consequences. Bob had once discussed this apparent anomaly with his mother, or rather attempted to discuss it, only to be told that the fate of those innocents hinged as much upon the temperature of the water as upon when and how much they had eaten.

Victoria was almost asleep, in a happy state of lulled consciousness, when a voice from above, sharp and insistent, roused her to immediate awareness.

"You've got to come home, Victoria. Albinia's arrived to take us to Grande Maison. Your grandfather is very ill."

A head and shoulders were visible, leaning over the stone wall. They all gazed in a bemused manner, while the import of the words sank into their sun-dulled brains.

"Hurry up, Victoria! Collect your things!" the voice said peremptorily.

Victoria obediently scrambled to her feet as her mother's words took meaning. Her Grandpa Lacy was ill and she had to go to him. He must be very ill if Aunt Albinia had come to collect them. What day was this? Oh yes, Thursday. He had been all right on Sunday. She had visited him on Sunday.

Her cousins were collecting her things together. She took them and shoved them into her picnic basket, plonking her straw hat on her head. Her mother was surveying the others.

"Helen, put a towel around your shoulders, they look red."

Helen obeyed.

Stephen said, "I'm sorry to hear about Mr. Lacy, Aunty. Is he seriously ill?"

"Albinia says he is," she answered shortly, reaching down a hand for the basket.

Victoria pushed her feet into her sandals. Bob and Stephen heaved her onto the wall. She called goodbye and her cousins chorused an answer in sad cadences, sorry for her as they settled back to their siestas.

Poor Vicky, Bob thought. Now I shan't be able to teach her to dive. Aloud he said, "Glad I'm not a girl," because it seemed to him that, if Victoria was a typical example, they were always being pushed around in a manner boys would not tolerate. Nobody answered him; the closeness of their relationship and their mutual knowledge enlightened the apparent enigma of his words.

2

VICTORIA followed her mother across the wide strip of coarse dune grass separating the beach wall from the busy road which they crossed, turning down another quiet one at right angles to it. Outside their narrow terraced house stood Albinia Lacy's staid black car.

"Is Grandpa going to die?" Victoria asked tremulously.

"He's an old man, Victoria. He hasn't been in good health for at least twenty years. It's amazing that he has lived so long. There was your father, hale and hearty—no, not hearty, he was never that, but in apparent good health anyway—dead at twenty-seven, and his father ailing to the age of seventy-seven. It makes no sense!" She spoke bitterly. Life had failed to make sense to her for years.

She unfastened the garden gate. Victoria followed her along the cement path between well-weeded borders of pansies and candytuft. The door opened as they reached it. Albinia Lacy stepped back into the cool obscurity of the small hall to allow them to enter. She was a tall, austere woman in her early fifties, her neatly coiled auburn hair turning grey in attractive streaks. She had an extremely smooth, unlined skin, supple and sallow, a long nose and fine hazel eyes, lacking softness. She seldom smiled or frowned; a gentle lift of well arched brows was her usual manner of expressing emotion. Her voice was evenly modulated and she was sparing with words.

Now she rested her calm gaze upon the attire of her young niece, a lemon two-piece swim suit, and suggested that she change as quickly as possible. Victoria ran upstairs to obey.

The house was dark and poky, filled with large, solid furniture that had belonged to Victoria's maternal grand-parents. Her bedroom was north-facing and, even on a day like today, appeared cool and uninvitingly neat. Monica was houseproud, obsessively so; a large untidy family would have cured or killed her. Fortunately her only daughter was naturally fastidious, although even she wondered sometimes how her father would have fitted into such an environment of lace doilies and lavender polish. It never occurred to her that her mother's obsession had grown after his death as a form of compensation. It had been five years after that event that his wife and daughter had moved into this house, soon after the death of Monica's last surviving parent, whose home it had been.

Victoria hurriedly pulled on T-shirt and shorts over her swim suit, brushed her hair and ran downstairs in time to hear her aunt ask, "What on earth is that child doing?"

The front door was opened to let in a momentary flood of blazing light and warmth into which they stepped, the door banging decisively behind them, as if the house was saying that enough was enough. Outside was where frivolous summer belonged, with its dust and insects.

As the car turned onto the beach road, Victoria spared a thought for her cousins, waiting indolently to be joined by the Bideau twins and Raoul Bellinger, Stephen's friend. All she could see beyond the beach wall was the sparkling sea and, a few miles distant, two islands, green and hazy against the indistinct horizon. She wished she were on one of them now and that they were as silent and remote as they appeared. In reality they would be over-run with visitors, taken to and from the main island by swift, noisy motor-boats. Where did one go to escape? Victoria knew from experience: within oneself; but even that retreat was unbearable with grief as a companion. Thoughts of her grandfather subdued all others.

"Who is with Grandpa?" she asked her aunt from the back seat.

"Mrs. Grey, but as you know he doesn't care for her company at the best of times. I'm afraid he was beyond caring when I left, but he may have taken a turn for the better and wonder where I am."

"He may indeed," Monica agreed, sardonically.

It was common knowledge that Albinia considered herself indispensable to her father's needs. That he did not care for Mrs. Grey, amongst a host of other personages, was a prejudice she actually encouraged, to boost her own importance to him. Only one other person would she acknowledge as having an equal place in her father's affections and that was Victoria, beloved by both of them as the daughter of a dead son and brother, who, happily, resembled him in both looks and temperament.

"Of course," Albinia conceded as a generous afterthought, "he may ask for Victoria. She is never far from his thoughts."

Monica glanced back at her daughter with a small, reassuring smile. The large, solemn grey eyes did not return it. The child is away again, her mother thought, putting a barrier between herself and the world. If only she were a happier child. Her introspective melancholy was a constant reproach.

In fact Victoria was back in the past, a little girl of seven or eight, re-living a typical Sunday afternoon, the pattern of which stretched virtually unbroken from her father's death when she was two until the present day—except that now she usually made the visit on her own.

It was a summer Sunday—most Sundays of her early childhood were remembered as being in high summer—and she was enduring the dreadful ordeal of getting ready. It seemed she would never be in a fit state to visit her Grandpa Lacy. First she was stripped. The clothes she had worn in the morning were not grubby, for Monica never allowed her to do anything that would soil her hands, much less her clothes. She was then washed as thoroughly as if she had not been bathed with the same vigour the evening before. Her mother searched anxiously behind her ears and beneath her finger nails, the flannel thick with scented soap, the basin half-full of warm water, frothy with rainbow bubbles. Inevitably the soap got into her eyes, which made her stamp and cry noisily, writhing in her mother's firm grip, while being reminded unsympathetically that it was her own fault for fidgeting.

Her mother's bedroom, over-crowded with hideous walnut furniture, was north-facing like her own and dismal even on the brightest day. Victoria stood in knickers and vest, wriggling her toes in what remained of the pile on the Indian carpet, waiting for what seemed ages while her mother searched the vast wardrobe for a dress. The yellow one would not do: the bows were crushed; the white one was too short for the frilly petticoat lying on the candlewick spread of the double bed. The pink dress would do, but the chosen hair ribbon was the wrong shade to go with it, necessitating a prolonged hunt for a freshly laundered white one. At last she was dressed, complete with the regulation two handkerchiefs: one for her coat pocket, the other to be stuffed up her knicker leg—unfortunately the pink dress had no pockets and was sleeveless. It was forbidden, by Aunt Albinia, the child assumed, to sneeze without covering one's entire face when taking tea with Grandpa Lacy.

Then Victoria was ready, standing in the dark hall, impatient to be off, waiting for the sound of her aunt's old car, watching her mother enact the last few minutes of ritual, prolonged because she was as loath to go as her daughter was eager.

Monica peered into the blackness of the hall mirror, from which it seemed her image was as vainly peering out, pale, floating, drowning in the depths of the alabaster oval. She smoothed her hair, dark and lustrous, straightened her cream silk cravat, brushed a speck from her shoulder, cocked her head to catch the sound of the motor, glanced sideways at her daughter's upturned face and nodded. The signal had been given. The child leaped at the door, struggling with the shiny brass knob. It turned reluctantly in her small fists and she was skipping down the path, smiling with pleasure in the light, radiant warmth at the sudden feeling of spurious freedom. Confined in the poky house all morning, she had not imagined that the sun was shining so generously for everyone else.

"Walk carefully, Victoria, you'll scuff your shoes."

Then the few miles into the island, sitting, as she was sitting now, in the back of Aunt Albinia's car, a different one, certainly, but as middle-aged and staid as its predecessor, indeed, as its owner.

Soon the little girl was ensconced on her grandfather's knees, one small hand stealing into his waistcoat pocket for his large, miraculously chiming watch. Tenderly she would hold the smooth, warm, golden thing to her ear, smiling in secret satisfaction at the magic of its rhythmic, insistent ticking, waiting expectantly for its melodious chime.

"When you are twenty-one, my darling, I shall buy you the most beautiful gold watch I can find," he had promised her, time and time again.

Brought back to the present by the car stopping in the drive at Grande Maison, Victoria was assailed by the realisation that she was only seventeen. The twenty-first birthday to which her grandfather had so often referred was likely to be celebrated without him. The thought of the gold watch was no longer a happy anticipation, but a sadness. Seized by an urgent need to see him, she jumped from the car, slamming the door in a manner that brought a severe rebuke from her aunt.

Mrs. Grey opened the door to them. She was the housekeeper, plump but not homely. She tolerated children and detested dogs. She had been a member of that household for more than thirty years; a strange, detached woman, conscientious in her work, living in the house yet managing to maintain an entirely separate existence.

"How is he, Mrs. Grey?" Albinia asked, rubbing her sensible shoes vigorously on the door mat at the top of the spotless white steps.

"The doctor is with him now, Miss. I told him you wouldn't be long." She spoke in a low, lilting voice. Her parents had spoken the island patois and, as a young woman, she would switch from English to Norman French and back again without a change in inflexion, so that uninitiated listeners had found it difficult to tell at what point her conversation once more became intelligible to them.

"Wait in the drawing-room, Monica," Albinia said, mounting the wide staircase.

They did as they were told. Monica went to her customary seat by the window. Victoria stood by her side, twisting a handkerchief in thin, nervous fingers.

"I sit in this awful chair from habit," Monica said. "After all these years it's still as hard and uncomfortable as the first time I sat on it. It's too tightly stuffed and entirely the wrong shape, not meant for the human form at all."

"Sit somewhere else, then, Mum," Victoria suggested.

Both looked round the room for an inviting alternative. There was the sofa by the wall, its velvet cushions plumped, yet not attractive in its distance from the fire; there was Albinia's chair, with her knitting still upon it; two straight-backed wooden chairs, old fashioned carvers with upholstered seats and, lastly, the old man's winged leather chair, the worn seat still softly dented from his bony old bottom. Monica stayed where she was, contemplating the many wearisome hours she had spent there, hoping that when the time came to say goodbye, the old man would produce a present in the shape of money for his grand-daughter. My God, how she had longed for that present, although its acquisition had been both a pleasure and a problem. The trouble lay in disposing of it satisfactorily; they had always needed so much. It was illogical because, had she hinted that she was hard-up, he would eagerly have given her whatever was needed and more—anything for the child. Monica smiled sardonically at the sacrifice she had made for the luxury of pride.

When first her husband, Leonard, had died, his father had been anxious to provide for the widow and her baby daughter, but Monica could not bear the thought of living at Grande Maison. She had stayed on in the rented cottage for two years until her father died and she could move into the family home. Leonard's father had wanted to be generous towards his daughter-in-law, despite his disappointment that she would not come to live in his large house with the small girl who was already his joy. His advances were met with cool reserve and he was gradually deceived into believing that financial help was not needed, it was so frequently spurned in the first years after his son's tragic death. As the child grew and her resources dwindled, Monica took seasonal, part-time jobs to provide expensive extras, determined that her daughter should enjoy the same advantages as her more affluent cousins. Her sisters, knowing her better than her father-in-law, pretended they were unaware of her comparative poverty and helped in subtle ways that called for no acknowledgement. Monica resented her father-in-law's gentle enquiries into her affairs and he, frightened that the precious weekly visits might cease if he persisted, had gradually lost interest as their material state never visibly deteriorated. The small amount of money that Leonard had left, Monica put aside for Victoria's future, intending, if necessary, to pay for her education, but here the old man had proved adamant, insisting that he pay her school fees and any future university fees. This meant she had attended the same schools as her cousins without additional hardship to her mother and, in substantial measure, lessened the loneliness of an only child's upbringing.

Victoria shivered. Monica glanced at her sharply.

"Are you cold?"

Victoria shook her head.

"Do you know?" Monica said. "This is the first time I have ever been in this room with the gas fire unlit."

They both looked towards the hearth. From there Victoria's eyes went to the winged chair. Usually when they arrived her grandfather was sitting in it, his long, yellow hands, mottled with age, resting on the arms, his thumbs rubbing nervously along the worn piping. Even with the fire out, the atmosphere in the room was still warm and stuffy. He liked it that way, he was too fearful of draughts. Monica complained that even a deep breath was enough to make him sneeze fretfully.

Victoria left her mother's side to look at a familiar photograph in its silver frame upon the bookcase. The young man smiled politely back at his daughter, as he smiled from every photograph she had seen of him. The fact that she was fast catching up with him in age made their relationship seem remotely incredible. It was the image of someone who, as far as Victoria was concerned, had never actually existed, without character or emotion, forever smiling; a person based entirely on hearsay to whom she owed her life, but of whom she had no affectionate memory.

"I have grown to resent that self-satisfied smile," Monica said.

Victoria glanced round at her reproachfully. Monica shrugged.

"I suppose bitterness has replaced sentiment."

"How can you say that, Mum?"

"Well, fifteen years is a long time, when

you consider I only knew him for five. I can't help thinking how much easier things would have been had he lived. His father and Albinia never wanted me to marry him, you know. If I had given them half a chance they would have taken you from me."

"That can't be true," Victoria protested. "Grandpa Lacy asked you to live here with him, you have often told me."

"It wasn't me he wanted, it was you. He has tolerated me all these years, because of you. If I had accepted his offer, in a few years you would have been a true Lacy, with no trace of Le Feuvre. As it is, you may look like your father, but I think you have more willpower, you take after me for that."

"Oh, Mother! What was he really like? Was he like Grandpa?"

"Heaven forbid!" Monica said involuntarily, then, relenting at the sorrowful expression on her daughter's face, "well, a little perhaps, but I fancy he favoured his mother."

"What was she like, then?"

Monica shrugged. "I don't know and neither did he. He used to say he could scarcely believe she had existed. They rarely spoke of her. It is difficult to imagine that Theodore Lacy ever had a wife, or Albinia a mother if it comes to that."

"What unkind things you say," Victoria murmured.

"Yes, I do," her mother cheerfully agreed.

The door opened and Albinia entered.

"You may come up now," she told them. "He wants to see Victoria."

3

"WHAT did the doctor say?" Victoria asked as she followed her mother and aunt's stately progress up the green-carpeted staircase.

"He was not hopeful," Albinia replied.

Theodore Lacy's bedroom was square and spacious, the heavy, oak Victorian furniture not intrusive in such dimensions. The heat was stifling. It enveloped them palpably as they entered, so that they faltered on the threshold. The mid-afternoon sun was upon the two bay-windows across which heavy gold curtains were partially drawn. Victoria noticed that the gas fire was lit and felt strangely comforted. It was as if the steady flame was a continuity of his feeble life. The dreaded moment when this fire would resemble the one in the drawing-room, grey and spectre-like, had not arrived.

The frail old man was propped up in bed upon snowy white pillows, edged with lace, which appeared scarcely to feel his weight. His shoulders were tucked about with a black cashmere shawl, accentuating his extreme pallor; a golden puffy eiderdown covered the double bed. His eyes were closed.

Victoria crept to the foot of the bed, nervously considering his intense stillness. He looks dead already, she thought, beginning to weep quietly into her mangled handkerchief.

Albinia inspected him at closer range.

"He's slipped away again. You had better wait awhile," she advised in a low voice, placing a chair beside the bed for Monica and motioning Victoria to sit in one on the other side.

"If you watch him, I'll go and fetch some tea. I have some arrangements to make with Mrs. Grey for the nurse Dr. Raines is sending. Let me know as soon as he comes round." She left the room.

Monica and Victoria sat in silence, regarding him. Unknown to Merle, Stephen had appropriated two bottles of red wine destined for the dinner of visitors with undiscriminating palates, and Victoria had helped her cousins polish them off on the beach, disdaining the orangeade provided by her mother. Now she had a headache, aggravated by crying, and felt strangely disorientated. From bright beach to shaded death-bed, without a period of mental adjustment, gave the day a bizarre twist and she wondered, shutting her eyes tightly, if when she opened them she would be mercifully awakening from a bad dream.

"You look peaky, Victoria," her mother said softly across the wide bed and its inert occupant.

Reluctantly, Victoria opened her eyes, smiling wanly in answer, fighting down a sudden desire to be sick. She fixed her eyes upon her grandfather's ashen face, willing him to look at her.

The airless warmth and the persistent tick of the silver travelling clock upon the bedside table began to have an overpoweringly sleepy effect upon the watchers. Monica fought the creeping drowsiness with an effort, surveying the room inch by inch as a form of mental exercise. Even in the muted sun light she found it forbidding. The shining areas of dark oak were bereft of relieving ornaments. She marvelled that they had ever known a woman's touch. The bedside table alone boasted impedimenta. There was an assortment of medicine bottles and pill containers, the travelling clock, a crystal water jug with matching tumbler, a medicine glass with a white sediment at its base, a spoon, a scuffed leather link box with the initials TEL, for Theodore Edward Lacy, in gold upon the lid, a tortoiseshell-backed hair brush and a crumpled linen handkerchief—but no photograph of Charmian Lacy. Was he lying there dreaming of joining her at last? Was he still able to dream? How strange to think he was so near to solving the one great mystery, or was there no solution, just oblivion?

Monica looked from the old man's face, the flesh falling away from the delicate bones, to her daughter, and was filled with pity.

"What is it?" Victoria asked under her mother's gaze, fidgeting uncomfortably.

"I was just thinking how like your father you look at this moment," she answered. She had seen him look like that, white and strained, many times when he had been emotionally hurt or upset.

Leonard had been sensitive, introspective, just like Victoria, too vulnerable without the desire to retaliate. His sole act of rebellion was in making Monica Le Feuvre his wife, thereby changing his dependence; but of course she had not realised that at the time, not until much later. She had never imagined when they were courting that his air of self assurance, of being accustomed to pleasing himself, was an act put on to deceive not her, but himself. It was when Monica met his family for the first time, when she had already committed herself by falling in love with him, that she perceived his reliance on them, his fear of their disapproval, and realised why he had delayed the meeting for so long. They had certainly disapproved. Albinia always blamed Monica for the marriage, convinced that she had snared Leonard. The truth, his passionate clinging to her, his eagerness to enter her own family circle with its satellites of friends and numerous acquaintances, was something his sister never suspected. Leonard had spoken little about his family, but somehow Monica had received the impression that they mattered little to him. All her efforts to draw him out on the subject had been in vain. She became nervous of meeting them. Knowing so little of his father and sister, of his home life, put her at a disadvantage. How was she to be the young lady they most desired for Leonard, when she had no idea of the type of person they would find most pleasing? She need not have worried, she thought bitterly. No woman on earth would have pleased them; the only acceptable one would have been someone who would not steal him from hearth and home, but docilely take her place there alongside him.

He had taken her home to tea soon after they became engaged. How well she remembered that afternoon. Pouring with rain! Sitting on the bus in headscarf and mackintosh, apprehensively making plans for befriending his sister. She had been thrown completely off balance on arrival by realising that she was not expected. They were expecting Leonard, but on his own. To make matters worse, they were unaware of the engagement. In fact he had needed her support to break the news to them. Theodore Lacy had rallied quite quickly from the shock of the announcement, made by his son with a pathetic air of bravado, and did his best to be pleasant and welcoming to the thin, dark-haired girl who was to be his daughter-in-law. Albinia remained cool and aloof, addressing her as Miss Le Feuvre throughout the visit, although repeatedly cajoled with words and smiles from her brother to be less formal. She said it would take time to get used to the idea. Monica had surmised she never would.

There was a slight, snuffling noise from the bed. Monica and Victoria immediately became alert, sitting forward on their chairs.

Suddenly Theodore Lacy's eyes opened. He turned them slowly onto his daughter-in-law without moving his head.

"Monica," he breathed softly, through apparently motionless lips.

"What is it?" she asked kindly, leaning nearer to catch his answer, but no other sound came, although it was obvious to an anxiously watching Victoria that he was trying desperately to speak. She reserved her own breath in a subconscious effort to aid him. At last, to her immeasurable relief, he uttered a sibilant sound which gradually resolved itself into a whispered, "You will answer to me."

Monica glanced quickly across at Victoria in surprise and doubt. She could not have heard correctly. Her eyes went back to his, unwaveringly upon her face.

"Answer to me," he repeated, softly but more firmly.

"For what, Father?" she asked gently, in the tone one uses to a child who cannot possibly realise the significance of what he is saying.

"Victoria," he sighed, his eyelids fluttering wearily. "For Victoria," he managed again, more weakly. His eyes closed.

"But I don't understand," Monica said patiently. "In what way? Why?"

His eyes remained shut. He lay like an effigy.

Monica waited a few minutes for some sign of life, then, exasperated, she said with an edge to her voice:

"She has always been my responsibility." She settled back in her chair, flushed and cross.

"He didn't know what he was saying,

Mum," Victoria whispered. "He could only manage a few words and he chose the wrong ones. Poor Grandpa! He was confused." Her eyes filled with tears again as she added, "He didn't even know I was here."

Monica did not reply. They waited, busy with their thoughts, hoping he would rally. After just a few minutes the passive face upon the unwrinkled pillows suddenly contorted, the figure writhed beneath the eiderdown then lay as still as before, but more bloodless, if that were possible.

Both mother and daughter rose in their seats. As he subsided again, so did they. Monica said urgently,

"Quickly, run and fetch Albinia."

Victoria sped from the room. Running along the landing she almost collided with her aunt at the top of the staircase, which she had just slowly ascended bearing a tray of tea.

"Is he awake?" she asked, then seeing Victoria's expression, "is he dead?" on a higher note.

"I don't know," the girl answered, hanging back as her aunt proceeded rapidly, fearful that her grandfather was familiar no more, just a recognisable dead thing.

Monica appeared at the end of the landing, beckoning to them.

"He has opened his eyes again," she reassured them, but there was no thankfulness in her voice.

As she once more entered the bedroom, Victoria's sigh of relief on seeing her grandfather to be conscious was almost enough to pluck the tenuous spirit and send it soaring.

"Grandpa," she breathed, going quickly to his side and placing her pink cheek briefly against his pale, sunken one.

He was unable to talk, but his eyes spoke his love, as hers did unhappiness and pity, his rheumy blue eyes endeavouring to remain focused upon the beloved young face, so close, yet so remote, slipping further away every second as he drifted back into unconsciousness, her name the last thing on his mind, but no sound issuing from his lips.

Victoria turned towards her mother who was standing at the foot of the bed, but Monica was lost in thought, unaware that his eyes had shut again. Albinia took her arm and beckoned to Victoria, who followed them out.

"I'll drive you home now," she said briskly. "He has seen Victoria and that was what he wanted. I will let you know if there is any significant change, although Dr. Raines thinks he will probably pass fitfully in and out of consciousness. It's a pity you're not on the telephone." Her father had offered to have it installed for them years ago, but Monica had refused, causing much inconvenience to Albinia over the years.

"You could 'phone Aunty Merle," Victoria suggested. "One of the boys would bring the message."

"Very well," Albinia agreed, wondering how Monica's sisters put up with the inconvenience.

"It may be good news," the girl suggested hopefully, yet without hope.

Albinia gave her a look of pity, not for her distress so much as for her self-delusion.

"I'm afraid not, Victoria. He is too weak to rally."

"Yes, but . . ."

"There are no 'buts', child. We must

face the worst. It's just a matter of time. You two get in the car, while I go and ask Mrs. Grey to sit with him until I return. It would be just like the nurse to arrive and take over while I'm away."

Victoria's cousins stayed on the beach until almost five o'clock. Soon after lunch they were joined, as Jill had predicted, by Prissy and Roy Bideau and Raoul Bellinger.

"Where's Vicky?" they wanted to know. Not because they cared, but because it was so unusual for her to be absent.

Raoul had sailed his dinghy round the headland from the harbour and the boys spent most of the time in her. The girls lay in the sun, gossiping and watching their antics, slightly resentful of the sleek beauty that was claiming so much attention. After an hour or so, Raoul left his friends to issue an invitation to the girls, his eyes on Jill,

"Anyone want a sail?"

"I do," Sandra said, jumping up eagerly, running down the beach and yelling to Bob to come in closer, as she was going to have a go.

"How about the rest of you?"

"Would you like to, Prissy?" Helen asked her friend.

"If you would," was the reply and they followed Sandra to the sea at a more leisurely pace.

Raoul sat next to the recumbent Jill, waiting, his eyes on his precious craft. They remained in silence, very aware of each other's presence. At last Raoul said:

"Let's have a day on the islands."

"Yes, let's," Jill agreed lazily, not lifting her head from her arms.

"We could sail across. You girls could take the ferry. It would have to be a fair day. Dad's pretty lenient about most things, but a bit sticky about suitable sailing weather. He had a younger brother who was lost at sea, caught in a sudden squall or something, so it's understandable, I suppose."

"Yes," Jill agreed again.

Raoul took his eyes off his craft and looked at her instead.

"I say, Jill, is anything wrong?"

"No, why do you ask?"

"Oh, I don't know. You seem a bit offhand, not very enthusiastic, not like you usually are. One would hardly guess from your manner that this is the beginning of the holidays. Are you sure there's nothing wrong?"

She did not answer.

"Jill?" he insisted.

She shook her head.

"I should hate anything to spoil these few weeks, the last holiday before we all disperse into the wide world."

"I'm not going anywhere," Jill said, sitting up.

"But you could. It seems such a waste, not taking up that university place."

"Higher education isn't everything," she said.

"You are restricted without it. I wouldn't be a doctor, for a start."

"That's different. If what you want to do needs special qualifications, then of course you must get them, but I don't believe in qualifications just for the sake of them."

"I don't agree, Jill. I think everyone should get the most they can from the education system."

"And I think," she countered, "that they should get just what they need. 'A' levels and a business course are adequate to go into my father's office. He will never make an architect of me, so he is content to have a secretary instead. A son would have suited him better, but never mind, he must make do. Perhaps Helen or Sandra fancy architecture. As far as I'm concerned, three years at university would be three years marking time. I should be no nearer fulfilling my ambition than I am now and financially no better off."

"What is your ambition, Jill?"

"Very modest, I'm afraid. It doesn't involve leaving home and acquiring letters after my name."

"Tell me," he urged her, but she shook her head, smiling teasingly at him.

"When I have what I want, then I'll tell you," she promised.

"It sounds most mysterious."

"In fact it's very simple, so simple that my mother would despise me for it." She stood up, stretched and then ran down the beach. He watched her, thoroughly perplexed, as she splashed into the sea and began to swim with strong, regular strokes towards the dinghy, where mutiny was breaking out amongst the new crew.

Suddenly he felt utterly miserable, as if she had said goodbye to him. The two months before he departed for London were not going to be as happy and carefree as he had anticipated; he almost wished them over.

4

"I'M going out, Mum," Victoria said quietly, putting away the last of the tea things, which she had just dried.

"Where are you going?" her mother asked, "not back to your grandfather's, I hope."

There was no answer. Victoria took off her apron and hung it behind the kitchen door.

"You'll only be in the way," her mother warned her. "The nurse will be doing everything necessary for his comfort and Albinia will be busy making sure the poor woman never forgets her place. Anyway, you don't look well. You ate practically nothing for tea. If you ask me, you'd be better off going to bed early."

"I feel fine, Mum. I thought I'd just cycle over to Aunty Merle's, to tell her to expect a telephone call. I feel like some fresh air. I won't be long."

"Merle will be giving her visitors their evening meal. You know how hectic it is there at meal times," Monica reminded her.

"I could help," Victoria said. "I have before, and she has always been grateful."

Monica relented. "Very well, go on, then."

Victoria escaped from the house with a sense of relief. Her mother's constant concern for her welfare was oppressive. She was always trying to put colour into cheeks that were naturally pale or happiness into eyes that were habitually solemn. She watched her like a hawk to gauge her mood, and thought, when Victoria obligingly smiled, that she had achieved an emotional breakthrough. Left alone, Victoria smiled a lot less, but felt happier in her own, quiet way.

She set off on her bicycle to Merle's home, which was situated on the elevated central plain of the island, above the main harbour and town. She went mainly along dusty lanes, winding their way between acres of greenhouses, filled with tomatoes or flowers, occasionally skirting small fields in which were tethered the distinctive honey-coloured cows. Pasture was scarce on this overcrowded island and the greenhouse had more than its fair share of space.

Merle Bienvenue lived in a pleasant square house of green granite with a slate roof. It was near three large public parks with tennis courts and bowling greens. It was not far from a library and a museum and even nearer to the Lacys' austere residence which was tucked away at the end of a drive leading from a cul-de-sac of very dull respectability. There was nothing dull about the street in which the Bienvenues lived, although it was considered just as respectable. It was wide and curving, containing a pleasant hotchpotch of domestic architecture lovingly preserved, surrounded by generous gardens, flower-filled and visible beyond low stone walls.

The most beautiful garden of all was certainly Uncle Karl's, Victoria thought as she alighted in front of it. It was filled with dahlias of every variety, for they were his passion. He grew other flowers as well, of course, but in the main the front garden was a glorious mass of dahlia colour, some of the staked flower heads so huge that they provoked comment from passers-by and won him prizes at the horticultural shows. He even grew flowers in the back garden where his wife would have preferred vegetables. He appeased her by growing salad stuff in a greenhouse tucked away at the far end, hidden from the house by fruit trees and currant bushes. There was also a narrow strip of ground given over to such things as cabbages, carrots, peas and beans, but his heart was not in them and they did not thrive as well as they should; Merle could have done with thrice the amount to feed her household.

As Victoria wheeled her bicycle along the short gravel drive, she noticed her uncle in the garden which at this time of the evening was engulfed in the shadow of the house. She called out a shy greeting to him, at which he looked up from close inspection of a yellow floribunda rose bush, to answer with his usual kindly smile. He was a large, loosely jointed man, with a shock of prematurely grey hair hanging untidily over his forehead and an unhealthy complexion which was at variance with the amount of time he spent in the open air. As Victoria passed him, he remarked upon the settled spell of weather they were enjoying. She answered him, but did not stay to chat. He embarrassed her. Today he was just friendly, gentle Uncle Karl, but she could never talk to him without being overcome with the timidity she felt when he was "not himself." She could not like the other Uncle Karl, he frightened her.

Victoria propped her bike against the wall, entering the house by the side door which gave onto a narrow passage leading to the rear garden. Half-way along its length was the kitchen door. The kitchen was a vast room, having been extended when Merle found it expedient to take in paying guests. It had two large windows, one at the end, facing southwards and overlooking the garden, the other at the far side from the door, over the sink unit, looking along the length of a flower-filled conservatory. It was almost like looking into a huge bowl crammed with water weeds with, here and there in the shape of a flower, the bright hues of tropical fish.

It was a beautiful kitchen, especially now, filled with early evening summer sunlight and the delicious aroma of dinner.

The substantial pine table in the centre was piled with dishes and plates. On the cooker next to the sink, three large pans simmered gently. The sliding glass doors to the breakfast room were open, but there was no sign of her aunt or the girl, Doreen, who helped her.

Victoria crossed over to an easy chair by the rear window and plonked herself down in it, gazing at the garden with pleasure. It was a place where she had spent many happy childhood hours with her cousins, playing games like pirates and cannibals. The boys had usually ended up victorious, tying the girls to the apple trees with lots of clumsy knots, while they prepared to cook them on the fire, a meagre bunch of smouldering twigs around which the cannibals pranced with fiendish abandon.

The window was open. The scent of vegetation and freshly mown grass drifted in to mingle with the smell of dinner.

Suddenly Merle rushed through the breakfast room towards the cooker, exclaiming angrily about something. She smiled briefly as she caught sight of Victoria. She lifted first one pan lid, then the other, sniffing delicately at the contents, then turned to her niece.

"Now, you know better than just to sit there, Victoria."

As Victoria apologised and got to her feet, another girl, not much older than herself, almost ran into the room.

"Help Doreen carry the plates through," Merle said.

"But, Aunty, I don't like serving. Can't I help in the kitchen?"

Merle was busy piling warmed plates onto a wooden tray.

"If you want to be useful you must help Doreen," she said.

Doreen smiled encouragingly at the shy girl. Victoria resigned herself to the unpleasant task and held a tray while vegetable dishes were placed upon it. Meanwhile her aunt was ladling soup into ten plates.

"Take these first, silly child," she said testily. "Oh heavens, the children were supposed to have fruit juice."

Reluctantly Victoria followed Doreen through the breakfast room, across the hall and into the dining-room, which smelt of suntan lotion and cologne. At four round tables sat an assortment of adults and children, whose appetites had perked up as the sun declined.

Victoria placed her tray upon the sideboard, leaving Doreen to hand it round, and hurried back to the kitchen for the second consignment, carefully avoiding the eyes of a girl who looked about her own age and was sitting near the door. This girl watched Victoria's subsequent comings and goings with interest and some amusement, much to the latter's discomfort.

Back in the kitchen, while the roast beef was being consumed, Doreen quickly rinsed the soup plates and stacked them ready to be washed. Merle cut wedges of loganberry pie and Victoria poured thick yellow cream into four dainty jugs with a blue and white design. While this was going on, Bob came in through the conservatory. When his mother was not looking he helped himself to a slice of roast beef from a dish set aside for the family meal.

"I wish you would not pick at the food," his mother said over her shoulder.

"And I wish that you did not have eyes in the back of your head," he answered good-humouredly. He was very hungry, but it was useless to say so. The visitors had to be fed first and, while this operation was in progress, nobody who was not actually helping was welcome in the kitchen. He left to go up to his room. In the hall he passed Doreen, returning with a tray of dirty plates.

"Rush it through, Doreen. The sooner that lot are fed, the sooner I can fill the aching void in my stomach."

"My God, it's all rush in this place," she said. "If they scoff the stuff any faster they'll choke their bloody selves!" She smiled at him broadly. "Not a bad idea, eh?"

"All except the pretty one called Natalie. I've got my eye on her."

"You would," she replied, carrying on into the kitchen, her generous hips swaying seductively in the navy-blue dress, over which she wore a diminutive white apron edged with lace. She accidentally banged the tray against the breakfast table as she passed, by no means for the first time. Merle shouted at her to be more careful.

"Sorry, dearie," sang the irrepressible Doreen.

"Perhaps you would set the table for us now, Victoria," her aunt suggested. "Put a place for yourself." And when Victoria answered that she had had tea, she said, "Have some more, you are far too thin."

Victoria did as she was told. The last of the dishes from the dining-room were scraped, rinsed and stacked. Merle ladled soup into six green bowls and carried them into the breakfast room, while Victoria went to call the rest of the family. Karl was already taking off his gardening shoes in the side passage. He timed meals to a nicety: never too soon, when he would be in the way, never too late, when he would be a nuisance.

Victoria went upstairs to fetch the boys. During the summer months they shared an attic bedroom. The door to the attic was at the far end of the main landing, opposite the shower room. She climbed the almost vertical wooden staircase in darkness, the door banging shut behind her on strong spring hinges, entering the attic by a door in the floor, like ascending to the deck of a ship. The upper landing was well-lit by a large dormer window, beneath which was a camp bed, stacked with a pillow and blankets, for Uncle Karl, when he was "not himself". There were two doors on the left, leading into bedrooms of identical size. The door of the first room was open, as it usually was, to give an illusion of more breathing space. Stephen was lying on his bed beneath the window, reading. Bob was behind the door, combing his hair, looking into a square of mirror balanced precariously against a pile of books upon a chest of drawers. As well as the twin beds and the chest, the room contained a narrow wardrobe and a wooden chair, which was practically hidden under clothes and books. There was worn blue linoleum on the floor and a multi-coloured rag mat between the beds, made by Merle's mother during the long nights of the German occupation when the curfew kept people indoors. The walls were distempered a biscuit colour and were in need of redecorating, as was the grey, patchy ceiling. It was altogether too small and cluttered to be comfortable and Stephen hated it. He resented having to relinquish his spacious room downstairs every summer, but more than the comfort, he missed the privacy. Sharing with Bob was the greatest inconvenience.

Bob, on the other hand, tolerated it all with patience and good humour. Unlike Stephen, he was not used to having his preferences taken into account. He was aware that Stephen was his mother's favourite son and, being a perceptive young man, he guessed the reason. His own character was too much like his father's and his mother feared it held the same flaw. She watched and waited for some evidence of it, which meant she worried and could not be entirely at ease with him, whereas Stephen was more like her own family and she felt she could always rely on his judgement and dependability. During the tourist season, Stephen found it difficult to adjust to losing priority to the host of strangers who invaded his home. Bob and his father, for different reasons, were glad of the respite it afforded them.

"Dinner's ready," Victoria announced.

"About time," Bob said, replacing his comb in the pocket of his jeans. He left immediately.

"I'll just finish this chapter," Stephen said.

Victoria caught sight of a magazine, on which was a picture of her favourite pop star. Edging her way between Bob's bed and the chest of drawers, she reached over to take it from his pillow.

The door at the foot of the stairs swung shut after Bob and a few seconds later thudded again as someone ascended the staircase. In a few moments Doreen stood on the threshold. Victoria could neither see her nor be seen, as she was effectively concealed by the open door. She heard her announce jauntily,

"Grub's up!"

"So I believe," Stephen answered coolly, not raising his eyes from his book.

Doreen caught sight of the mirror which Bob had flung at the foot of his bed. She picked it up and, looking into it, began to fiddle ostentatiously with her hair, pursing her lips as she considered the effect.

"You'll crack it," Stepen said, without turning his head.

"Cheeky devil," she said cheerfully. She re-arranged a lock of hair over her forehead, glancing surreptitiously at him to see if he was watching, but apparently the book was still claiming his attention.

Doreen abandoned the mirror.

"Your mother's waiting for you. The soup is getting cold," she told him, leaning with one hand upon the door handle in what she considered a seductive pose.

"I'll come when I'm ready," he said shortly and, catching sight of Victoria in the corner, blushed at the discovery.

Victoria followed Doreen downstairs.

"He isn't always so disinterested," Doreen said, then grinning broadly she added, "poor boy, he doesn't know what he's missing."

It was humiliating to offer oneself and be tacitly declined; Victoria felt sorry for her. Stephen's dark, arrogant good looks obviously affected her. Doreen was plumply pretty and vivacious in a boisterous way that Victoria did not think would appeal to someone like Stephen. She loved attention from the opposite sex and was used to receiving it without begging. Bob flirted with her outrageously, in a manner she appreciated as being flattering but meaningless; in return she teased him about his many girl-friends, pretending to be jealous. Stephen, on the other hand, appeared to ignore her, but she was aware that his eyes were often upon her when he thought she was not looking. In fact the difference between the two brothers was never more marked than in their behaviour towards Doreen. Bob was easy-going and pleasant mannered, with a light-hearted sociability that hid a deep sensitivity; Stephen was withdrawn and studious, thinking before speaking, judging people by his own strict code of behaviour. He was as aware of Doreen's physical charms as his younger brother, but despised himself for it. Essentially a romantic, to lust and not to love was a betrayal of his code. When Doreen read derision in his eyes, she was mistaken in thinking it was aimed at her.

As soon as the family had finished the meal, Merle went straight from the table to her bedroom next to the boys'. Everyone else joined forces in clearing the table. Doreen filled the dishwasher with the first load, then began washing up the many things it would not hold, mainly pots and pans. Victoria and Bob dried, Stephen and his father tidied everything away. In a short time the kitchen was clear. Victoria wiped the table and the work surfaces, while Doreen skimmed round her feet with a sponge mop, the men having made themselves scarce. Stephen went back to his book, Bob said he was going swimming and Karl went into the sitting-room to watch television.

As soon as she was finished, Doreen thanked Victoria for her help, collected her handbag and took herself off to the ground-floor bathroom to freshen up her make-up before going home.

Victoria went upstairs in search of her aunt, recalling that she had not yet mentioned the telephone call.

She knocked on the bedroom door and was invited, none too cordially, to enter.

"Oh, it's you, Victoria." Merle was lying in the middle of the double bed, fully clothed but for her slippers which were on the floor. She patted the bed. Victoria obediently sat beside her—there was nowhere else to sit. She glanced around the cluttered room. Merle laughed shortly, saying,

"I little thought, when I put this old furniture up here, that one day I should be up here with it and, although I hate to admit it, grateful for it. When I used to send you all up here to play on a rainy day, I half-hoped you would wreck it. Now I'm glad it proved indestructible. It's amazing the amount of stuff it will hold. When we clear out every summer, all our stuff has to go somewhere. Mind you, I think most of it is under the beds."

"You look tired, Aunty," Victoria said, noticing the dark smudges under her eyes. "I'll go so that you can get some sleep."

"Sleep! Oh no, that would never do. Tell me what's the matter. I can see something is wrong. You are even quieter than usual."

"My Grandpa Lacy is dying," Victoria said, in a mournful voice.

"He's an old man," Merle reminded her.

Victoria sighed in exasperation, "Everyone says that, as if it makes a difference. It doesn't mean I love him any less. Love doesn't dilute with years, if anything it gets stronger."

Merle patted her hand.

"Of course, dear. I only wanted to remind you that no one lives forever, no matter how much they are loved. We have to grow accustomed to the idea, it helps."

"I shall miss him dreadfully. Death is so final, it's like infinity, difficult to grasp. Do you ever think about dying, Aunty?"

"No, child," Merle answered firmly. "I have enough problems here, without troubling about the hereafter."

"Not about after death," Victoria persisted, "about actually dying. I feel so sorry for Grandpa, alone in that big house. Well, not actually alone, but you know what I mean, he would still be alone even if the rest of the house were full. I wonder if he's frightened. I hope someone will stay close to me when I'm dying."

Merle sat up.

"For goodness sake, Victoria! Stop being so morbid. I refuse to encourage it. How are you with a paint brush?"

Victoria stared at her, not following the sudden change in the conversation.

"I'm quite good at art at school," she said.

"No, no! Before we come up here next year, I am going to have this attic redecorated. Stephen will be away and I can't rely on your Uncle Karl, so that leaves you and

Bob. I can bully Bob into it, but how about you? Do you think your talent extends to murals?"

"Murals?"

"Well, flat emulsion then."

The side door banged, followed by the scrunch of hurrying feet on the gravel drive.

Merle sighed once more.

"I'm grateful for a lot of things now—Doreen, for instance. What a clumsy, unlady-like creature she is, but what a treasure: utterly reliable, always cheerful and willing. Mind you, I don't say I wouldn't swop her for Margaret's Annie Figgus, given half the chance, especially when I remember that hefty swipe she gave the breakfast table this evening. Margaret doesn't appreciate Mrs. Figgus enough. She actually looks after their furniture as well as their stomachs. I often wonder what Margaret does with herself all day, apart from gad about and complain, of course."

Merle swung her plump legs to the floor, groping around with her feet for her slippers. Victoria knelt and put them on for her.

"Thank you, dear. Now we shall have to go down. I've been up here too long already. It's a good job that you came up, you stopped me from dozing off. I feel as fit as a flea all day, but as soon as the evening meal is over, I can hardly totter upstairs from sheer weariness. This hour lying down is becoming a bad habit."

"I could come and help more often," Victoria suggested willingly.

"Oh, I don't know what Monica would say about that. Mind, you could help Doreen with the bedrooms on Saturday mornings. That's always a busy time. It would give you a little pocket money, if you are interested."

Victoria went downstairs with her, waiting in the hall as Merle glanced briefly into the sitting-room, then the dining-room, hurrying after her into the kitchen.

"Go and see if your uncle is anywhere in the garden, will you, dear?" she asked lightly.

Victoria made a search of the front and the rear gardens, not forgetting the green-house and the shed, with a thoroughness that would have seemed ludicrous to anyone considering the situation as a casual observer. When she returned to the kitchen, she could see Merle poking her head round the door of the lavatory at the end of the conservatory. Always a risky thing to do, without whistling or singing loudly on approach, because the door would not shut properly, despite repeated efforts to persuade it over many years. There was a worried look on her face as she retraced her steps between the shelves of pot plants, but when she joined Victoria her expression was one of unconcern.

"I couldn't find him," Victoria said.

"We shall have to have a cup of tea without him, then," Merle smiled. "Put the kettle on. I have to run upstairs for a moment."

Victoria filled the kettle and set out two cups and saucers. When Merle returned, about ten minutes later, it was obvious her journey had been unsuccessful. She sank down wearily in the armchair, accepting a cup of tea with an air of preoccupation.

Victoria could think of nothing comforting to say. At last she suggested lamely that perhaps her uncle had slipped out for some cigarettes.

Merle shook her head.

"I knew this would happen sooner or later," she said, with tired resignation in her voice. "I thought an hour to myself after dinner wasn't a lot to ask, but of course it was too much. A watch-dog should never sleep, and that's what I have become. It's such a hateful thing to be, but what else can I do? Usually I can tell when this is going to happen—there's something in his eyes, a silent appeal to me to be more vigilant; but I never suspected this time, probably because it's only a few weeks since it last happened."

She slumped back in the chair, gazing into the garden with unseeing eyes, twisting the sapphire engagement ring round and round her plump finger. Victoria regarded her uneasily, sorry for her and unable to comfort her.

Stephen entered the kitchen wearing his jacket.

"Don't worry, Mum, you know it's no use. I'll try his club first. Is Bob about?"

"No." Merle answered crossly. "Trust Bob to be away when he's most needed. Stephen, please don't make a scene if you find your father, you can't make him come home if he refuses. Knowing where he is always helps."

Stephen left, looking grim and determined. Victoria drank her tea, resenting her aunt's remarks about Bob. It wasn't true. He was always around when she needed him and far more approachable than Stephen. How was he to know his father was going to disappear this evening? After a few minutes she asked,

"Do you know where Bob went?"

"No, he is becoming as elusive as his father," Merle snapped, picking up her cup from the window ledge and beginning to drink. Then she remembered. "Yes, I do. I heard him tell Doreen that he was going swimming."

"He didn't say which beach, I suppose?"

"No, dear, but he went without his bike, it's propped up against the conservatory. I saw it just now."

"Oh well, it doesn't matter," Victoria said, standing up to go. "I think I'll look in at Grande Maison on the way home."

"Is that wise, Victoria?"

"I want to," she said stubbornly, adding, "that reminds me. Aunt Binnie is going to 'phone you if—that is when—anything happens to Grandpa. Would you mind sending one of the boys with a message?"

"Of course I will," Merle assured her, thinking what a fool Monica was to resist having the telephone. "Shall I tell Bob you want to see him when he gets home?"

Victoria shook her head. She did not want him for anything in particular, just reassurance, a smile and a promise she had come to rely on over the years, that everything would be all right.

She left her aunt sitting in the golden light of the evening sun which was streaming through the window, with worry and misery for companions.

She cycled the short distance to Grande Maison.

5

VICTORIA leaned against her bike in the deep shadow of a group of beech trees, gazing towards the windows of her grandfather's bedroom. It was not possible to tell whether or not a light burned behind them, the curtains were too thick.

The house looked as it always did, uninhabited, as if it were waiting for the occupants to return from a lengthy sojourn abroad. The garden was overgrown, the shrubs in need of pruning, yet it was a tame mass of growth, as if nature deferred to the maiden lady who cast occasional appraising eyes upon it, willing it to remain as manageable as her own existence.

It was chilly standing beneath the trees. Victoria buttoned up her cardigan. She propped her bicycle against a tree trunk and walked slowly across the lawn towards the lobby door, where she hesitated. Her mother had warned her that she would not be welcome; perhaps she should postpone the visit until tomorrow. She knew she should, yet somehow she found herself inside, through the lobby and standing at the back of the hall near the kitchen door, which was ajar. Her aunt's voice came from beyond it, the subject of her conversation almost ludicrous when Victoria recalled what her mother had said before she left home.

"No, I couldn't possibly do that. She is far too young, Mrs. Grey. I can't imagine what Dr. Raines was thinking about, sending such a flibbertigibbet. I'm unable to leave her alone with an easy mind, which is ridiculous. The main reason for having a nurse was to ease my burden, not add to it."

Mrs. Grey replied soothingly, her quiet words unintelligible. Victoria was about to enter the kitchen, when there was the sound of someone descending the stairs, almost skipping down them, and a figure in white swung into view around the newel post at the other end of the hall.

"Hello," the nurse said with a big smile. "Do you live here?"

Victoria barely had time to shake her

head, before Albinia appeared on the scene.

"I thought I made it quite clear, nurse, that Mr. Lacy is not to be left alone for a moment," she said, eyebrows raised haughtily.

"He's quite peaceful," the young woman answered mildly. "I came to fetch some water." She held up the crystal jug, which Albinia positively snatched from her hand, saying,

"That could have been done upstairs, surely."

The nurse stepped back involuntarily at the suddenness of the movement.

"Mrs. Grey will bring the water. Please ring for anything further you may require."

With a rueful half-smile at Victoria, the nurse turned and ran lightly back upstairs. Albinia turned her attention upon her niece.

"What are you doing here, child?" she asked in a more kindly manner, for she knew that if she were abrupt Victoria could become infuriatingly inarticulate. Monica's fault, of course. She was too soft with her, allowing her to indulge in moods and fancies. What Victoria needed was a brisker, more practical approach.

"I've been visiting Aunty Merle, helping her a bit with the visitors' dinners. I thought I'd drop in on my way home, just to see if Grandpa is any better."

"He's sleeping and has been since you left."

"May I go up? I shan't disturb him."

Albinia's bright hazel eyes regarded her niece sympathetically. "No, you won't do that," she assured her, adding as she turned to go, "only stay a few minutes, mind. Wait, you can take the water."

Victoria knocked gently on the bedroom door and was answered by a cheerful but subdued voice bidding her go in. The nurse was sitting by a window in a pool of yellow light cast by a standard lamp. She had an open book upon her lap. Her eyes went from Victoria to her patient and back again. She smiled encouragingly. "Put the water on the table, will you?" Then she continued to read.

Victoria stole to the side of the bed and deposited the jug, then she stood looking at her grandfather. He lay as she had left him, pale and inert. He was no longer swathed in the black cashmere shawl and the eiderdown was folded on top of the blanket box at the foot of the bed. The atmosphere in the room had altered considerably from the afternoon. The hot fustiness had changed to a cooler, fresher air, sharpened by the tang of disinfectant and a sweeter, floral smell that emanated from the trim figure of the nurse.

Victoria was overwhelmed by a feeling of utter uselessness. She glanced with envy at the bowed head in the starched white cap. That person was only a few years older than herself, yet so competent, so serene; her love of duty worth far more than love alone, no matter how intense. To be a nurse suddenly seemed to Victoria the most worthwhile profession in the world and became her greatest desire.

Her eyes filled with tears as she thought of all the things she would like to tell her grandfather and never would. Even this sudden wish to be a nurse, he would never know. If she did become one, it would be without his constant encouragement. She was so used to him taking an interest in everything she did, no matter how trivial; so used to his gentle support on which she had always relied, a buffer between her own pliant nature and her mother's immense will-power. A barren plain stretched before her, where once there had stood a fence against which she had leant gratefully, like a sapling in the wind, while insistent gusts were persuading her with relentless logic that it was easier to lie prone. When the wind desisted, it had made it easier to stand upright again.

"Don't upset yourself," said the nurse. "There is nothing you can do and he isn't suffering, you know."

No, but I am, Victoria thought. She whispered that she had to go, but that she would be back the next day.

As one prop was slipping from her life, it became imperative to make sure of the other one. She left the house without seeing her aunt. Sympathy did not lie in that quarter, nor from her mother, whose advice she had deliberately ignored.

She ran down the drive, grabbed her bicycle and pedalled fast towards the beach which she knew to be one of Bob's favourites.

He was not there. She cycled round the headland to the next cove and then on to the next, walking along each beach in turn, sandals in her hand, scuffing her toes in the damp sand, throwing pebbles into the water, scrutinising every group of swimmers, few and far between at this time of the evening, every beach comber, in vain.

At the fourth beach there was a group of youths a long way out to sea, playing with a large yellow ball. She stood watching them for a while, trying to pick out a familiar inelegant crawl, one voice amongst the shouts and laughter. After a few minutes her presence was noticed. They began to swim inshore, calling and whistling. She set off hurriedly along the sand, convinced they were all strangers. She returned to her bicycle, her spirits falling even further with the failing light. At this rate she would circle the entire island. What was the use? He had probably changed his mind about swimming and was at the cinema with one of his girlfriends. Even if he had gone swimming, he could have been home long ago.

She was cycling across the grassy headland not far from the home of her Aunt Margaret and three girl cousins. It was a bleak stretch of coastline, its wild loneliness matching her mood. She got off her bicycle, throwing it down beside the road as if it had done her an injury and started off along a sandy track towards the sea, across rough grass and heather, completely absorbed by her thoughts.

I must not feel sorry for myself. Aunty Merle says it's self-indulgent to wallow in one's own misery to the exclusion of other people's troubles and, goodness knows, she has trouble enough. Why does Uncle Karl continually make her so worried and himself into a stranger whom everyone despises? Mother says it's because he is sick and cannot help himself, but she says it in such a way that I don't believe she really sympathises with him. Stephen certainly despises him, which is a dreadful thing, considering he's his father. Stephen lives by such a strict set of rules himself, as if fate were ready to take advantage of the slightest lapse. He's a bit of a fanatic, actually, even about cleaning his teeth. You would never catch Stephen smoking or getting drunk. He's a bit like Aunty Margaret and neither of them is very fond of me. Uncle Larry's nice. I wonder how he came to fall in love with Aunty Margaret? Not that I know him very well, really; I don't see a lot of him, but when I do he's always kind, listening to anything I have to say as if it interested him. He never ignores people, he's far too well-mannered. I think the girls are jolly lucky to have him for a father. Helen and Sandra are cheeky sometimes and quarrelsome, but they never argue and fall out with Uncle Larry. Jill sometimes has differences of opinion with him, but they remain good friends. I wish I were like Jill, in fact sometimes I wish I were Jill. She's so lovely and clever. She's not shy of anyone, not even the staff at school, she's not even afraid of her mother. I would have given in by now about going to university, but once Jill has made up her mind, no one can bully her into changing it. I wonder where Bob is?

She was climbing to the top of a rocky outcrop against a stiffening onshore breeze. She pulled down the sleeves of her blue cardigan to cover her cold wrists. Once at the top she sat down, dangling her legs over the steep drop to the beach, gazing out to sea at the small craft barely visible near the horizon which was merging into the evening sky, closing in on the world.

She wriggled her toes in the red sandals to keep them warm, wishing the summer would go on forever, dreading the end of it, because it would mean change. Grandpa Lacy would probably be gone forever, Stephen far away in England and Jill working for her father. At least the other three would still be at school.

Bob and I will be taking our "A" levels, she thought, then, turning her head slightly, why is that man looking at me? Is he looking at me? He must be, there's no one else. Do I know him? It's difficult to make out his features in this light, he's too far away. I wish he wouldn't stare, he is making me feel uncomfortable. I'll pretend I'm not aware of him. Goodness, I feel so conspicuous perched up here in these silly shorts. He can't be looking at me, he must be watching a seagull or something. I wish there were some other people around, the road's such a long way away. I can hear the traffic on it, mingling with the sound of the waves and the breeze in the tall grasses. To get to it I have to cross a large expanse of undulating dune—undulating—that's a lovely word, large expanse of undulating dune; very expressive, I could work it in to my next essay. Oh heavens, what am I doing? I can't sit here forever. Perhaps he has gone. No! There he is, absolutely still, hands in pockets, staring at me. It's getting darker every minute. I shouldn't have stayed so long. I shouldn't have come in the first place, it was a stupid idea, typical of me, acting on impulse. I shall have to climb down; if I tried jumping onto the beach I'd probably break my neck or something from this height. I'll go down casually and then, when I've reached the bottom, run like mad. Now, draw my legs under me, stand up very slowly, keep looking at the sea as if something out there is holding my attention as much as I am holding his; now, turn, nonchalantly, another lovely word for heaven's sake, start going down, glance at him casually—oh, God! He's coming towards me!

Victoria scrambled inelegantly down the last of the rocky slope, her eyes fixed on the face of the rapidly approaching man. He can't know me, she decided in alarm, otherwise he would smile. She reached the narrow track through the dunes and immediately turned away from him, running in the general direction of the road. She heard him break into a run behind her and ran harder, her heart pounding with effort and agitation. He was close, getting closer. Her foot twisted on a stone, momentarily checking her progress; as she stumbled she cast him a beseeching look over her shoulder, was alarmed anew at the tense expression on his face and fled again, but was checked almost immediately by his hand in the waist-band of her shorts. She opened her mouth to protest, too weak to scream—no one had ever mentioned how much strength one needs to scream. His hand closed hard over the lower half of her face, smothering her nostrils so that she was fighting for breath now as much as freedom. He was pulling her back along the path towards the obscurity of a dip in the dunes. She had the irrational thought that this could not be happening to her as she grunted and twisted in terror, kicking at his shins with her sandalled feet. He was pulling her relentlessly to the ground, struggle as she might. His strength seemed inexorable; her form was slight and much weakened; her knees gave way; she fell with a thud with him on top of her. He wound his hand in her long, blonde hair to clamp her to the ground. She could fight no more, just sob in fear, wriggling weakly beneath him, exciting him the more. She shut her eyes tightly as his face closed on hers. The quieter her body became, the wilder raced her thoughts. Terrified, she whimpered pitifully under his crude hands.

Then he was there no more. His weight was gone, so was his smell. She whimpered on, her eyes open now, staring at the sky. Quite suddenly she reacted to this inexplicable release, springing to her feet, racing unheeding past her deliverer, a small terrier bounding through the tussocks of grass towards her, followed by a man and two children, talking animatedly as they jogged along in tracksuits.

Mindless, breathless, she ran until she reached her bicycle. She was about to mount it, rather haphazardly, because she was shaking so much, when she saw Bob.

"Bob," she croaked weakly on a joyful note, then again, more strongly, "Bob!"

She dropped her bicycle and ran along the grass verge towards him, suddenly realising he was not alone. She stopped. In the first moment of incredulous relief, she had only been aware of him, now she saw he was holding the hand of a girl, that same girl who, earlier in the evening, had been sitting in his mother's dining-room, watching Victoria with such interest. Victoria paused for a moment, then spun round and ran back to her bicycle.

"Vicky, wait! Come back!" Bob called, dropping his companion's hand and running after her. But she was away, cycling along the coast road as if pursued by the hounds of hell.

She could not face him in someone else's company, not after what had happened. There was only one thing to be done: return home like a wounded animal to hide.

Monica met her in the hall.

"Where have you been?" she greeted her as she entered. "Not to your grandfather's, I hope. I told you not to go." Then she noticed how upset the child looked. "Victoria, you have been there, haven't you? Is it bad news? Is he dead?"

Mutely, Victoria shook her head.

"What is it then? You're limping and you look a mess."

"I've twisted my ankle a bit. It will be all right, Mum, really. I fell off my bike, but I've only a few bruises, nothing much. I'll have a bath and go to bed. I feel a bit tired and shaky."

"Tired? Exhausted, more like it! You should have stayed in this evening. You look positively washed out. Are you sure you feel well? Perhaps you have hurt yourself more than you realised at the time."

"No, I'm all right, honestly, just bruised and shaken. I'll go up now."

She edged past her mother with a reassuring smile, which was too tremulous to be convincing.

Monica watched her go upstairs, noticing the dirt on the back of her cardigan and shorts. When she reached the landing she called,

"I'll bring you up a hot drink when you're in bed."

"Thank you," Victoria answered, thankful to have got away so easily.

Once in her room, she sank onto the bed, shivering and shaking as if she had a fever. What would have happened to her if the joggers and their dog had not come along? She must not let her imagination dwell on that, it was bad enough recalling what had happened. The man's expression haunted her, it had been so cold and fixed. He had looked at her as if she were an object, not a human being, and now that was exactly what she felt like—a dirty object. She jumped to her feet, tearing her clothes off and dropping them on the floor. Wrapping herself in her towelling robe, she went to take her bath, transforming it into a ritual cleansing, a scrubbing and lathering with soap and water with which she endeavoured to purify not only her flesh, but her innermost being.

Why do I feel guilty? she kept asking herself. What have I done?

After her bath and hot drink, and the effort of once more getting rid of her over-anxious mother, she lay in bed like a limp rag doll that was exhausted after a day of being played with, washed and dressed, combed and petted, laughed over and cried over, abused and discarded.

That morning—what an age ago that seemed!—Stephen had recognised the woman in Jill. There had been initial surprise, followed by a look of respect as he acknowledged the change in her. This evening, a stranger had, presumably, seen the woman in her and in his eyes there had been a look that had made her shrink with fear and self-loathing.

6

THE following morning Victoria paid another brief visit to Grande Maison, this time with her mother's consent. There was no apparent change in her grandfather's condition and she returned home feeling even more depressed, ready to mope in her room for the rest of the day, listening to her least favourite records. She had just lain down on her narrow bed, with her face to the wall, when the first out-dated pop song was unceremoniously interrupted by the entrance of her cousin Helen, who gave the door a perfunctory knock after opening it.

"Aunty Monica said I should find you here. What's up? Aren't you well?"

Victoria rolled over and sat up, making the excuse that she had a slight headache.

"I'm not surprised," answered her unsympathetic cousin, "listening to that row. Whatever possessed you to buy it in the first place?"

Victoria switched off the record player.

"I used to like it," she said, defensively.

"Oh, I see, a form of masochism," Helen grinned, sitting down beside her and examining the pile of records, one by one.

"When I feel miserable, I read poetry. That really makes me feel suicidal. It doesn't seem to matter what it is—sometimes I don't even understand it."

She dropped the records on the bed as she read their titles. When she came to the last one, she said,

"I can't stay long. I came to ask you to play tennis this afternoon. Honestly, if Aunty Monica would get the 'phone put in, it would save all this flogging backwards and forwards. It's a bit hot for tennis, isn't it. Still, it's all arranged, the usual lot you know. Will you come?"

"I don't think so," Victoria answered. "I don't much feel like tennis." She knew, even as she uttered the words, that she should have given a decisive no. Helen, like her mother Margaret, was used to making up other people's minds for them. She positively revelled in it, seeing it as some sort of challenge.

Now she surveyed Victoria critically, her head tilted to one side.

"You do look a bit peaky. Not that you ever have much colour, so it's difficult to tell."

It was true. Victoria had often wished that she had the same complexion as her more robust cousins, all of whom, with the exception of the one beside her now, were typical of the Le Feuvre family, good looking brunettes with deep brown eyes. Helen, although tall and thin like her mother, with the same long, slender neck, had the light brown hair and blue eyes of her father. Victoria, very fair of hair and skin with grey eyes, felt colourless in more ways than one beside the other five.

Monica called upstairs, "Lunch is ready, Victoria. Are you staying, Helen?"

"What is it?" Helen asked in a low voice.

"Vegetable soup, cold meat and salad," Victoria answered; smiling slightly at Helen's expression.

"No thanks, Aunty. Mother's expecting me," Helen called back, then to Victoria, "You seem to be on a perpetual diet in this house. I need fattening up, everyone says so." It was a comforting thought. She stood up.

"Look, if you don't feel like playing, you could umpire, or just watch and pour lemonade. It's not much fun staying in the house on a day like this. It certainly wouldn't get rid of my headaches. See how you feel after lunch. Much better, I expect, I usually do after I've eaten." She sounded cheerfully confident.

They went downstairs together, Victoria feeling mildly surprised that Helen had not been more pressing. Obviously they must be expecting an even number without her, in which case why had she troubled to come?

"Well, have you managed to persuade her?" Monica asked, as they entered the kitchen.

Oh, I see, thought Victoria. Helen's big gun, yet to be fired.

"Almost," Helen answered with confidence. "She's going to see how she feels after lunch."

"You'll be able to wear your new tennis dress," Monica encouraged her daughter brightly, setting her bowl of soup on the table.

An hour later, Monica discovered her in the living-room, engrossed in a novel. In fact, although her eyes were on the print, her mind was elsewhere, on the lonely dunes.

"I thought you were going to play tennis!"

"I don't want to go."

"Why not, for goodness sake?"

"I just don't, that's all."

"Do you still feel unwell? Is your ankle hurting you?"

"Yes, a little," Victoria admitted. "All I need to do is rest it for a couple of days."

"But Victoria, it's such a lovely day. It seems such a shame to spend it indoors. Why don't you go and watch? I know you feel unhappy about your grandfather. If you were with the others, it would take your mind off him a little."

"Very well, Mum." Victoria dutifully shut the book. It was useless to argue half-heartedly. She had learnt that it was strategic to surrender in skirmishes in order to win the more important battles, when the unpleasantness to be suffered in the fight would be judged to be greatly outweighed by the spoils of victory.

"Put on your tennis dress," Monica encouraged her. "I want to see what it looks like now I've finished it and you might as well wear it, even if you don't play."

When Victoria returned downstairs, a trifle sulky, her mother greeted her with a fond, exasperated smile. She had only completed the dress two days before, cleverly cutting it from a remnant of linen that had been a bargain. With ingenuity and industry, she managed to keep Victoria as smartly dressed as her cousins, albeit with a more restricted wardrobe.

"It's very nice, Mum, thanks," Victoria said.

"You don't need that cardigan, surely?"

"I may stay there for a while this evening," Victoria explained.

"Well, take it off now. I can't see the dress properly."

Victoria opened the cardigan, holding the fronts stretched out, and pirouetted round so that the short skirt flared out becomingly. Her mother was satisfied. A few minutes later she left on her bicycle, the novel in her saddle bag. She found she could not put much pressure on her right ankle, it was even more painful than when she had gone to Grande Maison that morning, so she made up for it by pushing harder with her left. Obviously her mother's constant worry about her health did not encompass wonky ankles, or she would not have been so insistent on her going. She wondered just what it did encompass, as she had rarely been ill in her life, except with the usual childhood complaints of chicken-pox, measles and tonsillitis, none of which had been very severe and to which Monica had reacted with judicious sympathy but no undue concern.

When Victoria was passing the front door of her cousins' home, the telephone was ringing. She was going to ignore it and cycle on to the tennis court; then, remembering that Mrs. Figgus was partially deaf, she paused, listening to it, and as it remained unanswered she reluctantly obeyed its insistent summons and opened the front door, stepping into the hall. It was beautiful, as was the whole house; Victoria acknowledged it every time she saw it. Larry de Valois was an architect rapidly acquiring an international reputation, so perhaps it was not surprising that his house was out of the ordinary, but it was his wife's consummate good taste that had turned the handsome shell into an elegant home. The fabrics were gorgeous, the gleaming furniture mirrored the strategically placed objects of rarity and antiquity. On the walls were pictures of all kinds, some of them by relatively unknown artists patronised by Larry de Valois because his wife admired their work.

To the left of the sun-drenched hall, an open-tread wooden staircase swept upwards in a gentle curve to a first-floor balcony. Halfway up the stairs, one hand on the ledge of a tall narrow, stained-glass window, the other held out towards the 'phone in a gesture of apparent supplication, rather like a heroine in a melodrama, stood the elegant lady of the house, as yet unaware of the presence of her niece.

The telephone went on ringing. Margaret remained motionless. Victoria stared up at her in wonderment. At last, stepping forward from the recessed door, she asked,

"Shall I answer it?" and it stopped ringing.

Margaret snapped out of her peculiar trance, but whether as a result of the question or the cessation of ringing, Victoria could not guess. Her aunt descended the staircase slowly, very upright, her loose dress of fine pale-green lawn billowing about her tall, thin figure, a peculiar half-smile of triumph lighting her dark eyes.

"I'll join the others," Victoria said, feeling distinctly uncomfortable.

"Yes, do, dear," Margaret said in her normal brisk manner, giving herself a mental shake. "Go through the kitchen. I think Mrs. Figgus has made some lemonade you can carry out."

Annie Figgus was busy at the stainless steel sink. On the marble-topped working surface near her was a tray upon which stood two tall jugs of lemonade, frosted with ice cubes, an assortment of plastic beakers and a tin of home-made biscuits. Victoria asked her in a loud voice if she should carry the tray into the garden. Mrs. Figgus turned round with a beaming smile of welcome.

"I hope I've made enough," she said.

"You are likely to be a thirsty lot on such a hot afternoon. You would have been better off on the beach."

"We spent yesterday on the beach. Tennis is a change."

"Young people always want a change," Mrs. Figgus remarked good-humouredly. "They are never satisfied. How is your mother, Victoria?"

"Very well, thank you, but my grandfather isn't, he's very ill."

Mrs. Figgus was instantly full of sympathy.

"Oh, I'm sorry to hear that."

She was fond of the girl. A thoughtful, sensitive little thing, always careful to speak loudly enough so that she could hear. It was one of her employer's failings, as far as Mrs. Figgus was concerned, that she did not like to raise her well-modulated voice. Margaret had rarely needed to do so to her children, only when either distance or danger made it absolutely imperative; for chastisement a look was usually enough, the ultimate deterrent being a softly spoken rebuke carrying an underlying threat of her mounting displeasure. It was Margaret de Valois' secret opinion, guessed and thoroughly resented by her housekeeper, that Mrs. Figgus' infirmity was selective; that in fact she could hear well enough when anyone but her employer spoke to her, as well as those things not intended for her ears. This was unkind. Margaret could be unkind, but only in her opinions, never in her actions. Mrs. Figgus was not fond of her, but she respected her. Her devotion she lavished upon Mr. de Valois and his three girls, for she had no one of her own. Her husband had been killed in an accident during her early years of service in the family. She had no children, although a more motherly looking woman it would be difficult to find. She was tall and buxom, with a benign expression on her round face, arising from contentment with her lot and satisfaction from a job conscientiously done. Upon her good management and excellent cuisine depended to a large extent Margaret's fine reputation as a hostess. In bolstering Margaret's image of herself as a perfect wife and mother, she was unwittingly making herself indispensable within the family circle and satisfying her own need to be needed.

Victoria left with the heavy tray. Mrs. Figgus held the door open for her, cautioning her to take care. She walked slowly across the lawn towards the tennis court, limping a little. She placed the tray upon a white metal table with a hole in the centre, through which protruded the shaft of a large, faded green sun-shade. On the court, Stephen, Bob, Raoul Bellinger and the boy twin Roy Bideau were playing a vigorous game, their enthusiasm, if not their prowess, boosted by the critical female audience consisting of Jill, Helen, Sandra and Prissy Bideau, sitting on a long wooden bench. They greeted the lemonade with cries of approval, shoving along to make room for Victoria.

"Good," said Helen, "now we can have a girls' double without Sandra."

"But that's not fair," protested Sandra crossly. "Vicky has only just arrived. It's my turn to play."

Victoria hurriedly interrupted. "You can play, Sandra. I've only come to watch."

"Then why are you wearing your tennis dress?" demanded a suspicious Sandra.

"To keep mother quiet."

"If you could cycle all the way here, you must feel fit enough to play," Helen persisted, eyeing her critically. Victoria's hair was sticking in damp tendrils to her forehead and her cheeks were slightly flushed, which was unusual.

"You wouldn't feel so warm if you took off your cardigan," was Helen's considered opinion.

Victoria's cheeks became even pinker. She went to the table to pour some lemonade.

"Are you going to play or not?" Helen called.

"No," Victoria answered.

The boys finished their game. They poured themselves drinks and lay on the grass, exhausted. When the four girls went onto the court, Bob joined Victoria on the bench.

"Why did you run away last night?" he asked her reproachfully. "What on earth were you doing out there on your own in the first place? I thought you must have been here, but Jill said you didn't visit them." His dark eyes watched her face for the truth, so that she was obliged to look away to conceal the fact that he was not going to hear it. Unfortunately it was a trick that Bob knew too well.

She said lightly, "I suddenly remembered I'd promised mother to be home early."

"It was already late, nearly ten, wasn't it? Where were you going?"

"Just for a ride."

"Honestly, Vicky, am I supposed to believe that?"

"Does it matter?" she asked in a weary tone, turning her wide grey eyes upon his at last.

"Something was the matter last night. One minute you looked pleased to see us, the next you were running away as if you'd gone crazy."

"I'd been to Grande Maison. I was upset. I wanted to be on my own."

"I see," he said, accepting this explanation, but he knew she had been looking for him, his mother had told him she had asked where he was.

"You didn't have to run away, Vicky," he scolded her gently, wondering why he always felt so responsible for her. After a few minutes of watching the game, he tried again.

"Mr. Lacy is very ill, then?"

"Yes. He's dying," she said quietly, almost matter-of-factly.

That was enough to account for last night. He knew how much she loved her grandfather. She sounded as if she was growing reconciled to the thought of losing him now. It still hurt that she had turned from him. He could not remember a time when he had not been the friend to whom she had confided her small anxieties and miseries. He supposed it was bound to happen sooner or later. He had noticed that their relationship was changing, although he could not tell in what way. He surmised it was because, as they were getting older, their interests were growing wider and further apart, diverging from the family circle. He was called by the other boys to settle a point of difference. He gave her a parting look conveying that he was not wholly satisfied. She pressed her lips together firmly, vowing to keep her sordid secret.

The afternoon wore on towards tea.

Raoul and the Bideau twins left for home. Stephen went indoors to telephone his mother. Victoria poured herself more lemonade from a replenished jug and fetched her book from her saddle-bag. When she returned, the last game, Helen and Sandra versus Jill and Bob, was just starting. She lay down on the grass with her drink and book. She had firmly resisted all attempts to get her to play, but had willingly kept score and given her opinion on all line disputes—an opinion that was by no means treated as decisive, it depended who was considered at fault. She had even retrieved the occasional ball that had sailed out of court into the herbaceous borders.

The game had been going about ten minutes when Larry de Valois approached. He greeted them all in his usual charming manner, to which they all responded warmly, his youngest daughter being particularly delighted to see him. She bounded across the court with all the exuberance of her thirteen years to tell him how she and Stephen had beaten the Bideau twins.

"Well done, darling," her father said

approvingly, smiling at her excited enthusiasm.

"Will you have a game with me, Daddy?" she implored.

"Another time. I particularly want a quiet word with Jill."

Sandra pouted prettily with disappointment. Her father tweaked her nose gently through the wire netting, against which she had pressed to be nearer him.

Jill had heard him. She left the court, handing her racquet to Victoria with the request that she take her place. Then she walked beside her father towards the trees at the side of the garden, wondering what on earth he was going to say.

Victoria, reluctantly, joined Bob on the court.

"Now we stand more chance of winning," Helen said to Sandra with satisfaction.

Bob winked at his new partner and Victoria was determined not to let him down. When it was her turn to serve, she peeled off her cardigan and threw it to the back of the court, tucking her long fair hair behind her ears to keep it from her eyes.

Enjoying herself in the fierce competition of the first few games, she ignored the occasional twinge from her ankle, but having landed heavily on it a few times, it began to give her more trouble and she could not help but favour it. In the end Sandra's energetic determination, coupled with Helen's cool expertise, won the match, for Victoria was of little help to Bob, being unable to move swiftly enough to intercept anything at a distance. As they left the court, Bob lightly caught hold of her arm, raising it for a closer inspection.

"Did you receive these at the same time as you hurt your ankle, Vicky?"

She pulled her arm away, blushing scarlet, limping back to retrieve her cardigan from the ground. He waited for her.

"I fell off my bike," she said.

"Was that before or after you saw me?"

"Before, I think. Oh yes, it was, I remember."

"Those bruises make an odd pattern, don't they? Almost like a hand grip, spaced like that."

She did not answer.

"When I asked you why you turned and

ran away last night, you gave me an accusing look. Why?" He stopped, detaining her by holding her elbow.

"You acted like someone in a blind panic. Had something frightened you? Someone, perhaps?" There was a pause, then he added wistfully, "I wish you would say something, Vicky."

When she remained mute and miserable, he turned from her in exasperation, swiping at a lavender bush with his racquet. Although she had said nothing to make him think so, he had the feeling that in some obscure manner he had failed her and it made him angry.

7

THEY had tea in the glass extension to the drawing-room. This was the favourite place for all meals during the warm weather. With the patio doors wide open, it was as pleasant as eating in the garden, with none of the inconvenience. When they did venture onto the terrace, Sandra spent most of the meal leaping around, screaming about wasps and daddy-long-legs, two things she feared even more than her mother's displeasure.

As Jill and her father approached across the lawn, they could see Margaret, half-turned from them, pouring tea at a long, low table. They were walking in silence, both feeling that there was nothing more to be said, both wondering if perhaps they had said too much already. As they slipped into the room, Margaret turned towards them and gave a start of surprise on seeing her husband.

"Larry! But I thought . . ." she began,

then catching her daughter's eye, she looked uncomfortable and fell silent.

"What did you think, dear?" he asked, kissing her lightly on the cheek as he accepted a cup of tea.

"Well, there was a 'phone call earlier and I thought . . ." again her voice trailed off. It had been about the time he often 'phoned to say he would not be in for dinner. She was now ashamed that she had reacted so irrationally; as if not answering the 'phone would bring him home. As it was, he had arrived even earlier than expected—most unusual.

"I'll just go and tidy up," Jill said.

"Are the others coming in for tea?" her mother asked.

"No, they're still playing, but I should love some." She left the room.

Margaret always had tea accompanied by sandwiches and biscuits at five o'clock, mainly for the benefit of the children, who found it a long wait until dinner at seven-thirty, especially after a day at school. She ate very little then herself, but was always grateful for a cup of tea.

When Jill returned she found her parents in animated conversation, discussing a small improvement to the house. Margaret was happy and vivacious, very different from her usual cool, reserved manner. It was always the same, Jill thought ruefully; her father had that effect upon women of all ages, even those in his own family. The change he wrought in his wife Jill always found strangely pathetic. She hated to see her mother so vulnerable. When Larry de Valois conversed with people, he gave them the benefit of his full attention. They were flattered by his good looks and perfect manners into believing they must be special. It was marvellous that he should still have that effect upon his wife after twenty years of marriage. Margaret was at her wittiest and prettiest in his company, cold and snappy when his work kept him from her, which was frequently the case, for he travelled a lot to London and Paris. She was ambitious for him and might have loved him less had he been a failure, yet she resented the demands that success made upon his time and attention. Her daughters existed on the periphery of her life with her husband; they knew it and grudgingly accepted it, basking in the warmth of her personality when their father was present, keeping out of her way as much as possible during his absence. It made them almost as jealous of his company as she was.

Now Margaret was laughing gaily at something he had said. Larry caught Jill's eyes upon him and, giving her a small smile, turned to his wife and said,

"Jill no longer wants to come into the office, darling."

Margaret's expression changed dramatically to one of astonishment.

"Really? What changed her mind?" she asked coldly, looking at her daughter. "I considered the matter settled."

"The more I thought about it, the less keen I became," Jill answered lamely, avoiding her father's eyes. "I've decided to do something else."

"What, for instance? Don't tell me that after all this time you have seen sense about going to university!"

Jill sighed. "No, mother, not university. It would be difficult now, anyway, having turned down the offers."

"You could go next year and fill in the time by working for your father."

"No, mother," Jill said again. "I'm definitely not going to university, even supposing I get the necessary 'A' level results, and I don't think working for Dad would suit me."

Margaret sniffed contemptuously, "Not suit you indeed. Madam, you are very hard to please. Many girls would give anything for the opportunity. Jobs are few and far between as you well know. Frankly, Jill, I'm amazed at your stubbornness over this, I just cannot understand you. It would help if you gave me some reasons, but no, you seem determined to waste an excellent education, expensive, too, I might remind you, and a good brain for some absurd notion which no one can possibly guess. You promised your father that you would train to take over when Miss James leaves. It's not fair to let him down."

Jill looked at her father.

"It's perfectly all right, Margaret. After all, Miss James is not leaving for another year, which gives me plenty of time to find someone with experience."

His wife turned on him. "You sound as if that is what you would prefer to do."

"Not at all, dear," he mollified her, avoiding his daughter's look of discomfort.

"So that is what you have been discussing in the garden," Margaret said, recalling their entrance together. That could also account for his being home at this unprecedented hour. She sat still for a few moments, watching Jill with a puzzled expression in her dark eyes, then she shook her head, as if acknowledging the incomprehensibility of the whole situation and switched her attention to Stephen, who had just come in.

"Are you staying to dinner, Stephen?" she asked him.

"No thanks, Aunt. As soon as Bob has finished this game, we must go."

"I thought perhaps it would help Merle if you both stayed here."

"Actually, I've just 'phoned her and she's rather anxious for us to get back."

"Oh, very well," Margaret said, wondering why, but knowing better than to question him.

Later that evening, soon after dinner, Jill asked Victoria up to her room to listen to her latest record. They played it through twice, then Jill switched it off and said, "Dad doesn't want me in his office, you know."

"Did he say so?"

Jill sat before her dressing table and began languidly combing her dark curls.

"Not exactly, but I can tell. You see it was mother's idea in the first place. What isn't? As soon as she realised that Miss James would be retiring next year and that I had no intention of going to university, she started scheming to get me into the office. Dad didn't say anything against the idea but, come to think of it, he didn't say much for it, either. Anyway, Mum kept going on about it and, as it suited me well enough, I considered it settled. Imagine my surprise this afternoon when he asked me if I still wanted the job. He suggested that I probably need more time to think about it, as it had been mother's idea and not my own. Then he began suggesting things I might like to do better, such as nursing, or teaching. He also asked me again why I am so dead set against going to university."

"Why are you?" Victoria asked, as puzzled as everyone else.

Jill looked round at her and laughed.

"Et tu, Brute?" She considered for a few moments, then said,

"I'll tell you, Vicky, on condition that you keep it a secret."

Victoria promised. Jill was satisfied. She crossed over to the window, looking over the garden and the cliffs beyond to the sea, sparkling beneath the low evening sun. She wished she could see into the future as clearly. Victoria, sitting on the edge of her bed, watched her patiently. It was not often that Jill shared a confidence and her younger cousin and fervent admirer felt very privileged.

Suddenly Jill turned, asking, "Do you know what you want to do when you leave school, Vicky?" and when Victoria shook her head, forgetful of her wish the night before to be a nurse, she said, "Well, I do. I've known for ages. I have one ambition—if you can call it that, mother certainly would not. I want to get married." She paused, anticipating a strong reaction from her listener. Victoria just returned her look solemnly.

"Well?" Jill demanded, disappointed.

"I still don't see why it should make any difference to going to university."

"I'll tell you why," Jill said, sitting down beside her on the bed. "I want to remain here on the island, until the man I love returns to it. When he thinks about home, I want him to think of me as part of it. I don't want to be educated up to the eye-balls just for the sake of it. If that makes me unique, so what! I'm sick of conforming. I know I'm intelligent. I expect to get good 'A' level results. I'm not modest. This last year I've grown fed up with people telling me how clever I am and what I must do because of it, remain a student for as long as possible and hope I'll be able to get a job at the end of it. Until a few hours ago I was confident about the immediate future; now that it's obvious Dad doesn't want me in the office, I'm not so sure."

"Plans for the future always make me feel apprehensive," Victoria confessed.

"That's because you're a little pessimist. I'm not. I always plan on the basic assumption that I can make things turn out the way I want them, if only I'm determined enough. Unfortunately this plan involves someone else. If one of the men I love doesn't want me, perhaps the other won't either."

The two girls sat in doleful silence for a while, then Victoria said comfortingly,

"I shouldn't worry too much, if I were you. Your father may not be too keen to have you in the office, but your mother obviously still thinks it's a good idea."

They digested this for a few moments, then they looked at one another and burst into laughter.

"Could I take the job, knowing he had been coerced into having me?" Jill asked, becoming serious again.

"I think you could," Victoria told her quietly. "You would make him a good secretary and his reasons for not wanting you may be trivial compared with your grand plans for matrimony. Anyway, in my opinion, it's not you he doesn't want in the office, it's your mother's proxy."

Jill looked at her cousin in amazement.

"Do you know, you could be right. Mum would certainly like to be with him every minute of the day. I suppose I'm the next best thing. Well, I'll be as cool and efficient as Miss James and as discreet. I'll do my best to keep mother out of that part of his life. That will certainly please Alex Stuart. Do you know, Mum would eat Dad, if it were socially acceptable." A ludicrous idea which started them laughing again.

8

IT was Saturday when Merle received the telephone call from Albinia Lacy.

It was early. She was in the middle of getting the breakfast. Saturday morning was a hectic time at the Bienvenues'. It was when Merle bade farewell to one lot of guests, while preparing to greet another. Noon was the deadline. By that time even the most reluctant had been ushered into taxis for the harbour or airport.

Doreen worked like a slave, unobtrusively clearing bedrooms and changing linen whilst the erstwhile occupants were in the bathroom or downstairs swallowing travelling pills with their coffee. By noon, all vestige of the personalities who had been temporarily inhabiting the house, cluttering it with their possessions and conversation—mainly trivial social chat about the scenery and weather—had been obliterated. Windows open wide, so that even the air might be changed, the house waited in ordered cleanliness to be annexed anew.

Victoria arrived early to collect a bunch of flowers which her aunt had promised for her next visit to Grande Maison. Merle was grilling bacon, frying eggs and making coffee. She waved a hand towards the conservatory, where a gorgeous bunch of flowers lay loosely tied with string upon a dusty shelf. Victoria went to collect them. They were wet with the morning dew. She gathered them up, cradling them in her arms, intoxicated by their moist, fresh scent, smiling over them at her aunt through the kitchen window, immensely grateful that, busy and preoccupied as she was, she had taken the trouble to pick them. There were carnations, asters, dahlias, sweet williams, love-in-the-mist and sweet peas, all bundled together with generous abandon. It occurred to Victoria that Uncle Karl might not have approved of such wholesale rape of his beloved garden. Merle winked at her, guessing her thoughts. Perhaps she felt it served him right for going off and worrying her half to death.

The telephone rang. Victoria went into

the kitchen expecting to be told to answer it, but Merle was in that state of rush and panic when it seems easiest to do everything oneself. She pulled a pan from the heat and hurried away. Victoria followed slowly, just to say goodbye and thank you.

Merle picked up the receiver in the hall with a worried expression on her face, a churning in her stomach, dreading that it was either the police or the hospital, as she always did when Karl was absent.

"Oh, it's you, Albinia," she said, relief flooding through her.

Victoria knew immediately that her grandfather was dead. Not waiting for confirmation, she hurried away to give vent to her distress in private, as was her way; her mother's happiness rested too firmly on her own for her ever to feel free to indulge openly in tears.

Merle hastened back to the kitchen with the bad news, but after a quick glance along the length of the empty conservatory, she forgot about it for a while as empty cereal plates were returned and it was time to serve the bacon and eggs.

Half-an-hour later, breakfast was over,

Stephen and Bob returned from a long fishing trip. Merle greeted their arrival thankfully, imparting the sad news.

"Victoria was here when Albinia Lacy 'phoned and I think she must have overheard. She disappeared without saying a word. I'm rather anxious about her, you know what a sensitive little thing she is and she loved her grandfather dearly. She probably went home, but I should like to be sure. One of you must go along to Monica after you have eaten."

"I'll go," Bob offered. "Put the coffee on, Steve, I shan't be a minute." He dropped his canvas fishing bag onto the floor and went back into the lobby, quietly shutting the kitchen door behind him. The long, narrow passage, lit by two small fanlights at either end, was dim on the brightest days. Today the sky was overcast with threatening rain clouds, intensifying the gloom. Bob took a few steps towards the back door, calling softly,

"Vicky?" There was no answer. "Mother wants you."

Victoria reluctantly emerged from amongst the clutter of winter coats and mackintoshes hanging on pegs along the wall, head bent, her face buried in the mass of flowers she was still clutching. Bob put his arms around her, holding her tightly for a few moments before leading her back into the warmth of the kitchen, away from her childhood retreat, where she had escaped when her cousins' unthinking cruelty had driven her to seek a refuge in which she could shed the tears that would have provoked derision.

"There you are," Merle said, slightly exasperated. "Pour her some coffee, Stephen, then you can drive her home."

Stephen was at the cooker, grilling bacon and sausages. He gave Victoria a sympathetic look.

"I thought Dad had the car," Bob said.

"I found it last night at one of his favourite haunts," his brother told him. "Unfortunately the bird had flown. I shouldn't be surprised if he turns up today. He will have spent all his money by now and be spongeing on his so-called friends. This time, Mum, it was partly your fault. I told you to hide the cash more efficiently."

Merle had just finished the washing-up. She dried her hands, poured herself some coffee and sat down. Over her cup, she said wearily,

"It's no good putting it where he will never find it."

"What kind of logic is that?" Stephen demanded.

She tried to explain. "When the urge is on him, he will get money one way or another. You simply don't understand, dear. Better that he takes it from me than from someone else."

"Good God, Mum, are you saying that he would actually go out and steal it?" Stephen asked incredulously, his cooking forgotten.

She answered him dispassionately. "When the craving is on him, he is tormented. Pity him, son."

There was no answer. Stephen turned the sausages in the pan.

Victoria, her own misery blunted as she witnessed theirs, placed the crushed flowers on the table and sipped her coffee. Stephen divided the food between two plates and handed one to Bob. The boys ate in hungry silence. She felt sorry for them. Death had taken her grandfather from her, but death, particularly in the elderly, one had to accept, however grievous. Subconsciously one knew this, even while crying out against it. Something else was taking the boys' father from them and, because they could see a remedy, they would never reconcile themselves to it. Salvation, they reasoned, lay in his own will to be saved; destruction lay in his lack of it. Whereas Victoria could weep and find ultimate solace, their sorrow held too much bitterness for tears and, in Stephen's case, humiliation. He despised his father. Proud and reserved, with a spartan side to his nature which he deliberately fostered as a safeguard against weakness, he was unable to comprehend his father's sickness and could not forgive what he considered a moral laxity. It was a shame that he could not continue to love him with tolerance and compassion, as Bob did, nor yet with resignation and despair, as Merle did. His father's behaviour, the frequent avowals of good resolution, the subterfuge and subsequent degradation, following as surely as night followed dawn's promise of day, was eating away at the fabric of the family. It was an ever-present shadow, lying across the hearth.

9

FOUR days later, Theodore Lacy was buried. There were not many people at the funeral. The last twenty years of his life had been too reclusive to retain friends of his youth and business life. There were two friends of his late wife, accompanied by their husbands and attending more from respect and curiosity than any sense of sorrow, their thoughts dwelling with Charmian Lacy in a past that included themselves.

Raoul's parents were there, Fiona and Richard Bellinger. The latter was the family solicitor, an acquaintance of long standing, his father having been a close friend of the deceased. Richard was the same age as Albinia and there had once been hope, overt on the parents' side, deep-hidden in the recesses of Albinia's mind, that the two would marry. That she would hardly have been his choice was apparent from the woman who now clung to Richard's arm. Small and pretty, with light blue eyes and wispy fair hair like a child's, Fiona was the antithesis of Albinia, both in looks and personality. Her light, scatty manner was in contrast to the firm decisiveness of Albinia's. Now her tears of sympathy overflowed for mourners she hardly knew, while the chief amongst them stood tall and unbending. Albinia had never clung to anyone's arm in her life; her fine hazel eyes were quite dry, there was not a hair out of place from its well brushed smoothness and her expression was one of calm rectitude.

Richard Bellinger considered, as he faced her across the open grave, how difficult it was to offer sympathy to one so self-contained, how impossible it would have been ever to have offered love. He patted the hand, resting so comfortingly upon his arm and the small figure reacted instantly by moving even closer to his side. Life had not been kind to Albinia Lacy, he was the first to acknowledge that; losing her mother when she was sixteen and her brother just six, then Leonard dying when he was twenty-seven. She was a civil servant, dedicated to her work, but apart from that her life had included little beyond her ailing father and her niece, Victoria—not enough for a woman, in Richard's opinion. At least now she was free to rise to the surface of her turgid existence, her father's frail arms no longer locked possessively around her proud neck. Was it too late for her to make something of her life? Would she want to? Mr. Lacy had left everything to Victoria, even the house, ultimately. Was she aware of that? Of course she would have the use of it for the rest of her life, but it curtailed her freedom. She might well have planned to sell the monstrosity and move into something smaller and more practical.

Standing next to Albinia were the three Le Feuvre girls. Richard Bellinger still thought of them as that, they seemed to exist as an entity; so alike in looks, if unlike in stature, uncannily intimate. First Monica, the youngest and least attractive of the three but well-looking for all that, of medium height and thin like her eldest sister. She was dressed in black, which was unbecoming to her sallow complexion, a mistake Margaret would never have made. A fine woman, Margaret, tall, regal in bearing, always elegantly, often unusually, dressed. Other women envied her sense of fashion. Today she was in dove grey, a mauve hat on her head, a silk scarf in gradated shades of mauve about her long, slender throat. Last was Merle, the middle one in years, the shortest and prettiest, plump with smiling eyes looking upon the world with a little more kindliness and tolerance than her sisters. Not that she was smiling today, far from it. She looked tired and preoccupied. Around the sisters were gathered their offspring, friends of Raoul's and well-known to Richard and his wife. It was strange that neither Merle nor Margaret had their husbands with them. He wondered why that should be. He had heard rumours concerning both of them, gossip to which he had paid little heed, but their absence gave some credence to it. In his opinion their place was by the side of their wives on such occasions. Heaven forfend a time when Fiona should stand alone at a graveside to weep uncomforted! The fact that, while his wife wept, Margaret and Merle remained dry-eyed throughout the service, he counted as irrelevant.

As the mourners were leaving, treading

carefully on the grass around the heaped earth and laid-out row of wreaths, as if fearful of waking the dead, he noticed a strange little incident, something to ponder over later. He glanced back at the graveside and saw that Monica Lacy was still standing there, head bent as if bowed with grief, a touching sight in a mere daughter-in-law and, he had to admit, unexpected. Victoria, walking with her cousins, suddenly realised her mother had not moved and went back for her, apparently persuading her to come away, gently pulling at her arm. For one wild moment he thought Monica was about to cast herself onto the coffin as her slender form swayed forward, her head bending lower, but she recovered herself and, with a shrug of her shoulders, the meaning of which he was at a loss to interpret, followed Victoria along the path to the cars that were waiting to carry them to Grande Maison.

In fact, Monica had heard a voice, Theodore Lacy's voice from the grave, admonishing her to take care of his beloved Victoria, or she would have to answer to him for the consequences of neglect.

Common sense told her that she had imagined it. It was not the voice itself, but her inexplicable capacity to imagine such an outrageous thing that was to haunt her for months with fears for her sanity. Why he should have said such a thing in the first place puzzled her. She had been dwelling on his words ever since, hence the reiteration today from her subconscious. She remained subdued for the remainder of the day; even the reading of the will which made her daughter an heiress failed to animate her. This had not been a formal affair. Richard had unobtrusively taken the beneficiaries into the library—Albinia, Monica, Victoria and Mrs. Grey—while the rest of the assembly tucked into tea, sandwiches and cakes which had been set out in the drawing-room. There were small bequests to Monica and Mrs. Grey, a slightly larger one to Albinia, considered by her father to be rich enough already, and the bulk of the money was to be put in trust until Victoria reached twenty-one. Why not eighteen? Monica wondered. Richard had asked that, but the old man had never become reconciled to this modern notion of young people coming of age so early. In fact, but for Richard's persuasion, he would have made Victoria, as a female, wait until she was twenty-five.

It was the first time that Monica's sisters, and their children had set foot in Grande Maison. They were impressed and depressed; it had that effect upon people. As she munched on a salmon and cucumber sandwich, Merle considered what an excellent small hotel it would make. Set in such large grounds it had definite possibilities, but of course it would need extensive modernising.

Margaret, idling around the room, a cup of tea in her hand, abhorred the wall-paper and furnishings—dreary beyond belief. There were ghastly pictures on the walls and the furniture was ugly, although some of it was worth a lot of money. She longed to scour the room until it became a clean, empty shell and start again upon it, giving prominence to the handsome fireplace and intricate plaster mouldings on the ceiling. Had the house belonged to anyone else but Albinia Lacy, she would have asked for a tour of it, curious to see what treasures it might hold, but she knew this request would be regarded as frivolous and intrusive. Margaret came to rest by Merle's chair.

"I suppose she will sell it," she whispered, presuming the house to be Albinia's now.

Merle nodded. "It's very grand, isn't it? I can understand Monica not being keen to visit the place. It should have had a large family living in it, not just an elderly recluse and his middle-aged daughter." She would have said more, but Fiona Bellinger approached to speak to them and soon after Monica and Victoria returned from the library.

"Will Albinia sell this house, do you think, Monica?" Margaret asked.

"She can't," her sister answered shortly, none too pleased, "it's in trust for Victoria."

"Good heavens!" Margaret said, her eyes upon her slight, unassuming niece, who from that moment was never to appear quite so insignificant to her again.

Albinia entered and came across the room to them.

"May I have a word with you, Monica? In the library again, if you don't mind."

When they were alone, she said, "I have a proposition to put to you. Please think it over carefully before you answer. Speak to Victoria and let me have your decision in a week or so, there's no hurry. It's this. I want you both to come and live at Grande Maison."

Monica opened her mouth to protest, horror-struck at the idea, but she was not given the opportunity, as Albinia hurried on.

"This house is huge, as you well know, far too big for one person to be comfortable in alone and far too expensive to run. It makes sense for the three of us to share it. It seems pointless for you to continue in that tiny little house when Victoria has this one. I know you wouldn't come when Leonard died. I don't know why, but that's your concern. I hope you will change your mind now. Sell your house and settle here."

"The house isn't mine," Monica said stiffly. "It belongs to me and my sisters." She resented hearing it described as a "tiny little house". It had been big enough for her parents and their three children. It was foolish of her sister-in-law to judge it against this edifice.

Albinia was undaunted.

"Speak to them about it, then. I'm sure they will see the sense of my proposal."

"But I should be without a home," Monica said involuntarily. "What I mean is, I should have nowhere of my own. I don't fancy living in someone else's home."

"Not even your daughter's? After all, it will be hers some day. I could say the same thing, if I wanted to be nice."

"It would be accepting charity," Monica complained.

"Nonsense! It's not as if you are destitute, Monica. You have the money that Leonard left you, presumably."

"That is for Victoria. I can't touch that."

"You have no need to worry about Victoria's future now, you have never had to. Her education is well provided for and in a few years she will be a wealthy young woman. Surely, just knowing you could buy a home of your own if you desired is enough to stifle even your pride."

Albinia opened the door.

"Think about it. See what Victoria says. Now we should get back to the people in the drawing-room. I particularly wish to speak to Dr. Raines. He has been so kind these last weeks. I don't know what I should have done without his advice."

10

THE day of the proposed trip to the small island dawned, shrouded in mist. According to the weather bureau, this would gradually clear, revealing a cloudless blue sky. But how soon? That was the important question. Should they postpone the trip until another day? Should they all go by motor boat ferry? The telephones between the respective houses were busy until such questions were resolved. The trip would go ahead as planned. Raoul, Stephen and Bob would sail across in the dinghy once the mist had lifted.

Margaret drove her daughters to the harbour, collecting Victoria on the way. The dithering about whether or not to go had made them late. Sandra was despatched along the path to fetch Victoria and explain the delay, for, having no telephone, she had been waiting in blissful, albeit impatient, ignorance and readiness. Monica stood at the door to wave goodbye.

On account of the mist it was cool and they were all wearing thick jumpers over their shirts and shorts. There was a cool atmosphere in the car also, nothing to do with the weather. Victoria sensed it as she got in. She judged it best to keep silent; however, Sandra, with the recklessness of extreme youth, spoke when her thoughts dictated.

"What time are we likely to get back? Not too late, I hope. Do you think we shall be back for seven-thirty?"

Jill, sitting beside her mother in the front, said that she thought it most likely.

"Why do you want to be back then?" Helen asked.

"Because there's a programme I want to see on the telly."

"How many times have I asked you not to use that word, Sandra?" Margaret enquired coldly.

"All my friends say it," Sandra said. "Their parents don't mind."

"I am not interested in what your friends say, nor in their parents' lack of concern. Please don't let me hear you say it again."

Helen and Sandra exchanged grins and

both said, "Telly", obligingly quietly so that it did not reach their mother's ears.

After a few minutes, Margaret said, "I wish I could just go off for the day." She was in a foul mood, because Larry was in Le Havre for four days on business.

"It must be wonderful to have nothing to do, no commitments, no work, no worries, no obligations, just the freedom to laze about and enjoy oneself. During my school holidays, I was expected to help in the house and do shopping before going out. You young people don't realise how privileged you are. At least when the time came to get a job, we were not afraid of the idea. Now youngsters seem to expect idleness to go on forever, subsided by their parents or the State."

Oh dear, thought Victoria, has Jill not yet made up her mind about the office? But apparently she had.

"It's not my fault, Mum, if Dad doesn't want me to start until September," Jill answered mildly.

"You might at least appear more eager when he talks about it," her mother said, then she turned her attention to Victoria.

"Has Monica decided whether to go to live at Grande Maison?"

"Not yet," Victoria admitted.

"I wish I had the chance," Helen sighed enviously. "It's so gloomy and romantic. Just the kind of house in which the heroine goes into a decline from unrequited love. She cries buckets of tears and gets thinner and thinner, yet still manages to look beautiful, even when she's lying in her coffin. When I cry, I look so ghastly that people lose sympathy."

They were now approaching the quayside. The mist was lifting a little and getting patchier. In another hour it would disappear. Margaret stopped the car opposite the steps leading down to the moored ferry boat. The girls got out and took their haversacks from the boot.

"I expect we'll be back about six," Jill told her mother.

"Very well," Margaret answered. "Have a good day," and she drove off.

"That means we'll have to get the bus home," moaned Helen.

The sea crossing from the busy harbour, crowded with small craft of every description, active with the summer traffic of visitors and cargo to and from the south coast mainland, took about twenty minutes. By the time they arrived on the small island the sun had broken through and was glinting on the water in a dancing pattern of brilliant light. As soon as they had trudged up the rough stone steps onto the narrow path, they pulled off their jumpers, tying them around their waists.

"Are we going to wait here until the boys arrive?" Helen asked.

"No," Jill said. "I thought we'd go round to the other side and find a secluded beach. Most of the trippers stay around here. We'll leave this path and cut across the middle."

"They may never find us," Sandra demurred.

"Too bad," said Jill, setting off in the wake of the other passengers. The rest followed her in silence. They continued for a while along the main path which circled the island, passing the one and only hotel and a handful of cottages, until they discovered a definite track winding up through the bracken to the island's summit. This they took, the sun's heat gaining strength as they climbed higher into the deepening blue of the sky.

"It's going to be a scorcher," Sandra said. "I hope we haven't got too much walking to do. I want to swim. Look at my feet, they're filthy." She held up one sandalled foot in disgust.

They were walking Indian file along the dusty track, Sandra in third place, followed by Victoria who was day-dreaming and bumped into her when she stopped, knocking her off balance into the bracken. As they waited for Sandra to get to her feet, Jill pointed out to sea. They turned and saw Raoul's boat about a third of the way across, making fair headway in the light breeze.

"Come on," urged Jill. "I agree with Sandra, a swim would be nice after this trek. We're nearly at the top, we'll soon slither down the other side."

They found a small deserted cove, with large rocks like stranded hulks on the sand. The chances were that in an hour or so many more people would have found their way there, but in the meantime, they were satisfied. They dumped their haversacks in the shade provided by one of the massive rocks and were soon cooling off in the sea, lazily swimming or casually floating, submitting ecstatically to the cool, intimate caress of the water on their languid bodies.

It was an hour and a half later when the dinghy appeared. Helen and Sandra ran to the water's edge to hail it, Jill and Victoria acknowledged its arrival with a mere look and returned to their books.

"I think they're cross," Victoria whispered a few minutes later, as the shouted conversation drifted back to them.

Jill only smiled. Victoria shut her book and sat up nervously.

"Why the hell didn't you say that you intended coming halfway round the bloody island?" Stephen was shouting.

"It was Jill's idea," Helen informed him, as the three boys towed the boat onto the beach.

He and Raoul strode across the sand to stand threateningly over the accused.

"Well?" Stephen demanded.

"You enjoyed the trip, didn't you?" she asked sweetly. "I thought that was the main attraction," she added, looking at Raoul.

"I enjoy other things besides sailing," he said with a grin. "Revenge is sweet." He bent down and grabbed her feet, Stephen took her shoulders and they carried her, resisting vigorously, to the sea, where, having attained a good depth, they dumped her, complete with sunglasses, holding her under a couple of seconds for good measure.

She came up gasping and furious. Stephen and Raoul made a quick getaway.

Bob said, "You asked for that," before diving to retrieve her sunglasses, which she snatched from his hand ungratefully. But she knew she had asked for it and by the time they had eaten their sandwiches and drunk their cokes, all was forgiven on both sides and tempers matched the sunshine.

They decided to explore the nearby cliffs.

"Oh, are you coming as well?" Jill asked Victoria in surprise as they got to their feet.

Victoria halted, uncertain now.

"Of course she is," Bob said, smiling at her.

"You don't usually," Helen told her. "You stay and read or sketch. If you come, there'll be nobody to mind our belongings."

Victoria glanced up and down the beach. There were not many more people on it, about ten in two distant, distinct groups. If she sat on the sea side of the rock, no one would know she was there unless they went swimming.

"I'll stay," she decided. "I don't mind, really!" as Bob began to object. "I brought my paints, so it would be a pity not to use them." She turned back immediately, but she was not happy. How could she tell them that she feared to be alone when she would not tell them why?

They set off eagerly, scrambling up the rocky cliff face, and were soon lost to sight around the headland.

A stillness settled around Victoria, a quietness broken only by the soft lapping and stirring of the incoming tide and the occasional piercing call of a sea bird. She did not sketch. She sat for a while with her back to the rock, knees hugged to her chest, wishing she were not alone, despising herself for giving in so easily. Every so often she cast a swift look to right and left, imagining that someone was creeping up on her. As her fancies grew, she could sit still no longer. Abandoning the clothes and haversacks, she climbed, quickly and heedlessly, to the top of the rock. On this vantage point she felt relatively secure and settled down to wait for the others to return, until, after about five minutes, she realised that the way up was also the only safe way down. Someone waiting below would have her as securely trapped as she had been on the dunes. She left the rock with even more careless haste than she had climbed it, jumping the last few feet onto the soft sand. She had to be somewhere where she could see, yet remain unseen, with an avenue of escape. She took her book and lay in the dinghy.

Meanwhile the others were hazardously climbing across a steep cliff face towards what looked like the mouth of a cave. They were all enjoying themselves, except Jill whose thoughts were too preoccupied with feminine strategy. How could she get Raoul to herself? It would be easy, she thought crossly, if he were as eager to be alone with her. Perhaps a slight accident, a twisted ankle or bump on the head from a fall would make her appear vulnerable and in need of his help and protection. She doubted it and did not feel inclined to hurl herself onto the beach below to find out. They had been friends too long for him to see her as anything other than independent and competent—for a girl. She wanted him to treat her like a woman, not a pal. Giving her a ducking because she had been naughty only showed how far he was from doing that.

They had reached a difficult patch of outcropping rock. The three boys, all tall, would manage it; the shorter legs of the girls might experience more difficulty. Stephen and Bob went up first. Raoul stayed to help from below. Jill hung back. First Sandra, then Helen was heaved and yanked upwards. Raoul turned to Jill.

"I can manage," she said stiffly, not wanting to submit to the indignity of the rough man-handling, but try as she might, she could not quite make it. Finally she gave up the attempt, resigning herself to being pushed on her bottom by Raoul and pulled on her arms by her cousins.

Twenty more yards brought them to the cave, which turned out to be no such thing, just an indentation in the cliff. They sat down to regain their breath and overcome their disappointment.

"Great view," Helen said. The others agreed.

"Let's go back along the top," suggested plump Sandra, who had endured enough climbing. "It will be quicker and Raoul says I can have a sail." Raoul looked at Jill, "Would you like to come out?" he asked.

She hesitated.

"If not, perhaps you would like to sail her home with me?"

"Just the two of us?" she asked in pleased surprise.

"If you like," he answered cautiously.

"I can handle her better than Jill," Helen said, then, seeing the look on her sister's face, added quickly, "but she could do with the practice, of course."

Jill looked at Stephen and Bob, to test their reaction to Raoul's suggestion. They showed neither pleasure nor surprise;

perhaps Raoul had told them of his intention to change crew. Jill's spirits soared. She smiled at Raoul and he smiled back, his blue eyes meeting her brown ones in a moment of warm intimacy. If he knew how much I love him, she thought, he would be nervous. I must get him used to the idea without frightening him off. I haven't much time, just until the end of September.

They set off in a group, chatting happily along the grassy path, fragrant in the light sea breeze, larks singing overhead, unseen, lost in an infinity of dazzling light. When the cove eventually came into view, there was no sign of Victoria, but there were a few more people on the sand and in the sea.

"She'll be behind the rock, reading," Sandra guessed.

"She said she was going to sketch. All she will be able to see from there will be water and sky. She's probably gone wandering off to find something more interesting to draw," Helen surmised.

Bob said nothing, but went on ahead. He reached the pile of belongings some minutes before the others. Victoria was not there He scanned the beach and the cliff shading his eyes from the sun. It occurred to him that she could be hiding. He turned to look at the dinghy. Sure enough, he could just see the top of her head. He crept up to the boat, leaned over and shouted.

"Boo!"

Victoria nearly died of fright. She leaped out with a shriek, realised it was only Bob and began to shake uncontrollably, her face as white as her cotton T-shirt.

His first impulse had been to laugh, until he realised she was disproportionately distressed. He ran round the boat to her.

"I'm sorry, Vicky. I'm sorry!"

She clung to him, unable to speak, trying hard to get a grip on herself before the others arrived. She could hear them clearly, laughing at something Helen had said. She turned away from Bob, giving him a small push of rejection as he tried to restrain her.

Utterly perplexed, he stood looking at her long straight hair, a silky curtain hanging almost to her waist. He put out a hand to stroke it comfortingly. At his touch she jumped away as if it had scorched her. Colour flooded her cheeks as he stammered an awkward apology.

"What's the matter with you?" he asked with impatience, while she fought for composure. He was used to hearing her troubles and making light of them, helping her with maths homework, mending her bike, admiring her painting, encouraging her when she felt shy, forcing the others to listen on the few occasions she ventured a contrary opinion or proposed a rare scheme. Now there was a barrier between them. Something had happened that evening on the dunes, the evening she had visited her grandfather on his death bed. She was nervous and withdrawn, more willing to be in company than was usual, yet, if anything, more apart from her companions. He did not think it was grief that had brought about this change, although it certainly contributed to it. Something else was worrying her. It troubled him and he did not know why it should; it almost made him dislike her. Now he shrugged at her silence, turning with relief towards the others as they came round the huge rock.

"Told you she would be here," Sandra

said triumphantly, going straight to her canvas bag for a drink. She took out a plastic bottle of diluted orange squash, but could not unscrew the cap.

"Will you get this off?" she asked Bob, holding it out to him.

"Ask Stephen," he said, ungraciously, walking off by himself along the water's edge.

Victoria watched him, mute with misery. She hated the estrangement as much as he did. He was her closest friend, but he was male. At one time that had made very little difference; she realised that now it made a lot. It was one thing to tell him her childish problems, quite another to confide problems caused by her sex. There would always be this gulf between them. The death of her grandfather had robbed her of one friend, maturity was robbing her of another. She had never felt so lonely in her life. Suddenly she had the urge to run after him and say something silly to bring the laughter back to his eyes—too late, Jill called her and the opportunity vanished.

Helen watched Jill and Raoul set off for

home in the dinghy with jealous resentment. She was a little in love with Raoul herself and a lot in love with the dinghy. Also she was cross that the very person who had insisted on coming to the far side of the island was not having to make the long trek back again.

"It's too bad," she said petulantly to her young sister. "Jill's as expert as mother at getting people to do what she wants. I wish I'd gone out with Prissy instead."

In fact no one seemed particularly cheerful as they made their way along the coastal path to the jetty. Nor did it help to discover that they had chosen the same time to catch the ferry as hordes of other people. Standing in the queue, watching full motor-boats depart, was a tedious business, when tiredness and hunger were making themselves felt.

Jill, on the other hand, her mind concentrated on love in both the abstract and its physical manifestation, had no thoughts to spare for anyone else's emotions; in fact when she was alone in Raoul's company, it was as if no one else existed.

"Thank you for asking me," she said, as they neared harbour.

"I wasn't sure you would want to come," he answered. "You never seem very keen to sail. As a matter of fact you have been so unpredictable lately that I haven't been sure of anything. Are you regretting your decision not to apply for university?"

"No. I start work in three weeks time. I'm glad. Everything is going to change soon, anyway."

"Yes," he agreed, thinking of the new life ahead of him in England.

"You will make lots of new friends," she said lightly, thinking of the same thing, "but I hope you won't forget your old ones."

"I hope they won't forget me," he countered.

"Six years is a long time. You will be twenty-four when you come back, *if* you come back, of course."

"I'll be back," he said over his shoulder, as the sails took his attention. "At Christmas actually. I'm only looking forward one term at a time."

That's what I shall do, then, she thought, just live a term at a time.

11

ALBINIA'S suggestion that Monica and Victoria should take up residence at Grande Maison, although initially received with dismay by Monica, held too much logic to be dismissed entirely from her mind. She found herself considering it, even when she had decided to consider it no longer and, although she always ended up rejecting the proposal, she would wonder if she was being wise. Had the old man had just such a scheme in mind? If they did not go, would she be brought before him at some heavenly tribunal to justify her decision? Would she ever have to answer to him for blighting Victoria's chances in life? Apart from the fact that Grande Maison was larger and more opulent, there were no other advantages that she could see, whilst the disadvantages were legion—Albinia and Mrs. Grey for a start, neither of them women Monica felt she could live with in domestic harmony.

She sounded out Victoria on the subject, with little success. She appeared completely apathetic. Yes, she would be happy to go if her mother wished it and just as happy to stay if she did not.

"Don't you care one way or the other?" Monica asked in exasperation.

"Not really," Victoria admitted.

She had been in a withdrawn frame of mind ever since her grandfather's death. Unlike Bob, Monica accepted it as a manifestation of sorrow and, for once, did not exert herself to shake Victoria out of it, thinking it would disappear naturally in a week or so, so long as she was not left alone too much to mope.

On the Thursday after the funeral, Monica called on Merle. The two sisters sat in easy chairs either side of the wide kitchen window overlooking the back garden, drank tea and gossiped lightly, both avoiding the subjects uppermost in their minds. They were expecting Margaret, but she was unpredictable, breezing in and out of their more settled existences, her personality vibrating on theirs, causing definite responses when she was present and a disturbing hum of latent interference in her absence. One could never ignore her.

She arrived when they had drained the tea-pot, but it did not matter as she preferred coffee anyway. She sat on the edge of the table, her slim legs crossed, and said to Merle, "How is Karl?" Margaret liked to come straight to the point.

"He's well," Merle told her. "At work."

"What are you going to do about him?" Margaret asked.

Merle sighed. "What do you suggest? Short of chaining him up, there's not a lot I can do."

"But he's ruining his health. He'll kill himself, Merle. He ought to be stopped now, while there's still time."

"He knows the consequences," Merle said wearily. "His doctor and I are sick of warning him."

Margaret gave up and turned to Monica.

"Have you decided yet whether to move to Grande Maison?"

"We're not going," Monica stated flatly. Both her sisters regarded her in silence. She knew they did not approve.

"I couldn't live there," she complained. "Imagine it!"

Margaret and Merle exchanged glances. Monica waited apprehensively. This had been discussed between them in her absence. She wondered why it should make any difference to them, then a light dawned.

"We would have to sell the house if I moved."

Margaret nodded. Merle asked, "Would that matter?"

So there it was, they wanted to sell it. This was something Monica had not considered. It altered everything. Perhaps they had been wanting to sell it for years.

"You would be much better off financially living with Albinia," Merle continued. "Your share of our house would be a nice little nest egg."

Monica assumed, as Margaret was saying nothing, that it was Merle who was keenest on the idea and guessed, with Stephen about to go to university and Karl's working life becoming more spasmodic, that Merle anticipated needing the money. That was it, then. There was no way she could continue to live in the house now. The sooner she reconciled herself to the awful prospect of existence at Grande Maison, the better; at least she would not have to contend with objections from Victoria. It was inevitable, she thought self-pityingly, that Leonard's family would win in the end, she could only be thankful it had not happened sooner. She could expect no sympathy from her sisters. They were envious of Victoria's good fortune and probably thought that living with Albinia Lacy was a small price to pay.

Margaret seemed to read her thoughts.

"Albinia's not that bad, surely? She always seems pleasant enough when I meet her."

Monica smiled ironically. "Oh yes, she's very pleasant," she said, thinking it would be another story entirely if Margaret were in her position. The idea of Margaret and Albinia living under the same roof was extremely diverting.

"She obviously dotes on Victoria," Merle said, trying to comfort, sorry that she had been obliged to force Monica to do something against her inclination, for she knew that she would go now.

Monica was amused. "It's not in

Albinia's nature to dote on anyone, but she is certainly very fond of her." The nearest she had ever come to doting was on her brother Leonard, but that was the beginning of the whole story, as far as Monica was concerned.

They left the subject then, two of them content to let matters take the course they had directed, the third resigned unhappily to the inevitable.

They discussed the children and their worries concerning them, each mother's anxieties countered by remonstrances and evidence of positive qualities in the children concerned, by the two supportive aunts. Margaret, as always, complained of the selfishness and wilfulness of her three girls, their lack of appreciation for all that was done for them, so typical of the youth of today. Merle worried because Stephen was too quiet and studious with little social life and, conversely, that Bob was never in, had a different girl practically every week and she did not know what he got up to. Monica, her mind too full of impending change, for once had little to say about Victoria, except that she wished she had more friends of her own.

From their own children they ventured on to criticising the children of their friends and acquaintances and were comforted to discover them to be far worse. Surprisingly, their faults could be attributed almost entirely to a bad up-bringing, either too lenient or too restrictive, by people who were not good examples to their offspring. Like many parents, the three sisters were under the comfortable impression that the permissive society was something to which other people's children belonged. It did occur to Merle, when Roy Bideau's latest exploit was being discussed, to wonder whether Bob had indulged in anything so foolhardy, but it was too dreadful to contemplate it, so she did not; after all, what could she do? It was better not to know.

When she returned home, Monica was vexed to find that Victoria had not gone swimming, as expected, but had spent the afternoon alone in the house.

"You could have come to Merle's with me," she said, "instead of being miserable here by yourself."

"I wasn't miserable, Mum. I've been reading."

"Something gloomy, I suppose."

"No, really. A novel, very light and entertaining," Victoria assured her, hoping her mother would not ask what it was, for she would not approve of it.

When they sat down to their evening meal, Monica said, "I've decided to go and live at Grande Maison after all."

Victoria was too astonished to speak. She had shown little interest when her mother had asked whether or not she wished to go, simply because she considered it a foregone conclusion that they would not move. Wild horses would not drag Monica to Grande Maison, she had said so many times. Now here she was going voluntarily. Incredible!

"I'll not pretend I'm keen on the idea," Monica admitted, "but I suppose I shall get used to it in time. At least it's a big house, big enough for me to see as little of Albinia as possible. She will be at work all day, so there are only week-ends and holidays to worry about. We'll take the television. I know she would never have one in the house, but we'll take it for our benefit and put it somewhere for our exclusive use, then she cannot complain. Mrs. Grey is the worst draw back. She will be there constantly, creeping about the place as if she owns it, complaining about the least change. We shall start as we mean to go on and take no notice of her grumbling."

"When will we be going?" Victoria asked, still dazed by the news.

"If I don't look forward to doing something, then I don't look forward. I get on and do it. We'll go as soon as possible, perhaps in a couple of weeks. It would be better if we were settled in before you start back to school."

"Mum, if you don't want to go, why are we going?" Victoria asked, perplexed.

"If this house were mine, I would stay, but I think we have been living on your aunts, generosity long enough."

12

RAOUL'S eighteenth birthday was four days after the "A" level results. Both he and Stephen had achieved the grades they needed for university. Jill was more than satisfied with hers: she could have gone had she wished; that mattered. So the birthday party that Fiona and Richard Bellinger were to give their only child was regarded in the light of a celebration for his friends as well. They were all light-headed with relief and in the mood to let their hair down. All except Sandra. She had not been invited.

"It's not fair," she said. "I was old enough to go to Jill and Stephen's. Why can't I go to Raoul's?"

"For one thing, he hasn't asked you," Helen told her triumphantly.

"Only because mother told him I was too young."

"Well, you are. I wasn't allowed to stay up late when I was thirteen."

"I stayed up late at Jill and Stephen's."

"That was different, it was a family affair. No one minded when you fell asleep in a chair."

"I could come home early," Sandra suggested quickly.

"Who would bring you? Someone else would have to leave early as well." Helen did not like the idea, she guessed it might be her.

"I'll ask Daddy," Sandra decided. "If he will fetch me, I know Raoul will say I can go."

"You can't ask him now. The invitations have all been sent out," Helen told her, but she spoke with little conviction, suspecting Sandra would get her own way as usual and deprive her once again of any advantage of her own two years' superiority.

Sandra spoke to her father very prettily at the first opportunity and Jill spoke to Raoul on her behalf. It was settled that she should stay until ten-thirty, when Larry would call for her. The others would be brought home by Stephen in his father's car.

The Bellingers' house was built into the face of the hill above the harbour. It was narrow and deep, with a garage and rear entrance on the harbour road and another garage and impressive front door on the second floor facing the steeply winding road that led up from the sea. There was a fine terraced garden at the side of the house. If the weather was fine, the party would be held mainly out-of-doors. There was to be a barbecue and coloured lights festooned the trees, ready for the dusk.

Fiona did not sleep the night before, worrying, amongst a host of other things, about the weather. Not that there was anything anyone could do about the weather; if there was, Fiona would ask them to do it, over the telephone, of course. She was one of those small, seemingly ineffectual women who appear to do nothing, just drift around voicing anxieties, carrying endless lists, or perching on chair arms piping into the telephone. She was so hopeless, people fell over themselves to help her, basking in her sweet smiles of admiration for their expertise. She was always so flatteringly grateful for every favour, it was a pleasure to grant them to her. It never dawned on anyone to wonder how anybody so useless could have such a well-ordered home, a husband and son who, whilst appearing to be the coddlers, were in fact coddled themselves into states of even-tempered, well-groomed manliness. The crises Fiona feared never happened; the entertaining she did was always a success of good management. She hardly recognised a duster, could not change a plug, was incapable of carrying a heavy basket of shopping, had not travelled on a bus since she was married, yet did not drive, was an absolute disgrace to the movement for women's equality. She had never had a job, was uninterested in politics, loved going to church but never considered religion, talking to God as if he were a personal, ever-present friend, but no miracle worker. Fiona did not worry if she could get somebody else to do the worrying for her. As soon as their brows were creased, she relaxed, comforted. Under her artless, pretty exterior, she hid the organising ability of a great general, with a dependence upon the field telephone as the easiest method of communication with his men.

On the morning of the party she was constantly being reassured by her husband and her faithful "daily" that everything would be all right. She fluttered from room to room with a piece of paper in her hand on which was a list of reminders for other people. The caterers received a last-minute telephone call, as did the disco band and the friend who was loaning an extra barbecue. The weather—there were too many clouds for comfort—was a constant source of anxiety, but her frequent glances from the windows as she passed swiftly to and fro, and her clucks of dismay, were rewarded after lunch with a definite improvement, more blue sky and a lessening of the breeze. She had, of course, 'phoned the weather bureau first thing in the morning for the day's forecast, but paid as little heed to recorded messages as she did to one-sided conversations of which she was the recipient.

Her small detachment of recruits, briefed and eager to please, arrived on cue to carry out their allotted tasks. As the last-minute preparations began, Fiona disappeared. After a leisurely bath, she took her time over making-up and changing into her new dress, with no intention of appearing on the scene again until the first guests arrived. Her bedroom was a haven of peace and orderliness in a house given over to festivities. When Richard eventually found time to dress, he discovered his wife writing a letter to her mother.

It is supposed, presumably by those people who send them, that party invitations are always received with a mixture of gratitude and eager anticipation. Alas, this is seldom the case, even amongst small fry, who fear having to eat food they find disgusting or play games they will never win. Teenagers, whilst no longer expecting to be force-fed or regimented into ghastly games, have worries all their own and often look forward to an evening of pleasure in other people's company with feelings of apprehension, even dread. No matter what one's age, parties can be hell!

Of the five cousins, only Stephen anticipated Raoul's birthday celebration with uncomplicated pleasure. He was not fond of parties, nor did he dislike them, provided he could take a back seat and watch others making fools of themselves. As he would be amongst people he knew well, he was confident of relaxing and non-participating as much as he desired.

Bob on the other hand, extrovert and gregarious, a lover of parties generally, had misgivings about this one. He had yet another new girl-friend, whom he suspected of being partial to someone else, and as that someone else was to be present, suspicion seemed likely to mar his evening.

Jill longed for the party as she did for every opportunity to be in Raoul's company, yet she feared it would be a disappointing evening; so much depended upon his attitude towards her. She was not comfortable in his mother's company. Fiona Bellinger was possessive of her only child, but subtly so, far too shrewd to alienate him by showing it. However, Jill knew that Fiona suspected she was in love with Raoul and was watching him for signs that his allegiance was no longer hers. It perturbed Jill that he had not yet given his mother real cause for alarm, for when

Fiona was certain that Raoul was in love, hostilities would commence between the two women for ascendancy. As it was, they were both watching and waiting uneasily, one determined to be the victor, the other suspecting that she would eventually have to accept defeat.

Helen's expectation of a fun-packed evening was lessened by her younger sister going as well. Sandra would be a nuisance. She would report back home everything that went on. Helen intended keeping out of her way as much as possible, especially when the time came for her to depart.

Sandra was worried that her father would arrive too early, just when things were getting lively or, that her mother would come for her instead. If there was one thing one did not want on the way home, it was criticism of one's behaviour or, worse still, of the party which one had been obliged to leave early very much against one's inclination. Margaret had the unpleasant knack of putting her heel through papered cracks, over which other people blissfully skated. Helen did Sandra an injustice when she suspected she would prattle artlessly about the goings on. If the favour was ever to be granted again, Sandra knew enough to prattle judiciously.

Victoria wanted to go least of all. There was nothing she liked about parties, they ran contrary to her retiring nature. She endured them, escaping thankfully as soon as possible. She even considered saying she felt unwell and leaving early with Sandra, but could not stand the thought of the anxious questioning she would have to undergo if she returned home unexpectedly.

By nine o'clock the festivities were in full swing. Guests both eager and reluctant had imbibed the party spirit, some more than others. Dusk was closing in over the harbour, casting into prominence the coloured lights festooning the garden trees and shrubs. There was dancing on the terrace to the disco band, arranged on a corner of the lawn. The neighbours who lived near enough to hear it, were present to save them the embarrassment of having to complain about the noise. The patio doors were open into the living-room, where the carpet had been rolled back from the parquet floor to allow an extra dancing area for those who found it too chilly outside as the evening wore on. Kitchen and dining-room had been given over to food and drink, the remainder of the house, with the exception of Fiona's bedroom, to the convenience and comfort of the many elderly guests, mostly Raoul's relations, including his paternal grandmother, who sat and drank tea, gossiping and smiling benignly upon the incomprehensible young, who were wandering about the place willy-nilly.

Events had taken a surprising turn for Victoria. For the first hour or so she had stuck close to Stephen, dancing with him a couple of times when he felt obliged to make the effort to satisfy his hostess's notion of what constituted enjoyment. Bob had eyes only for his girl, Debbie, a vivacious red-head who preferred to play the field. Fiona was determined that Raoul should not forget he was the host and had, so far with success, prevented him from devoting too much attention to any one person, so Jill was flirting outrageously with an admirer she had cold-shouldered for months. Helen was dancing non-stop with a young man about ten years her senior, leaving her dear friend Prissy to sulk in the boring company of her brother, Roy. Sandra was dancing and eating in about equal proportions, cramming fun and food into what little time remained for her.

Victoria left Stephen's side to go to the bathroom, something she did regularly at parties, spending as much time there as possible. When she returned reluctantly to the living-room, she found Stephen in conversation with someone who had been introduced to her on arrival as Raoul's friend, David, from London. She had immediately thought how much like Bob he was to look at, taller by about two inches and not as dark, but there was a definite similarity in features. Consequently, she had since glanced at him from time to time to confirm her first impression, only to find his eyes upon her. Now, as she entered, he left Stephen's side and, approaching her with an attractive smile, asked her to dance. His voice had a strong Home Counties accent which sounded strange to her. She accepted his invitation shyly, allowing herself to be led out onto the terrace with as much trepidation as if she were a contestant in "Come

Dancing". At least dancing nowadays for the young, and often for the not-so-young, is virtually a non-contact pastime, and she had not to endure the agony of being embraced and breathed upon by a stranger while trying to make conversation. The band was too loud to make the effort of speech very rewarding, anyway. With so little confidence in herself, she expected the first dance with him to be the last, but no, he liked her and continued by her side, either on or off the terrace, until it was time to cook sausages and beefburgers at the barbecues.

While putting butter on her baked potato, Victoria found herself next to Bob and Debbie, who were similarly employed. She smiled happily at Bob, but his answering smile was constrained. He and David exchanged the measuring glances of the competing male in female society.

"My cousin Bob," Victoria explained to David, thinking how unalike they were when one saw them together.

"Isn't this fun?" Debbie said to David. "Oh, where did you get the mustard? I didn't see any."

"I'll fetch some for you," he said. Debbie followed him.

Bob watched them go, then, turning to Victoria, he said,

"Shall we find somewhere to sit down to eat this lot?"

They found a bench beneath the trees. They balanced the cardboard plates on their knees and set to with plastic cutlery. Soon they were joined by Jill, Raoul and Stephen.

"Where's Debbie?" Jill asked.

Bob shrugged, as if he did not care.

"Over there, talking to that fellow who seems so smitten with Vicky," Stephen said.

"Oh dear," Jill laughed. "Poor Vicky. If Debbie fancies him, you don't stand a chance."

Bob glared at her, but she just grinned back at him. No one took Bob's girls seriously.

"You're wrong. That fellow, as you called him, is coming back to chat up Vicky," Raoul said.

Victoria blushed. Sure enough, David was returning, but there was no sign of Debbie.

"Come and be introduced properly, David," Raoul said. "This is David Strang, a friend of mine. He's here for the season at the Regency Hotel. He's from London."

"Enfield, actually," David corrected him, as he sat down next to Victoria, "and I'm working at the Regency, not staying there."

Victoria immediately moved nearer to Bob, shying involuntarily from the contact. Both young men were aware of the movement. Bob had been about to go and find Debbie, but thought better of it. This was a novel situation, someone interested in Victoria. He was not sure he approved of it, yet he could not think why; perhaps it was because, up until recently, he had regarded her as his responsibility to protect and neglect as the inclination took him. She had always been his faithful disciple, admiring and grateful for any attention he could spare. Gradually, over the past few weeks, he had felt her to be slipping away from his influence, making him realise how accustomed he had become to his role of comforter and protector, how necessary it had been for his self-image, even how much he had enjoyed it. Seeing someone looking at her with dawning attraction, he knew his role might well be usurped. The fact that she had instinctively moved closer to him when David Strang sat down, called forth his old protective impulse. He could not leave her until she released him with a word or look of dismissal.

A short, plump figure detached itself from the throng around the barbecues and came hurrying towards them through the half-dark.

"I can't find Helen," Sandra informed them with a mouth full of sausage. "Prissy thinks she's gone off with that man she's been dancing with."

"Gone off where?" demanded Stephen, getting to his feet.

"I don't know," Sandra admitted. "I've been looking for her everywhere. She's got my hanky in her jeans pocket. I lent it to her. Now I want it back."

"You can't share a handkerchief," Jill told her severely, "it's unhygienic."

"She didn't want to blow in it. She had an eyelash in her eye and I hadn't used it, honestly."

"Are you sure they've gone off together?" Stephen asked.

"Well, I can't see either of them. Anyway, they were all over one another," Sandra added with disgust. "Helen will be sorry if she misses the supper."

"Oh, dear," Jill sighed.

Raoul said, "I'll go and find them."

Stephen left with him.

"I bet she told him she's eighteen," Sandra said to Victoria, her eyes on David Strang. "She's always pretending she's older, otherwise she only gets coke to drink. I've tried it, but it doesn't work. Luckily I like coke."

"You've got butter on your chin," Jill told her. It was dripping off the baked potato she was swopping from hand to hand to avoid burnt fingers.

"I told you I needed my hanky," she answered, wiping her chin with the sleeve of her blouse.

Jill looked at her watch. Thank goodness it was ten past ten, Sandra would be leaving soon. Sandra saw the action.

"I'm going to look for Helen," she said and was away before Jill could stop her, determined to disappear for a while herself.

David took Victoria's empty plate and dropped it with his own into the rubbish sack provided for that purpose. He returned and asked her if she would like to dance. To Bob's surprise, she jumped up with alacrity, placing her hand upon his shoulder fleetingly as she left in what he took to be a gentle gesture of release. Raoul and Jill also left to rejoin the dancers. Bob stayed where he was. Let Debbie find him, when she felt so inclined. He ate a second potato with thoughtful relish.

Sandra duly departed with her father. Night had set in with secret intensity. The garden glowed and pulsated with light and sound. Raoul and Stephen gave up the search for Helen, who appeared back on the scene about half-an-hour later, refusing to say where she had been. The hectic gyrations of the early part of the evening were giving way to smoochier, more traditional dancing, in which some of the older guests were happy to join. Jill was blissfully contented in Raoul's arms.

Debbie had returned to Bob. Only Victoria was not relaxed in the heady atmosphere. Now that David Strang's hands were upon her as they danced, she was nervous and on edge, wishing fervently for the party to end. Each time she saw Bob watching her, she smiled back at him with bravado, but her eyes told another story. He felt unaccountably irritated, doing his best to ignore her by giving his whole attention to his partner, who for the time being was giving him the full benefit of hers.

When at last it was time to call a halt to the dancing, simply because the band was determined to pack up after their last frenzied assault on the ear-drums and emotions, David asked Victoria if he could see her home. She was about to say no, that she had to return with her cousins, but she knew Debbie had overheard and found herself saying yes, if somewhat hesitantly.

As the girls were collecting their handbags and jackets, she told Jill, who was being escorted home by Raoul in the car he had received as a birthday present from his parents. That left Stephen with Bob,

Debbie and an unusually subdued Helen. As they were all shouting farewells and thanks amongst the press of leave-takers, Bob took hold of Victoria's arm to hasten her towards the car.

"I'm not coming with you," she explained, drawing away from him.

He was astonished, "Of course you are," he said, looking coldly at David.

"It's all right," David said, in his loud, twangy voice, "I'm taking her."

"It's not all right," Bob countered, "her mother expects us to deliver her safe and sound."

Victoria began, almost without realising it, to gravitate towards him, preferring that arrangement. Debbie then intervened.

"Honestly Bob, she's not a child. What does it matter who takes her home?"

Helen, waiting aloof and silent, suddenly became anxious to go home and agreed with her,

"She'll be all right. Come on, Bob!"

Stephen shouted for them to hurry up. Victoria watched them go on a rising tide of panic. David smiled at her and said,

"Shall we go?" and she followed him to his car like a lamb to the slaughter, mentally scolding herself out of her nervousness by reminding herself that she was seventeen, and most girls her age were not as sexually retarded.

It was too soon for her to worry about getting into a situation with which she would not be able to cope. For all his brash, confident manner, bred in the sophistication of city life, he was mature enough to play the game as this shy, nervous girl dictated. First he wanted to get to know her. He loved her looks, he always fell for the fragile type.

Monica welcomed her daughter home, unaware that the car outside was an old mini and not her brother-in-law's new estate.

13

SEPTEMBER came. Monica and Victoria moved from their cramped home to the stately proportions of Grande Maison; not without tears and regrets on both sides, the former for her loss of independence, the latter purely from sentiment.

Jill began work in her father's office under the tutelage of his efficient, very plain secretary, Miss Gwendoline James. Every Thursday and two evenings a week, she attended a secretarial course, which she liked well enough. The office was a revelation to her. She began to see her father in a new light, that of the successful, highly respected architect. Out of the sphere of his wife's embracing influence, he had a stature, an importance, she had not imagined. He was very much in vogue in the world of architecture, especially on the continent. Jill was proud and, for the first time, glad she had joined him in his world. She supposed that most children only know the domestic side of their father's character, judging his worth in their mother's balance of power.

Gwen James was loyal and protective. She was the unseen wall keeping Margaret de Valois at a discreet distance, aided and abetted by Alex Stuart, Larry's junior partner, who resented every attempt by Margaret to interfere in the practice. Jill sided with Gwen wholeheartedly, determined to copy her subtle technique when it was her turn to act as liason officer.

At home she kept her mother's questions to a minimum by pretending only a grudging interest in the work, knowing Margaret would be afraid to be too insistent, in case she decided to give it up in protest.

With her attention so securely fixed upon her handsome husband, Margaret did not notice signs of unhappiness in her girls. Sandra, craving attention from her, knowing she would not get it, ate too much and was growing plumper. Helen, who had always eaten a lot, was losing her appetite and going out too much. Her school work was suffering, but her parents would not know that until she brought home her report. She kept out of Jill's way as much as possible. When they were together they quarrelled. Jill was concerned about her. Helen resented her careful questions, seeing them only as interference, not as a desire to help. It seemed they would never be able to agree again, except in the old game of placating their mother with half-truths, at which they excelled.

Annie Figgus watched the domestic drama, powerless to intervene. Her part was to remain firmly in the wings, pampering and loving the girls in her own way, through her scrupulous care for their home and table. She was the one who listened to Sandra's chatter about school friends, she was the one who found Helen sobbing in her bedroom and held her close until she ceased, and she was the one who guessed why Larry did not want his eldest daughter in his office and who dreaded Jill finding out.

"Sandra is getting too fat," she told her employer over a menu discussion.

"Yes, it's disgusting," Margaret agreed. "I think we'll have beef after all."

A little later she ventured the opinion

that Helen was unhappy. Margaret said that girls at that age often were. They fancied themselves in love with the most impossible older men—little knowing how near she had come to the truth.

While Sandra suffered from too little attention, Victoria was enduring too much. She felt besieged on all sides by people desiring her happiness. For someone who was not naturally of a cheerful disposition, it was daunting. Her mother alone had been bad enough; now she had her Aunt Albinia and even Mrs. Grey to contend with as well.

She saw David Strang only twice more before he returned to England. She made the excuse that she was too busy studying for her "A" levels. As the schoolgirl in her had been all too apparent during the times they spent together, he was not sorry to leave it at that. The first afternoon they had gone walking along the cliffs. She had been ill at ease, not knowing what he would expect from her, feeling very young and gauche. At one point he had put his arm lightly around her waist; immediately she had become tense, hesitant in her speech and awkward, missing her step continually on the rugged path. He had not persisted, but taken her hand instead, intending to gentle her as one would a frightened young animal. This had been no better. He let her walk free, aware that she drifted a little further from him, warily keeping her distance. The next time they met he had taken her to the cinema. The film was a comedy. She was relaxed and happy, laughing and sharing the fun with him, but as soon as they were alone afterwards, there was a change in her. He had not kissed her goodbye. When he suggested meeting again she had mumbled something about lots of homework. He watched her run along the path to her home with strange sadness. Time and patience might have rewarded him with her confidence, but he had possessed too little of both. He said his final goodbye to her on the telephone, with promises of seeing her the following year, but they rang hollow in the gulf between them. If she had been eighteen, if he had been allowed more time, he told himself, things would probably have been different. As the ship sailed, he watched the island recede, imagining her at school, solemn grey eyes intent upon her books, long fair hair falling over her shoulders. He sighed, leaving the rail to get himself a beer and sandwich. Next year, perhaps!

Stephen and Raoul sailed the following day, which was a Saturday. It was raining dismally and there was a strong wind blowing as they were seen off by friends and relations, with good wishes and anticipation of their first vacation.

"See you at Christmas," rang on all sides, as Merle and Fiona surreptitiously dabbed their eyes. Of the two mothers, Merle felt the more forlorn, for although they were both accompanied by their husbands, Merle knew Karl's support to be illusory and that she was losing the person upon whom she had depended more and more of late. Contrarily, Fiona felt that in saying a temporary farewell to her son she was securing a respite, holding on to him at least for the six years he would be at medical school. There was triumph beneath her tears.

Jill, standing beneath a red umbrella a little apart from the rest, kept her eyes fixed on Raoul with an unsmiling intensity. It was dreadful to be so much in love and so insecure. She had no hold upon him, no right to him. If he never returned, she could not say he had betrayed her. It mattered very much who was to receive his last look of farewell, so much in fact that she could not bear to watch and turned away from his diminishing form, leaving his mother full-stage for the finale, so that it was Fiona who was aware that his eyes followed the red umbrella as it retreated along the rainlashed quay.

Nothing momentous happened between then and Christmas. Jill wrote to Raoul regularly and received prompt replies. He had soon settled down in his room in halls and was busy. He gave her the impression that he would miss her very much, if he were not so engrossed with his new life. She had no reason to suppose that anything other than his studies and rugby occupied him and grew reconciled to his absence, adapting as she was herself to a new life of independence as a working girl.

Stephen phoned home once a week to start with, but as the term progressed the intervals between the calls became longer. He never wrote, although his mother occasionally wrote to him. She was careful to speak lightly, if at all, of any family problems, sensing that he would not want to know, being impotent to help. He supposed she would now turn to Bob for support, but she did not. Bob longed for the opportunity to show that he could take Stephen's place adequately. Karl was steadily and secretly drinking himself into ill-health, but had not gone off on one of his prolonged binges, so they had not had to face a crisis of that nature.

Gradually the fabric of the family of cousins, once so tightly knit, was being stretched and frayed. The one who felt it most was the one who had always appeared to feature least in the design. Cycling home from school with Bob one dismal December afternoon, the street lights glowing subdued in the murk, Victoria said to him,

"Everything's changed, hasn't it?"

"In what way?" he asked. Then, while she was considering her answer, he added, "You have."

"No, not me, just circumstances. I used to think that things would go on the same forever. Then suddenly something happens, like my grandfather dying, and it triggers off other happenings. I wonder where it will end."

"It won't end, Vicky. It's not happenings outside you, it's inside you. You're no longer a child and life, instead of slowly creeping by uneventfully, leaps from event to event, gobbling up time. It wasn't your grandfather's death that set life leaping for you, was it?"

She slowed down, wobbling a little, to let him get ahead at a busy junction. He was right, of course. The attack on the dunes had done that. She never let herself think of it, only occasionally in nightmares did she relive it, but one fear persisted, that she would meet her attacker again. It was a small island, if he were a resident the chances were high. She prayed he had been a visitor.

Bob looked round and gave her a shout. The lights had changed to green, but she was day-dreaming and had not noticed.

"Do you ever hear from David Strang?" he asked, when she caught him up again.

"No," she said, blushing. That was something else she did not like to think about, it was too humiliating.

When she reached home, she found her mother sitting in the bay window in the drawing-room looking out onto the front garden, where there was nothing to be seen but bedraggled winter shrubbery and lawn. Victoria switched on the light as she entered. Monica turned to her with a look of surprise, she had not realised it was so late.

"You shouldn't sit in the gloom, Mum. I'm surprised to see you in here, you always said you hated this room."

"I do," Monica admitted, looking round it with distaste, "but as I hate the whole house, it really doesn't make much difference where I sit."

Victoria had heard similar complaints since they had moved, but they were becoming more frequent, spoken in a doleful, self-pitying manner which was at variance with Monica's character.

"Let's find somewhere of our own to live, then," Victoria suggested briskly, not for the first time.

"It wouldn't be fair on Albinia," Monica said.

Too astonished to answer, Victoria offered to fetch the tea instead.

"Yes, that would be nice, and bring me something for my headache, will you?"

"Headache? Again?"

"Yes, I feel rather out of sorts. I don't seem to have the vitality I used to have."

It was a strange thing, but having so little to do did not agree with her. She had mentioned it to her sisters but they had been unable to sympathise, Merle because she could not imagine a life of indolence, so thought it must be luxury, Margaret because she filled her extensive leisure time with demanding social activities.

Monica loathed Mrs. Grey. If it were not for her, she could have found plenty to occupy her, but she was made to feel her help was superfluous. Monica insisted on cleaning and tidying the rooms set aside for her and Victoria's exclusive use. They consisted of two bedrooms with adjoining bathroom and a sitting-room on the opposite side of the passage over looking the back garden. At the very top of the house there was a room which Victoria used as a study-cum-studio, north-facing with a dormer window and skylight. What Monica missed most was a kitchen. Mrs. Grey ruled supreme in the one at Grande

Maison and did not welcome visitors there, much less interferers. Instead of it being the hub of the house, as it was at Merle's and Margaret's, somewhere where even the most unsociable inmate gravitated occasionally for a coffee and a chat, it was out of bounds to everyone—except for Mrs. Grey's friend, a woman of her own age who called every Tuesday afternoon to spend an hour over tea and cakes.

Mrs. Grey was not there when Victoria entered. On the table was a large tray set for tea for two, with a plate of biscuits and another of ham sandwiches. She switched on the warm electric kettle and, while it came back to the boil, fetched a bottle of aspirin from a shelf containing medicines, mainly cough cures and vapour rubs—Albinia had a weak chest, Mrs. Grey a bad back. As Victoria was pouring water into the tea-pot, Mrs. Grey returned, appearing as if from nowhere. She was a very quiet person, almost stealthy in her movements.

"If you'd waited a minute, I could have done that," she said softly.

Victoria immediately became apologetic,

"I didn't know how long you would

be," she said, picking up the tray to make a prompt escape.

"I'm never far away," Mrs. Grey answered, with what sounded like a warning in her tone as she held the door open.

"I only had to boil the kettle," Victoria muttered as she left, thinking what a fuss it was about nothing.

"Let's take it upstairs," she said to Monica, who agreed.

Once in their own cosy sitting-room, with the gas-fire lit and the tea poured, Victoria suggested that they should keep an electric kettle up there and some biscuits, so that they could have a cup of tea when they felt like it without having to bother Mrs. Grey.

"Margaret phoned," Monica said. "She wants to know if we are going there for Christmas."

"Well we are, aren't we?"

One year they went to Merle, the next to Margaret, staying over Christmas and New Year. It was a practice started when Victoria was small, so that she should have the benefit of her cousins' company at a time when families often feel the desirability of being together.

"I don't know what to do this year. I thought perhaps we could just spend Christmas Day there. What do you think?"

"But why?" Victoria asked in consternation.

"Well, your aunt, of course. We can hardly leave her in the house on her own for ten days, especially so soon after your grandfather's death."

Victoria gazed at her mother, at a loss for words. Monica had never liked Albinia, she had never made a secret of it, nor had she ever before cared about her welfare. Now she was talking about staying at Grande Maison, which she also disliked, to keep her company. If Victoria had suggested any such scheme a few months ago, her mother would have scoffed at it.

"Perhaps she could come with us to Aunty Margaret's," was Victoria's tentative suggestion.

"I'm afraid Margaret won't have her. She says she hasn't the room, but she can spend Christmas Day there and come to the New Year's Eve party."

"Well, that's all right then, isn't it? Please, let us spend ten days there as usual, Mum. I see so little of Jill and the others now."

Monica agreed. She was relieved. She hardly knew why she was so concerned about Albinia. Pity, perhaps. Seeing her every day, having to share this awful house with her and Mrs. Grey, made her realise how dreary her sister-in-law's home-life had been for many years, but at least while her father had been alive it had held meaning.

"Perhaps one of Aunt Binnie's friends at work will ask her to visit them," Victoria said, hopefully.

Monica hoped so, too, but did not think Albinia had many friends at work, not of the kind intimate enough to ask her to share their home.

"It would make more sense if she asked a crowd of people here, to fill the place up a bit, give it some life,' Monica said. "Mrs. Grey would have a fit, of course. If she didn't like the idea, she could always leave." Getting rid of Mrs. Grey was becoming an obsession with Monica.

14

AT Christmas, because of the emphasis on tradition, both cultural and family, everything seemed much as it always had been. Margaret had her usual large party of friends to supper on Christmas Eve, the day that Monica and Victoria arrived. Margaret and Larry's friends were a glossy set, not the kind to let their hair down, except verbally, when after a few drinks they became a trifle indiscreet and catty. They came unaccompanied by children. Jill, Helen, Sandra and Victoria ate their supper in the kitchen with Annie Figgus. This was as much a part of Christmas for them as hanging up their stockings when they were small; far more enjoyable than being part of the assembly in the dining-room. Jill, officially an adult now, was told she was at liberty to be part of that assembly, but declined. After her more congenial meal in the kitchen, Raoul called to take her out. He had been home a fortnight and when she was not in his company she was downcast. Already she was dreading his departure, making every minute they spent together bitter-sweet.

Merle, Karl, Stephen and Bob arrived after church on Christmas Morning, a service the whole family had attended. Jill had invited Raoul for the day, but his mother would have been hurt had he accepted, expecting to have him to herself on that special day. Consequently, Jill entered only half-heartedly into the festive spirit, longing for the next day which she was to spend at the Bellingers'. She was not the only member of the family to be less than content. Merle was anxious about Karl. He was his affable and amusing self as far as the rest of the family could tell. Signs of his constant drinking were visible in his bleary eyes and mottled complexion, if one needed to look further than the glass always in his hand, but his manner remained open and friendly. However, Merle knew there was something wrong. For the past week or so his manner towards herself had been constrained and wary. It was not just evasiveness, the constant waiting for her back to be turned;

she was used to that. He was troubled. He had barely spoken to Stephen since his return and even Bob found it difficult to converse with him. Today he seemed determined to appear normal. Merle applauded his efforts at sociability with smiles that hid her concern.

Albinia arrived an hour before dinner, traditionally eaten at six o'clock. Margaret, as always the perfect hostess, managed to make everyone, including Albinia, feel that their presence was essential to the perfect enjoyment of the occasion by the rest. Larry "chatted up Albinia", as Helen vulgarly called her father's accomplished conversational seduction. Albinia succumbed to it, despite unconscious resistance, as utterly as an ingenuous teenager; she even found herself promising to attend the New Year's Eve party. When she had let Victoria persuade her to come on Christmas Day, it had been with the understanding that nothing would induce her to accept the second invitation.

Whereas the Christmas Eve supper party had been attended only by Margaret and Larry's closest friends and the dinner on Christmas Day had been a family affair, the New Year's Eve celebration was a more gregarious occasion to which all and sundry were invited, even friends of the older children.

Unfortunately two things were to mar it. Karl had disappeared—perhaps escaped would be a more appropriate word—to his club during the course of the afternoon. Merle would not leave the house in his absence, so Stephen and Bob reluctantly went without her, the latter with a new girlfriend called Chloë.

Raoul arrived with his parents. Fiona had been planning to have her own party, but for reasons of strategy decided instead to accept the invitation to this one. She did not want Raoul to have to choose between the events, she preferred to go on deluding herself that her interests came first with him. The very fact that she was there was a tacit acceptance that they did not.

Margaret drew her nephews to one side soon after their arrival for their version of the story of their father's defection, although Merle had been on the 'phone earlier, tearfully explaining that Karl had eluded her and she would have to stay at home. Margaret could not see why. Merle said he might return in a few hours and she needed to be there just in case he did. Margaret had answered that he never returned in a few hours—a few days more likely—but Merle insisted there was always a first time. She would stay at home by the telephone.

"If your mother knows where he is, why doesn't she send you to bring him home?" Margaret demanded of Stephen.

"You mean I should walk into his club and drag him home like a naughty child?" The expression of disgust on Stephen's face was unmistakable.

Bob tried to explain. "Mum has to live with what's left of his self-respect. She wouldn't want to inflict more humiliation on him."

"He's destroying his health," Margaret pointed out for the umpteenth time.

"He's destroying everything," Stephen answered shortly, turning away from her.

"It's difficult to protect someone from themselves, Aunty Margaret." Bob spoke gently, trying to compensate for his brother's rudeness. He knew she was worried about his mother. "He knows what he's doing, he just can't stop."

"Poor Merle," Margaret sighed. It was really too bad of Karl Bienvenue, going off like that on New Year's Eve and putting a damper on her party. If he were her husband, she did not think she would be as long-suffering as her sister. Thank God Larry was not so weak. Suddenly she was overcome by the urge to be near him and be enlivened by his presence. She left Bob, winding her way eagerly through the guests until she found him, talking to a tall, blonde woman in a figure-clinging gown of blue silk jersey.

It was then that the second incident of the evening occurred, unremarked by anyone except Jill. She was with Raoul, talking to Alex Stuart and his young wife. There was something she wanted to say to her father, so every now and again she glanced across to see if he had finished his conversation. She was both impatient and amused by the way her father seemed to have been trapped by the beautiful blonde. It was not uncommon to find him in such situations. Women found him attractive; it was a fact of life about which his family constantly teased him, except his wife, who pretended to ignore it. Jill saw her mother approaching the pair and smiled. This was a common occurrence also. She never left her husband's side for long. Jill could hardly blame her. She felt the same way about Raoul.

Margaret called, "Darling!" as she approached, to gain his attention. He heard her. Before he turned there passed between him and his companion a look of total intimacy, brief yet unmistakable, excluding the rest of mankind; then both assumed the withdrawn air of mere acquaintances and casually drifted apart. The woman walked away towards a thickset man standing in a group by the window, whom Jill recognised as Gerald Frobisher, a business associate of her father's. Jill continued to watch her with growing dislike. How dare she look at her father like that! How could he return it! With misery in her heart she looked across at her parents. For a few moments everything seemed back to normal, until Larry glanced swiftly, guiltily towards the window, receiving a slight smile in reply, before giving his attention once more to his elegant, doting wife.

For the remainder of the evening, Jill

was acutely conscious of the relative positions in the room of her father and the blonde Mrs. Frobisher, a casual question to Alex Stuart having established her identity. When they were in close proximity, she watched for signs of flirtation. Ominously, there were none. If anything they avoided one another. She could not fault their behaviour. It drove her to the conclusion that matters between them had progressed beyond mutual attraction to something more settled. She was so shocked by this that she could not even attend to Raoul wholeheartedly.

The evening rushed on towards midnight in a confusion of gaiety and excitement reaching towards fever pitch, until Jill felt she would scream for silence. Trays heaped with food were placed in her hands. She struggled round with them like a smiling zombie, urging people to lighten her load. Several times she found herself in front of the blonde, looking into her blue eyes, hating her, asking her to have a sandwich, a vol-au-vent, a sausage roll; wishing she would take one and choke.

In between handing round food, she danced and drank, accepting full glasses of wine without recalling what had happened to the previous ones.

"Steady on, Jill," Raoul expostulated, as she drank the latest one as if it were lemonade.

"Oh sorry," she answered abstractedly, not knowing what she was apologising for, but, having caught Albinia Lacy's disapproving eyes upon her, she knew she must be behaving badly.

As they linked hands for "Auld Lang Syne", she looked round at the circle of glowing, happy faces, thinking, everyone's happy except me. Opposite her, Margaret smiled into her husband's eyes with perfect trust and love. Jill swallowed a huge lump in her throat and had difficulty singing as her hands were pumped up and down with energy by Raoul on one side and Roy Bideau on the other. Afterwards she hung back as her father kissed his family one by one to wish them a Happy New Year.

"Where's Jilly?" he asked at last, looking round eagerly for his eldest daughter. She emerged from her hiding place behind Stephen to fling herself into his arms and as he said, "Happy New

Year, my darling," she burst into tears on his shoulder.

He led her quickly from the room, before many people had noticed her distress. Margaret followed. In the quiet of his study, Larry took her gently by the shoulders and looking into her eyes, asked gently,

"What's the matter, Jill?"

Margaret answered, "She's had too much to drink. I'll take her upstairs."

Jill agreed, wiping her eyes with her father's handkerchief.

"Yes, yes, I've drunk too much. Sorry, Daddy, awfully silly of me," and she let her mother lead her from the room, but in the hall she stopped, insisting on saying goodnight to Raoul.

"I feel a bit better now, honestly Mum. His mother will think it very odd if I just disappear."

"Well, go into the kitchen and get some coffee. I'll send Raoul in to you, but for heaven's sake make yourself look presentable first."

Feeling that her legs would not carry her upstairs, Jill tottered into the cloakroom to splash water over her face and comb her hair, absolutely wretched in more ways than one.

When morning came, she still felt wretched. As she lay in bed, she could recall very little of the party and what she did remember was jumbled out of context, all rather woolly with the exception of the look of loving intimacy exchanged between her father and Mrs. Gerald Frobisher, which remained in her mind with startling clarity. Jill buried her face in her pillow, but it could not smother her mind, which, despite feeling as if it were working on half-power, was producing items of information at an alarming rate, incidents from the past which she had hardly noticed, but which now assumed significance: like the occasional look of unease Gwen James would dart at her as she answered the 'phone, as if Jill's presence was an embarrassment, so that she would pretend to be engrossed in whatever she was doing, however trivial, trying not to overhear the stilted, one-sided conversation, which had always seemed innocuous enough. Then there were the times her father had not come home to dinner, although she could not think, despite his excuse to her mother, what in his business affairs had kept him. Usually those evenings were carefully, casually explained away by his secretary, but not always; no doubt there were times when even she was at a loss for words. Poor Miss James was rapidly assuming the role of the villain of the piece. No wonder Larry had not wanted his daughter to work for him, it made Miss James' job even more difficult.

Jill turned over impatiently and was reminded immediately by head and stomach that she was unwell. Uncle Karl must be mad to drink so much, she thought, if he feels like this afterwards. I wonder what makes him do it!

15

KARL was returned home at lunch-time three days later, sodden and morose. Stephen helped his mother to put him to bed. Neither spoke a word. What was there to say? People only feel the need to talk about a problem while they have some hope, however faint, of a solution. Today even Merle was without hope. A friend had driven him home and had left without showing his face, leaving Karl to shuffle along the path in isolated degradation.

Merle had greeted him wooden-faced. There was no point in looking reproachful; that was for the past, when he had wrung out of her every emotion of which she was capable. Now she was wrung dry of everything except misery.

"I won't sail tomorrow, Mum," Stephen said, as he followed her across the landing from the spare bedroom.

"Of course you will," she answered briskly. "There's no point in staying.

Once he has slept this lot off, he'll be all right again for a while, perhaps for months. After all, this is the first long session since you went away at the end of September."

If only he could have waited until Stephen had returned to England, she thought, then he need never have known. As it was, he had ruined Stephen's vacation, just as he ruined everything now. He had reached the stage where he seemed not to care for anything or anyone; so long as he could procure drink, the rest of the world did not matter.

That evening, while Bob was out as usual and Stephen was doing his packing, Merle sat in front of the television shedding tears of self-pity. It would have been preferable, she thought, if Karl had died young, like Leonard, still loving me. At least Monica's memories were of coming first with her husband and being needed by him. Merle envied Margaret even more. If ever there was a woman who did not know when she was blessed, it was that one! She had everything. Three lovely girls, a beautiful home, plenty of money, Annie Figgus and, to crown it all, a handsome, loving husband. The comparison was too much for Merle to bear; her tears fell copiously. What have I done to deserve it? she asked pitiously. Have I driven him to drink? God knows I'm not perfect, but at least I used to be relatively content, I did not nag continually, or ask him to accomplish the impossible. If only I knew why he drank, but then he does not know himself. How could a person choose alcohol rather than affectionate involvement with his wife and children?

She heard Stephen descending the stairs and hastily dabbed her eyes and blew her nose. It did not help to know that he was going tomorrow and that she would not see him again until Easter. At least when he was at home he kept some kind of curb on Bob. He was another worry. What was going to become of him, left to his own devices, with no father or elder brother to check him from behaving foolishly?

Stephen put his head round the door, offering to make cocoa. She accepted and, by the time he returned with the two mugs, she had herself well under control, feeling ashamed of pitying herself when her husband was so much more in need of it.

She and Stephen talked quietly together for almost an hour, in a light, inconsequential manner, deliberately ignoring family worries and problems that could not be resolved in the short time they had before his boat sailed; each trying to save the other an emotional leave-taking. Bob came in just before eleven o'clock. They greeted his arrival with relief.

"Where have you been?" Merle asked automatically, knowing she would have to believe whatever he told her.

"To a friend's," he answered, then catching the expression of irritation on his mother's face, added, grinning, "what did you think, that I was mugging old ladies?"

She thought, some mothers' sons have been doing just that, and thanked God that was not one of her fears.

"Your father's home," she told him.

"That's good." He crossed over to her side and put his hand comfortingly on her shoulder.

She shook it off impatiently, saying, "It's a good job Stephen was here to help me put him to bed. How am I going to manage when he's away?"

"Oh, I doubt whether Dad will have a binge in his absence."

"What makes you say that?" Merle asked him sharply.

"It's a theory I've got," Bob told her.

"Explain it!" Stephen ordered.

Bob proceeded to do so.

"We all know there has to be a reason why Dad drinks. Mum thinks it's her fault," and at Stephen's angry expostulation, said, "oh yes, she does. She feels guilty."

"Of course she doesn't," Stephen declared with vehemence, looking at his mother.

Merle sighed, admitting in a low voice that in fact she did.

"But why?" Stephen asked, amazed.

"I don't know. Perhaps I make him feel inadequate, but then that's exactly how his drinking makes me feel, as if I've failed him in some way. He can't be happy."

"It's not your fault, Mum. It's Stephen's."

They both stared at Bob. Stephen leaped to his feet in anger.

Bob took two steps backwards, but when his brother showed no sign of approaching nearer, continued.

"Dad finds you so bloody difficult to live up to. We all do. I know how he feels. You set yourself such impossibly high standards."

"I don't find them impossible," Stephen argued.

"No, but the rest of us do. You have the knack of making people feel inferior, of making them aware of their own shortcomings. I don't suppose you can help it, but you might try a little more tolerance towards us lesser mortals. You can't find a girl who meets your standards, perhaps you never will. It can be a lonely business, being too critical of human imperfections."

"That's enough, Bob," Merle cried, grieved to hear him speak like that of his exemplary elder brother. She was shocked by the implication of his words. Could there be some truth in them? Was it Stephen who made Karl feel the need to escape from his responsibilities towards them all? No! Bob had to be wrong. Stephen was not to blame, he was everything a son should be, dependable and loving, someone in whom his parents could take pride. Bob was jealous. She was sorry, very sorry that it was so, but he had guessed, despite her efforts that he never should, that he came second in her maternal affections. Was Karl jealous of Stephen as well? If so, she must reassure him, let him know how much love she still had to give him, if only he would let her. A husband must always be best loved, otherwise, when the children left home, a woman had nothing to cherish.

"It's easy to blame someone else," Stephen said. "That's half the trouble. Everything, everyone must take the blame, except Dad. In fact it's his own weakness, his own fault that he drinks. He does it because he can't face up to himself, he falls short of his own measure. He drinks because he hasn't got the guts to stop."

"Stephen," Merle moaned.

He apologised, but it was for causing her pain, not for what he had said. How could he be expected to forgive weakness in someone else when he would find it unforgivable in himself?

"It's your unspoken criticism that Dad

can't stand," Bob told him. He knew from experience that it is difficult to defend oneself against reproachful silence. Words, however harsh, present a healthier target for retaliation.

"Please don't let's quarrel any more," Merle pleaded. Karl is doing this to us, she thought. He's tearing us apart. "Stephen goes away tomorrow. I don't want you to part in anger."

"I'm not angry, Mum," Bob said, "just fed up with being the one always in the wrong. I have sympathy with Dad, that's all. We are both very aware of our imperfections, but I think I can live with mine."

He said goodnight and went upstairs. While he cleaned his teeth, he thought, Stephen's like Dad, too, in one way. Neither will ever be really happy. One is always striving against temptation, the other has given up the struggle. It's Stephen Mum should worry about, not me.

16

THE months passed by towards another summer. As they progressed, uneventfully on the surface, cross-currents and eddies swirled and shifted what had seemed a solid base. The family structure, already trembling, began to loosen at the joints.

In May, Margaret accompanied Larry on a business trip to London. Helen invited herself to Grande Maison; she had been waiting for an opportunity to stay there. She persisted in regarding it in a romantic light and would have swopped her ultra-modern home for its old-fashioned gloominess any day.

She had submerged her troubles of the previous summer beneath a froth of normality and appeared more the old Helen, full of her own importance, with a waspish sense of humour. She got on well with Albinia, who liked someone with spirit, and she was not intimidated by

Mrs. Grey whom she described to Victoria in private as a "creepy old bag".

Victoria was glad to have her. She hoped Helen would bring her up to date with the happenings in the rest of the family, because she was feeling sadly out of touch. Helen did. They shared a bedroom and gossiped far into the night.

"Stephen's got a girl, did you know?"

Victoria had not known. Unfortunately, Helen could add very little to that particular item of information. She had overheard Merle telling her mother. Stephen had imparted the news in a letter. All he had said, apparently, was that he was occasionally going out with a girl called Alison. Merle suspected the information was for Bob's benefit. Stephen had resented the jibe that he would never find a girl who matched his exacting requirements.

Helen's next item of news was that Jill was looking for a flat.

"She can't stand living at home any longer. I don't blame her. As soon as I leave school, I'm going as well. She should have gone to university, then she could have left without all the fuss. Mother is furious and keeps telling her that she doesn't know when she's well off. It doesn't make any difference what she says and she knows it. If Jill has made up her mind to go, she'll go. She takes over from Miss James soon, then she'll be getting more money. I can't wait to have some money of my own. I shall spend most of it on clothes. I'm sick of school uniform, aren't you?"

"I shan't have to wear it much longer," Victoria reminded her. Next month she and Bob would be sitting their "A" levels. Helen would be taking her "O" levels.

"If you want some money, why don't you ask Aunty Merle for Doreen's job? She leaves school this year, so she'll be wanting something permanent."

"I've already asked her," Helen said. "Unfortunately Doreen is going to continue until she finds something else. Let's face it, she may not. It's not easy to get a job now, even if you have qualifications."

Doreen worked for Merle full time during the Easter and summer holidays, and dinner-times and Saturdays during the period between.

"What are you going to do when you leave school, Vicky?" Helen asked and, while Victoria considered her reply, continued, "I'm going to teach. I think I would be quite good at it. I don't like children much, that is one thing in my favour."

"But surely you should like them," Victoria protested.

"No, if teachers liked children, they would not want to inflict so much misery on them. In my experience they enjoy it. They're a sadistic lot. I shall spend all my holidays abroad—which reminds me, Jill is going to Austria with Raoul this summer. They are going with some of his friends from medical school."

Helen's appetite had returned with her good spirits. At breakfast the next morning she devoured the last piece of toast and asked if she could fetch some more. Albinia looked surprised at such a request. It was more usual in that house to send excess food back to the kitchen. Monica told her to go ahead. They waited with interest for her return. She was not long. She breezed in with four more slices and proceeded to apply butter and marmalade liberally to one of them.

"Did she mind?" Victoria asked.

"Who, Mrs. Grey? Well, she seemed to think that I was too dozy to put sliced bread in a toaster, but I quickly demonstrated my aptitude. She was quite amazed." She and Victoria exchanged looks and giggled. Monica smiled slightly. Albinia could not see what was amusing about such a trivial incident, so ignored the whole thing, wiped her mouth carefully on her napkin, folded and rolled it, inserted it into her battered silver ring and left the table, saying goodbye to them as she went.

Twenty minutes later the two girls left for school. Monica went upstairs to clean and tidy her rooms. Albinia had always let Mrs. Grey decide on what they ate, so Monica did not even have to think about food, but shopping was often required and she willingly, even thankfully, undertook this, something which, previously, Albinia had managed in her lunch hour. This morning Monica had arranged to meet Merle in the town. As soon as she had cleaned and tidied to her own exacting satisfaction, she went down to the kitchen. It was as much as she could do to refrain from knocking before she entered.

"Do you need anything from the town, Mrs. Grey?"

"We'll need some more bread," Mrs. Grey answered, pausing in the act of slicing carrots. "The visitor has a healthy appetite."

"Helen enjoys her food," Monica admitted. She wondered how Mrs. Grey would react if Bob or Stephen came to stay.

"Will she be here long?"

Monica answered sharply that she had no idea, but in fact the visit was expected to last until Margaret and Larry returned in ten days' time.

Mrs. Grey recommenced slicing carrots. Monica turned to go.

"The toaster is broken," Mrs. Grey said quietly over her shoulder.

Monica stopped in her tracks. "Really? What's wrong with it?"

"It won't toast," was the succinct answer.

Helen's toast had been all right; that meant it had stopped working later. The implication being, no doubt, that Helen had broken it.

"Oh, I expect it's just the plug," Monica said airily, escaping, but not before getting in a parting shot. "Helen will fix it, she enjoys doing things like that."

However, when Helen cheerfully offered her services that evening, it was only to be told that it had been fixed, thank you, the retired gentleman who did the garden on a part-time basis had obliged.

An hour later Monica was relating the incident to a sympathetic Merle over coffee and cream cakes.

"Why don't you suggest to Albinia that you get rid of her as a sensible economy measure? You could get someone to come in for just a few mornings a week to clean the place and you could manage the rest."

Instead of jumping at the idea, Monica demurred.

"To tell you the truth, Merle, I don't know whether I would cope. I haven't as much energy as I used to have. Some days I feel positively unwell. Just when I make up my mind to see a doctor, I feel better for a few days. Even if I did see the doctor, I don't know what I would tell him. It doesn't seem enough to feel just off-colour."

"Of course it does," Merle argued. "There must be a reason." She regarded her sister closely for signs of poor health, but could see none. The idle life she was leading had caused her to put on a few pounds in weight, which was becoming to someone who had been too thin, almost gaunt, before.

Merle leaned across the table to impart a confidential piece of news.

"Monica, what do you think? Larry has another woman." She waited while her sister's shock subsided a little, then went on. "Bob saw them together the other night, having dinner at Smithson's. You know that couple who were at the New Year's Eve party, Gerald and Sadie Frobisher? Well, it's her!"

"There was probably a good reason why they were dining together," Monica said. "Probably Margaret knows all about it."

Merle disagreed.

"Actually Margaret thought he was somewhere else that evening. Bob told Jill he had seen her father at Smithson's, not who he was with, of course, and it was Jill's reaction that made him think twice about it. Anyway, she asked him not to mention it to her mother. It's my opinion that he was going to meet this woman in London, because Margaret had a difficult time persuading him to take her. In fact, it was only when she showed signs of becoming suspicious that he agreed."

Monica digested this information along with her cake, which she ate in silence. Merle sipped her coffee. It was a novelty for her to discuss a problem relating to someone else's husband. It was five months since Karl had indulged in a heavy drinking bout. Stephen had been home for Easter and his presence had not affected his father adversely. Bob had been wrong.

"I don't believe it," Monica concluded. "Larry wouldn't be so foolish. What does he need another woman for, for heaven's sake? Margaret worships him, all she really cares about is making him happy. If she can't satisfy him, who could?"

Merle gave her an old-fashioned look, agreeing half-heartedly.

Monica said, "Well?" encouragingly, but Merle would not express the reservations she felt and deftly changed the subject.

"I expect it's all a storm in a tea-cup," she agreed. "Have you finished your shopping? Perhaps you would come with me to choose a jacket. I've seen one I like, but I'm not sure about the colour."

That evening, when the girls had finished their homework, cosily closeted in Victoria's own little studio at the top of the house, they washed each other's hair, adding a colour-rinse for fun; Helen ready to face the world the next day with bravado, Victoria with trepidation. As it happened, the results were disappointing and they reckoned they would be lucky if anyone even noticed.

"As soon as I've left home, I shall dye mine," Helen announced. "You're all right, being blonde, but I'm just in-between." It certainly did not suit her nature to be mediocre in anything.

They went to bed and enjoyed a lengthy discussion about school and its staff before falling asleep. About an hour later, Helen was jerked into wakefulness by a prolonged scream. Heart pounding, she groped for the light switch, giving it a hard jerk that nearly pulled it from the socket above her head. Victoria was moaning and tossing about in her bed, in the throes of a nightmare. Helen ran to her and, grabbing her by the shoulders, commanded her to wake up instantly. As Victoria opened her eyes, their horrified expression mirroring the world of her dream, her mother rushed into the room.

"Darling, not another nightmare!" she cried, hurrying to her side.

Back in the land of conscious thought, Victoria calmed herself, holding one hand to her mouth to stifle her sobs.

"Does she have them often?" Helen asked, appalled.

"Quite often," Monica admitted.

"I remember you used to have them when you were little," Helen said to Victoria, "but I thought you'd grown out of them."

"I thought I had," Victoria answered, smiling ruefully through her tears to set her mother's mind at rest.

"Are you all right now?" Monica enquired anxiously, hovering about in her long white nightdress like a distressed ghost. "Would you like me to make you a hot drink?"

"No, I'm fine. Please go back to bed. I'm sorry I woke you both."

It was some minutes before Monica could be persuaded to leave, but at last she went, reluctantly, convinced that Victoria was feverish and sickening for something unpleasant. Helen went back to her own bed.

"Shall I leave the light on?" she asked.

"Oh no," Victoria answered, knowing that Helen would find it difficult to get back to sleep if she did so.

After a short while, Helen asked in a whisper, "Vicky, are you asleep?"

"No."

"What was the nightmare about?"

"It's always about the same thing," Victoria confessed.

"What?"

"I relive something awful that happened to me."

"Tell me," Helen urged and because Victoria was upset and vulnerable, she found herself telling her cousin about the attack in the dunes.

"It's what almost happened that

frightens me, of course. What would have happened if those people had not come along. But that's not the worst of it, Helen. It's what it has done to me." In the intimacy of the darkened bedroom, Victoria blurted out her innocent fears. "I don't think I shall ever be able to get married. I can't bear to be touched. The thought of being at the mercy of a pair of hands fills me with horror."

There was silence, then she added in a distraught whisper, "Helen, what can I do about it?"

Sixteen-year-old Helen had no idea. Her thoughts leaped from Victoria's problem to her own. That's what's the matter with me, she thought. Memories of the evening of Raoul's party came flooding back. She shuddered beneath the warm bedclothes, blushing and screwing up her eyes in shame.

Because she was tall, with an assured manner, the young man had not realised she was only fifteen. She squirmed again as she faced the truth. She had deliberately led him to believe that she was older. It was easy while they were dancing and flirting, but when, at supper-time, he inveigled her out to his car, parked off the road in an unlit driveway, his love-making had alarmed her. Not at first, of course. Through ignorance of his intentions, she had been happy to be kissed and petted a little. She had allowed boy-friends from school similar liberties. It was when she realised that he was not content just to kiss and fondle her that she had panicked. "No," she had gasped, struggling away from him in the confines of the back seat, "I'm only fifteen."

He had shot away from her as if she had said she was suffering from leprosy. She could not tell Victoria of her experience, because she was ashamed for a different reason. She had invited what had happened, she had even enjoyed it, until she discovered his hands were merely preparing the way for another part of his anatomy. The scare had had the effect of a warning. She thought, like Victoria, that she would never allow a man to touch her again, for next time she might not be able to control the situation. There must never be a next time. As she slipped into sleep, she was wondering if perhaps it would have been pleasurable. Now she would never know.

"I'll never get rid of my spots," was her last coherent thought.

Victoria fought against sleep, considering how odd it was that of all people, it was Helen in whom she had confided. She hoped she would never regret it more than she did already.

17

THE change that Victoria had feared as inevitable and for the worst was well under way by the time August came round again.

It seemed incredible to her that merely a year had passed since she lay dreaming on the beach and had been brought abruptly back to reality by her mother bearing bad news. That moment had triggered off a slow disintegration of life as she had previously led it. Before her mother's arrival, she felt she had lain in a mental cocoon, with everyone around her behaving predictably according to her imperceptive view of their positions relative to herself. She nestled securely in the familiar structure of the family hierarchy; within it, yet detached from it, as an unborn child at the end of its umbilical cord.

The news that her grandfather was seriously ill had been the first tug at that cord, starting the gentle movement that was gradually to increase in momentum, swinging her further and further out from the protected centre of her immature world to that hazy horizon where other adults stood, vainly groping inwards towards the lost cell of childhood, reached now along tenuous threads of memory; everyone building and destroying new relationships, searching eternally for the love that would establish their identities in the bewildering complexity of human anonymity.

It was just after nine o'clock on the second Saturday in August. Victoria had eaten breakfast and was in her study, putting the finishing touches to a painting she had started a week ago. She stood in front of her easel in an old shirt and jeans and deftly applied a few highlights to the still life before her. She stepped back to judge the effect, the end of the brush between her teeth. The picture was finished. There was nothing she could do to improve it; whether it was good or bad, pleasant or unpleasant, it would remain so forever. She set about cleaning her palette and brushes, moderately satisfied with her achievement. In an hour she was going to help Doreen with the beds at Aunty Merle's.

There was a soft knock on the door and Monica entered. She glanced perfunctorily at the painting and said, "Very nice," before coming to the purpose of her visit.

Fortunately her art was the one thing in which Victoria had confidence in her ability. Her mother's cursory dismissal of her work was too habitual to cause her pain. Monica had no interest in art, only in so far as it amused her daughter. She saw it as a harmless pastime, which kept Victoria happy. The gift was inherited from Leonard, Albinia said. Monica had been unaware of it in her husband and supposed it could not have amounted to much.

"Merle's just 'phoned," she said. "She wants you to go there as soon as possible. Everything's in a bit of a turmoil. Karl's gone off on one of his binges again, after all these months. She's very upset."

"I'll go as soon as I have finished cleaning up. How long has Uncle Karl been gone?"

"Just yesterday."

That meant he was unlikely to return

for a day or so, judging by past form. Victoria did not want to be there when he came home "not himself".

Monica looked round the spartan room, ideal for a studio with its large north-facing dormer window and skylight. The floor was bare boards, stained light oak, with a brown rug in the centre. Behind the door were Victoria's desk and chair with an angle-poise lamp beside them.

"Mrs. Grey begrudges you this room," she said.

"Why on earth should she? Anyway it's not hers to begrudge."

"She used it as a store room and has had to find somewhere else to put the junk."

Victoria laughed. "Well, that can't have been difficult, can it? There are three more rooms like this one."

"You know how awkward she is," Monica said and began moaning on about Mrs. Grey and how difficult she made life at Grande Maison, until Victoria, who had heard it all before, gave up making sympathetic noises and said she must go.

"Not in that shirt, I hope!"

Victoria looked down at it. There was

Prussian blue paint on the front and white on the cuff.

"You have paint in your hair as well. It seems such a messy occupation to me. I don't know how you can stand the smell of the turps."

Monica followed Victoria from the room and down the first flight of stairs to the main landing.

"Don't stay there for lunch. I don't want to eat mine alone with Albinia."

Victoria was disappointed. She had hoped to stay all day.

Doreen was glad to see her, greeting her with a big smile. They were a contrast in looks and temperament. The only thing they had in common was their age, yet they got on famously together. Merle was nowhere in sight when Victoria arrived, so she went straight upstairs with Doreen to start on the bedrooms. As they worked they gossiped, with Doreen doing most of the talking and Victoria, cheerfully scandalised, most of the laughing.

"How on earth do you stay so skinny?" Doreen wanted to know, pretending to be envious when in fact she was perfectly satisfied with her own more generous figure.

"I see you've been streaking your hair again. Funny colour to choose, mind."

They were discussing Doreen's lack of success in finding a job and Victoria's chances of getting the necessary "A" levels to take an art and design course at the polytechnic, when Sandra bounced in, leaping straight into the middle of the bed they were making.

"I've come to help," she announced.

"Well, get off, you ghastly child. Go and clean the bathrooms," Doreen told her, but Sandra had no intention of doing anything on her own, there was no fun in that.

"I've just been to visit Jill," she said. "She's going to Austria with Raoul next week. Helen says she's going to move out as well, as soon as she leaves school. I'm not. I'm never going to leave home. I like Mrs. Figgus' cooking too much. I bet Jill will get fed up and come home to live again. Now Helen can't quarrel with her, she keeps picking on me."

She kept up a non-stop flow of chatter, but did nothing useful. Doreen suggested that she make them some coffee. She left quite willingly, but was back empty-handed in a couple of minutes.

"Bob's making it," she told them. "Aunty Merle's crying and Stephen is angry."

"Oh God," Doreen sighed. "Happy families!"

When they entered the kitchen ten minutes later, Merle was preparing vegetables at the sink, her back to them. Bob was pouring out six mugs of coffee and Stephen was reading a newspaper. There was an uneasy silence, the kind that follows after too much has been said.

Victoria and Bob exchanged smiles. They were always happy to see one another.

Sandra reminded Bob that she liked lots of milk in her coffee. At the sound of her voice, Merle looked round.

"Are you still here? I hope you're being helpful. We are far too busy to have someone getting in the way."

"I am helping, aren't I?" Sandra asked Doreen appealingly, then she remembered something and, turning to Victoria, said, "Guess who I saw in the town yesterday?

That man who took you home from Raoul's party, David somebody."

"Oh," Victoria said, blushing crimson. Everyone was looking at her.

"What's he doing over here?" Bob asked, almost accusingly.

"I don't know," she told him. "Probably on holiday. He said he might come over for a holiday."

"No, he's working here. I asked him," Sandra informed them.

"Temporarily?" Bob enquired.

"No, for good. He's been here a week."

Merle went back to washing lettuce. Stephen resumed reading the paper. Doreen and Sandra helped themselves to biscuits. Victoria accepted her coffee from Bob's hands, avoiding his eyes.

"Have you heard from him since last summer?" he wanted to know.

"Only a Christmas card," she admitted.

He wondered why she had been startled and embarrassed at the news. He knew she had been out with David Strang a couple of times and that the affair had fizzled out. He wondered why; Strang had seemed keen enough at the party. He supposed Victoria had been the one unwilling to commit herself. He knew her shyness and reserve so well, it seemed the obvious answer, yet looking at her now, her cheeks still pink, her eyes downcast to her coffee mug, he could tell she was disturbed, as if she expected, or even hoped, that David's arrival would affect her.

Actually Bob was wrong, as people so often are who know us so well that they confidently interpret our reactions in the light of our characters. Victoria was remembering, not anticipating, and did not expect to meet David Strang again except casually and by accident.

"Have you got a job yet, Bob?" Doreen asked him.

"I'm going into the merchant navy," he said.

The bottom fell out of Victoria's world. She raised her eyes to his and he was stricken by the reproach in them.

"I've only just heard that I've been accepted. I go at the beginning of next month," he told her gently, realising the news had come as a shock.

Oh God! Victoria thought, is there nothing I can hold on to, no one who will remain constant in my life? She had expected Bob to get a job on the island. It had never entered her head that he would leave.

"Both my sons are deserting me, Doreen," Merle said lightly, over her shoulder.

Stephen folded the paper, crossing the kitchen to put an arm affectionately around her shoulders.

"Only temporarily, Mum," he said. "We've got to get on in the world, otherwise we won't be able to look after you in your old age." He smiled as he spoke, but it was significant that he did not mention his father. No one with any sense expected Karl to reach old age.

"I'll take the car and have a scout round again," he told her, kissing her cheek.

"I'll come," Bob offered and they left together.

"Shall I wash up the coffee mugs, Aunty?" Sandra asked.

Merle nodded. "I've almost finished here. How are you two getting on upstairs?"

"We've almost finished as well," Doreen informed her, gulping down the last of her coffee. "Come on, Vicky!"

Victoria followed her, plunged in misery. How could Bob have taken such a momentous decision without even mentioning it to me? she wondered. We haven't seen very much of each other this last month, but there have been opportunities when he could at least have hinted at his intentions. She considered the family as it had been a year ago, a close-knit unit with her mother and her two sisters as the central figures, in control of their domestic fiefdoms. Admittedly, Uncle Karl had been a weak subject, slipping in and out of thraldom according to his state of sobriety; but Aunt Merle, with Stephen in support, had always coped, forgetting and forgiving. The children had been at home in each other's houses, frequently together and aware of every event that concerned any member of the family, however trivial.

All that had changed, as it was bound to. It was the extent of the change that so alarmed Victoria.

As she cycled home for lunch, through a thick drizzle that gave everything a partially rubbed-out look under water-colour, she considered life at Grande Maison and the strange effect it was having on her mother. There was no doubt in her mind that they had made a mistake in moving, although it puzzled her to fathom out why. Monica had begun life there defiantly, determined not to be intimidated either by the house or its two ensconced inmates. She was going to make the best of a bad job for Victoria's sake, she said so many times at first, but the more she said it, the more Victoria realised that she was losing the will to battle; indeed, although she still considered Mrs. Grey an enemy, she was gradually, almost without knowing it herself, beginning to side with Albinia and not against Mrs. Grey but against—of all people—Victoria. They were united in wanting what was best for her. Victoria shuddered at the thought. Both were watchful of her health and eager to promote her happiness. They wanted to know where she was going, how long she would be, whom she would be seeing.

It was an ironic laugh, really. Her mother's solicitude had been powerless to prevent her from nearly being raped, and she did not suppose that, now it was bolstered by her aunt's, it would be any more effective. All this fussing is pushing me further from them, not holding me closer, can't they see that? Aunt Binnie and Grandpa had the same effect upon my father. He became secretive about his private life and suddenly produced mother, like a rabbit out of a hat, as his means of escape. I'm just biding my time, until I can do the same thing. They are smothering me between them until I can't breathe. I would never be able to get a flat of my own like Jill; just the thought of the opposition is too much to bear. The only way I shall ever make a life for myself is by finding someone who will take me away from them, someone to marry me. I wouldn't be brave enough just to live with a man. I would need the security of marriage. You can't be a feminist without a strong character, no matter how sympathetic you are to the cause. I'm the kind of person who seems very moral, simply because I haven't the nerve to be anything else.

Then she remembered that she had inhibitions about marriage. I shall be at Grande Maison forever, she moaned, an old maid like Aunt Binnie.

She saw her mother standing at the

drawing-room window as she turned into the drive. She glanced at her watch. Five minutes to one. Just made it.

Monica greeted her in the hall, issuing from the drawing-room to tell her she was wet through and must change immediately and dry her hair. As Victoria meekly turned to obey, Albinia appeared from the kitchen.

"Oh, you are wet, Victoria. I'll tell Mrs. Grey to wait another ten minutes while you change."

"No, don't! I shan't be long," Victoria called as she raced upstairs.

She heard her aunt say, "Well, at least it's quite warm outside. She shouldn't get a chill."

When did I last get a chill? she thought crossly, stripping off her shirt and jeans, which she quickly replaced with similar items of clothing. She rubbed her hair with a towel and dragged a comb through its tangled length, grimacing at the sight of its damp lankness.

As soon as she sat down at the table, to forestall any comments about chills and wet hair, she asked her mother, "May I have the money for a curly perm? I'm sick of my hair."

"Certainly not," Monica said. "You have beautiful healthy hair, a perm would ruin it. If you want to do something different have it cut. You have a small face, it would suit you shorter."

Albinia fixed her piercing hazel eyes upon her niece and begged to disagree.

"I think she should wear it in a chignon, or plaited round her head. It would be a shame to cut such lovely hair. Now you are a young woman, Victoria, you should not wear it hanging down your back, but do something positive with it. There are many possibilities."

"I'll think about it," Victoria said. She very much wanted to alter her image and her hair seemed the easiest way to go about it. Wouldn't it be wonderful if a new hair-style could alter me fundamentally, really make me a different person, she mused, instead of being just a surface transformation. Perhaps I will get it cut very short. Bob won't like it, but who cares what he likes, he won't be around much longer to bother one way or another. She felt a perverse satisfaction at the thought of causing Bob annoyance and decided to make an appointment at the hairdresser first thing on Monday morning. In the meantime, she would visit Jill and get her opinion.

Jill was in the bath when Victoria called later that afternoon. She came to the door wrapped in a large blue towel, shouting through the letter box to ascertain the identity of the caller. It was the first time that Victoria had been to the flat and she looked around it with envious interest.

"Don't say it's small," Jill advised her. "Be original, for heaven's sake."

"It's cosy," Victoria said.

"That's better," Jill laughed. "Sit down while I get dressed."

The flat consisted of an over-furnished bed-sitting room with adjoining bathroom and tiny kitchen. The furniture and carpet were shabby; there was far too much pattern in the room, on the walls, easy chairs, bed and floor, with no colour co-ordination, so that the overall effect was messy and gave Victoria a distinctly uneasy feeling. She sat in a capacious arm-chair covered loosely in worn, faded cretonne,

IOG17

watching rugby football on a black and white portable television on the sideboard, and waited for Jill to reappear from the bathroom.

"Well, I made it," Jill said, emerging triumphant in bra and pants and flinging her arms wide to indicate emancipation,

"Mother hates it, of course. She put her fastidious nose round the door once and withdrew it almost immediately in horror. It offends her aestheticism. Needless to say, she's hardly speaking to me. I have hurt her deeply, wounded her maternal pride or something equally ridiculous. Why would anyone want to escape from such an ideal mother, I ask you?"

"Why did you want a place of your own, Jill?"

Jill paused in the act of stepping into her skirt.

"I don't know whether I can tell you, Vicky. I wish I could. As it is, everyone is giving their own reasons and they are all wrong. Mother considers I'm doing it to spite her in some mysterious fashion, Helen is envious and dislikes me for leaving her to defy mother on her own, Sandra resents me for leaving her to defy

Helen on her own. Fiona Bellinger thinks I'm setting up a web like a female spider to ensnare her darling son. She imagines that we shall be able to do here, what we shall not be able to accomplish in Austria or in his car, for that matter. Silly, isn't it? Have you come to see the flat, or did you have another reason?"

"Both, actually. It's ages since I've had a chance to talk to you. I feel so cut off from the family since we moved to Grande Maison. Mother feels it as well, I think, even though she visits her sisters quite often. It's just that everyone has started to go their separate ways, branching out on their own, and I feel isolated. For the first time, I'm feeling the disadvantages of being an only child."

"Poor Vicky!" Jill commiserated. "I know what you mean about the family. Everyone is becoming so immersed in their own concerns that they haven't time for anyone else. Worry isolates people. Look what it's done to me. I've cut myself off from home, simply because I need to escape from other people's problems and unhappiness. I have to cope with my own and I will."

"I don't understand," Victoria told her, surprised at the turn the conversation had taken. She recalled the trivial reason she had come.

"Let's have a cup of tea," suggested Jill.

Victoria followed her into the cramped kitchen. They stood shoulder to shoulder at the sink as she filled the kettle and plugged it in, reaching up into a cupboard on the wall for cups and saucers. Jill came to a sudden decision.

"I need someone to talk to, Vicky. I'm glad you came. Do you remember that Dad wasn't keen to have me in the office and tried to dissuade me? Well, I found out the reason why he didn't want me. He has another woman. Gwen James had been covering up for him and it made things very difficult for both of them when I started work there. Once I realised what was going on, I wanted to leave home before mother found out. I was in an intolerable position, knowing who he was with when she thought a client had kept him busy, even knowing that woman had accompanied him when he flew to London or Paris for a couple of days. Luckily he had never been in the habit of taking mother with him, although she had tried to persuade him a few times, when her own commitments made it possible, but he keeps her out of his business life as much as he can, partly to oblige Alex Stuart, partly for his own sake. She has gobbled up so much of him, he stubbornly resists being entirely demolished. You know what mother is like, so possessive it makes the people she loves tip-toe around her, rigid and with their arms out straight, so to speak."

Jill made the tea, placing a packet of biscuits on the tray. They took it into the living-room and sat side by side on the bulgy couch.

"It took me two months to find this bolt-hole. I was becoming a bundle of nerves. There were times, when mother was going on at me, hurling recriminations about ingratitude and selfishness, when I almost blurted out the truth, or went and strangled Sadie Frobisher. I was desperate to get out before Gwen leaves in September, because then I'll have to take over the job of deception; at least I've done it so far only by default, so to speak. Well, I've made it with a few weeks to go. Every night I pray Dad will stop seeing Mrs. Frobisher, but the truth is that he's getting more besotted and reckless. Mother is getting suspicious. Either he's less attentive to her now or he's overdoing it. What a mess, Vicky! I'm so unhappy. I love Dad, but I hate what he's doing. I don't know how he can. We all love him so much, but he can't care about us any more, only that blasted woman." Tears gathered in her eyes.

Vicky, miserably sympathetic, poured the tea and mutely handed her a cup. I only came to ask her to recommend a hairdresser and get her advice about which style to choose, she thought.

"Does Uncle Larry know you know?" she asked and, to her astonishment, Jill began to laugh through her tears.

"Don't you start that," she said incomprehensibly. "It's a game I used to play in my head every morning in the weeks before I left home as he drove me to the office. Does he know I know and, if so, does he assume that I know he knows that I know?"

"I can't follow that," Victoria admitted.

"Never mind, I'm not sure I can either.

Sadie Frobisher has never been mentioned between us, but he must guess I know about her. I would need to be a half-wit not to suspect something was going on. There is a constraint between us now. He can never be sure I won't tell mother and must realise why I've left home. It's an awful mess, Vicky." She wiped her eyes, blew her nose and took a big gulp of tea.

"I always thought they were so happy," Victoria said.

"On the surface, yes, but I suspect mother is sexually inhibited."

Victoria looked at her older cousin, wide-eyed with incredulity. What would she say next?

Jill continued, unabashed. "It's no good being generous with your emotions in marriage unless you are physically generous as well. Mother never petted or cuddled us, your mother was the same and Aunt Merle, for that matter, although I've never suspected her of being frigid. Mother and Aunty Monica always shy away from bodily contact. They hate having their hair messed up, or their clothes rumpled, and loathe sticky fingers and damp kisses. You know what I mean."

Victoria nodded. She did indeed.

"Perhaps Sadie Frobisher enjoys the kind of things that mother loathes," Jill said. "Then perhaps I can understand a little. Dad has betrayed his children as well as his wife, rejected the whole family."

"I think I am like Aunty Margaret and my mother," Victoria confessed in a low voice, not looking at Jill now.

Jill took her hand and squeezed it sympathetically. "Helen told me about that awful experience you had," and as Victoria protested, added, "yes, I know, she broke a confidence, but you know Helen, you should not have told her. I don't think she's told anyone else. Anyway, Vicky, my advice is to try and forget it. Don't let it spoil your life, keep telling yourself that you are not like your mother, that you are like your father, generous in mind and body, loving and giving in every way."

"But I don't know what my father was like," Victoria reminded her.

"That's an advantage. Lucky Vicky,

you can have the perfect father. He will never be able to let you down, deceive your mother, love someone better than you."

The novelty of the idea enchanted Victoria. What she had always considered as her great loss could now be looked upon as a positive asset when set against the fathers of her cousins, both with feet set firmly on courses designed to cause sorrow and aggravation to their children.

Jill poured them a second cup of tea.

"Have a biscuit," she urged.

Victoria accepted. She decided she ought to say something comforting to Jill, who was always so understanding and kind to other people. All she could think of saying was,

"At least you have Raoul."

"Thank God. I intend to keep him, too. I'll go to any lengths, Vicky."

"You must be careful. You sound like Aunty Margaret. You mustn't be too possessive," Victoria cautioned her.

Jill shook her head.

"I shall be as unlike mother as possible. I'll be generous with my love, not only to him, but also to my children, and not resent their independence. I miss Raoul dreadfully while he's away, but I let him go without feeling guilty about leaving me and wishing he could change the next five years. By the way, I'm having a wine and cheese party, a sort of belated house-warming, on Wednesday evening. Will you come? There won't be many here, it's too small. I've spoken to Bob about it. He said he would take you home afterwards, so there's no need for your mother to fuss."

Victoria thanked her. It would be almost like old times, with all the cousins together again with their friends. She left as soon as she had finished her tea, forgetting about the hairdresser until she was half-way home.

Wednesday evening, so eagerly anticipated, turned out to be a disaster.

The hairdresser had taken her at her word and savagely cropped her hair. A small, waif-like face viewed the result with secret triumph, muttering a subdued thank you in answer to the question whether or not she was satisfied. She left the salon feeling re-born, her hair a shining pale-gold cap without weight. As if miraculously free of all oppression, she travelled home with a light heart, to be met with disbelief, followed by angry dismay.

"But you said it would suit me short," she protested to her mother.

"Not that short! I had no idea you meant that short. It's more like a boy's cut than a young lady's."

Albinia, at first shocked beyond words, managed to say that nowadays one would not even find a boy with hair that short unless he was a skin-head.

"Well, I like it," Victoria cried mutinously, running upstairs to escape further criticism.

However, the worst was still to come. Bob hated it. As he drove her to Jill's party in angry silence, she kept telling herself that she was glad he hated it, but she felt unaccountably miserable; smiling defiantly every time he glanced at her with his dark, smouldering eyes, which usually held a more tender expression.

"What made you do it?" he asked at last, as they left the parked car, slamming his door with vexation.

"Do what?"

"You know very well!"

"Oh, you mean commit the crime of the century?"

"I think you deserve a good spanking. You are thoroughly spoilt!"

"Spoilt?" She stopped in her tracks, dumbfounded.

Bob stopped also, looking down at her as if he could break her neck.

"Yes, spoilt. We have all spoilt you. Because you're quiet and gentle, we don't argue, we let you win."

"That's unfair and untrue," she blazed at him. "I never win."

"Never, Vicky?"

"No, never," she repeated, but of course that was an exaggeration. It was just that her victories were few, her defeats many. How could Bob be so unjust? He didn't have to live with her mother and Aunt Albinia. He didn't need courage just to express an opinion, nor feel loath to say he was tired or had a headache. He didn't know what it was like to have continual fusses over trivialities. Now he was getting as bad as the rest of them, making a melodrama out of a stupid hair-cut. She could tell by the way he was watching her that he was expecting her to become tearful and demand to be taken home. Guiltily she acknowledged that she had beaten him a few times with that ploy. It was childish and she would not stoop to it again. She tilted her chin instead and he found himself facing a cousin grown even more unpredictable than he had realised.

"Soon you'll be far away," she said sweetly, "too far away to know or care what I do."

Swiftly she moved past him to mount the steps of the Victorian terraced house in which Jill lived. He watched her go, partly enlightened. He was deserting her. So far you have always won with me, Vicky, he thought, but not this time. I have to go.

Not all the cousins were at the party. Stephen, Helen and Sandra were absent. However, there was someone there who greeted Victoria's arrival with a warm smile of pleasure and moved to her side like an old friend—David Strang.

18

BY mid-October it was as if a large sieve with irregular holes in it had been thoroughly shaken and everyone had fallen through their matching shapes onto a strange plateau, where they set about recreating their lives in intricate designs upon its unmarked surface.

Now Bob, as well as Stephen and Raoul, had departed on a fine filament of influence from the centre, which was the island, to spin an existence elsewhere. Those who were left spun hard to fill the gaps they had created, with varying degrees of effort and success.

Margaret and her family were the least affected by the absence of the three young men, so had the least to do to live comfortably without them. Had Margaret not been so preoccupied with her own concerns, she might well have spent more time worrying about Merle's; instead of which her mind was concentrated on proving the one thing she could not bear to contemplate, that her husband preferred another woman. On the surface nothing had changed in their relationship. He was as charming and attentive towards her as always and his absences were as frequent, but not prolonged.

The three weeks she had spent with him in London had been a bitter-sweet interlude. Her suspicions had been aroused before they left and began to spread like sea mist, impossible to stifle, feeding on next to nothing. The image she had created of her perfect marriage was losing substance, yet she clutched at it futilely; anguished as it slipped through her fingers. By the time Jill moved into her flat, her mother's resistance had been replaced by a dawning understanding, although Jill was unaware of the change because by that time, they were scarcely communicating, both afraid of what the other might know.

In a household in which the atmosphere was unpredictable and difficult at times, influenced as it was by the mood of the mistress, the occupants trod warily. Helen spent a lot of time away from home and when indoors kept to her room as much as possible, missing her older sister who had been an ally, if an interfering one. Sandra, having been petted and pushed aside by her mother with bewildering inconsistency since birth, found comfort as always with Annie Figgus, reliably warm and practical, while her mother's indifference grew with the preoccupation with her own unhappiness. Larry came and went much as before, behaving towards his wife and children with the same, slightly amused, wholly tolerant attitude he had always used; pretending not to notice the warning signs on the explosive ground he was negotiating with such apparent ease. Mrs. Figgus watched and said nothing. Like Jill, she knew Margaret's faults, yet could admire and respect her with little love. Also like Jill, she adored Larry de Valois while deploring his conduct. She had known about Sadie Frobisher almost from the start of the affair, from a remark she overheard him make on the telephone.

Jill counted herself lucky to be away, living on her own. It made being impotent to change things more bearable. She found the job as her father's secretary completely satisfying and challenging to someone of her tender years. It was spoilt only by the unspoken secret between them, a secret that she struggled to hide from the rest of the staff, in particular his junior partner Alex Stuart, not realising that Alex knew all about Sadie Frobisher. It was a small island, all the discretion in the world could not hide the facts forever. It was a small world, so Larry's trips to any part of it were fraught with chance encounters. Jill kept the engagement diary without comment; only she and her father knew some of it was fiction, but *how* much of it, only he could say.

Merle, occupying her own room again after the usual summer residence in the attic, lay in bed each night courting reluctant sleep and wondered what was to become of her life. Lonely and confused, she wept for what she had once possessed, a husband, two dependent children and a home. Now she was left with a husband who cared more for whisky than he did for her, two absent sons and a guest house, surrounded by a garden also feeling the effects of neglect. The next thing would be that she would have to employ a gardener.

It was incredible that she should even be contemplating such a thing. Karl had been so proud of his flowers. Now he had no interest in anyone or anything except his drink. Her hopes of the spring and summer had been dashed. In August he had succumbed again, going off on a drinking spree and, when he returned, continuing to drink heavily, unlike previous times when he had only tippled moderately between serious bouts. Now they had separate bedrooms all the time. He did not object. The thought of his indifference bedewed her pillow with fresh tears.

At Grande Maison the liaison between Monica and Albinia was strengthening about the only thing they had in common, Leonard's child. Monica, absorbed into the vast house like a fly in an extensive web, allied herself with the spider against the praying mantis, the stealthy Mrs. Grey. Victoria, caught also like a fragile butterfly, fluttered in vain for freedom, a victim too tender to do other than love her oppressors.

She had started a two-year art and design course at the polytechnic and was enjoying it as she had never enjoyed school, where she had been a conscientious but mediocre student in most subjects. The novelty now was that she was amongst her peers, studying only subjects she liked. David Strang had re-entered her life at Jill's party. She had found herself shyly welcoming him to her side. Her initial surprise and embarrassment had rapidly disappeared as they conversed. His outspoken admiration for her new image, which he likened to a wistful urchin, was infuriating to Bob, but balm to her wounded self-esteem. She wanted him to find in her the woman he had looked for in vain a year ago and when he asked her to see him again, she thought she had succeeded.

Since then she had met him regularly once or twice a week, unconsciously turning to him for the affection and support she had previously received from Bob. In this way she missed her cousin less. However, as she saw more of David so, proportionately, opposition to him formed at Grande Maison. When he had called for her the first few times, his reception had been cordial enough, a trifle affected perhaps, as Monica and Albinia sized up the novel situation, but that was to be expected. Victoria's apprehension had been unnecessary. As she began to relax with relief, she realised the situation was changing, making her tense and nervous again whenever he called, so that she was ready long before he was due, meeting him at the door in her anxiety to get him away from the house. There were times, of course, when she was beaten to it, mostly by Mrs. Grey, who led him, confident and unsuspecting, into the drawing-room, like an insect into a Venus fly trap, to be partially sucked dry and spat out for the pleasurable anticipation of the return visit.

Her mother and aunt were growing hostile towards him. As they saw more of David Strang, their curiosity about him grew. Careful questions were answered by him with disarming frankness and a slight cockiness which was considered unbecoming. Victoria was given to understand that they did not approve of what they learned. In his absence they deplored his accent, his brashness, his line of work, his family background—his parents were divorced—the poor quality of his clothes and, unkindest cut of all, his lack of culture. None of this was stated openly, of course, the two women were far too clever to be overtly censorious. His faults were pointed out by way of subtle comparisons and innuendo which Victoria, oversensitive on the subject, could not fail to understand and resent. As their thinly trickling poison formed a bitter cupful, she dashed it aside rather than taste, becoming contumaciously more loyal to him. With so many faults in her mother's eyes, he could not help but evoke her protective instinct and a tenderness that would have delighted him, bold and confident though he was, had he only suspected it.

As it was David was content that his cautious advances were being met without rebuff. Victoria was different from his other women and had to be treated differently. He had returned to the island simply because he had been offered a job there. It afforded him the chance to meet her again, otherwise he would not have sought the opportunity. The girl in London was left behind with few regrets. Victoria, shy and unawakened to the delights of love, presented a challenge he could not resist. Time was not limited as it had been last year. He could be patient and savour the conquest of a prize which was to be hard-won. She had arrived at Jill's flat flushed with annoyance, her grey eyes sparkling with anger at something her cousin Bob had said. He guessed it was because of their quarrel that she had remained in his company most of the evening, ignoring Bob as much as possible. For David that quarrel had been providential, as was Bob's absence now. If he did but know it, he had something else for which he could thank Bob. As Victoria stood passive in his arms, letting him kiss her, she was calming her fears by imagining it was Bob's hands that held her, and her tightly closed eyes were shutting out the hateful image of a stranger's face, grim with lustful intent, seeing instead dark brown eyes, smiling with fond amusement.

19

ONE Wednesday afternoon in November, with the wind blowing icily across dead vegetation and evening already drawing away the parsimonious daylight although it was not yet four o'clock, the three former Le Feuvre girls, even handsomer in early middle-age than when they had graced their father's name, were sitting in Margaret's drawing-room—she would not own to anything so vulgar as a lounge—watching in dark-eyed silence as Annie Figgus set out the tea-cups on the occasional table before the fire. Although her house was ultra-modern, Margaret had insisted on a fireplace for its dramatic effect, and those people on whom the drama was lost gravitated towards it for more basic reasons: warmth and cheering comfort.

The sisters kept up the habit of a weekly meeting, although the day on which they held it varied, mainly according to Margaret's diary. When Merle had visitors, they met at her home, otherwise they took it in turns, with a decided reluctance to visit Grande Maison where, for some indefinable reason, they felt inhibited; Monica's conversation there centred mainly on the ghastliness of the house and Mrs. Grey's insidious liberties.

This particular afternoon each one had a specific worry to be diffused amongst her siblings. Monica and Merle had greeted Annie Figgus cordially on arrival. She was a trusted friend of the family who knew her own worth, kept her own council and, above all, knew her place in the household. Now they waited patiently while she completed her task. She surveyed her handiwork, checking she had forgotten nothing and, with a smile that was readily answered by the two visitors, left the room. Margaret, sitting furthest from the table on a green silk couch, said, "Pour the tea, will you, Monica?"

She lit a cigarette, sitting back to smoke it in a jerky, nervous manner, unlike her usual slow, smooth savouring.

"I'll wait until you've finished smoking," Monica said reprovingly.

Merle, who might at one time have

warned her about damaging her health, never gave the matter a thought, she was too used to watching Karl destroying his. Instead she said, "I had a letter from Stephen yesterday," in a light, inconsequential tone, which did not fool the others. Their eyes focused upon her, waiting for her to continue.

"He's bringing his girl here for Christmas."

They thought about this. He must be serious about her, was the silent assumption.

"Won't her parents want her to go home to them?" was Monica's question.

Merle's eloquent eyes spoke first, then her voice said, "She has no parents."

"Oh, I see," Margaret said. They all did. Stephen had found someone for whom he had assumed responsibility. Doubtless he was now lost to the family as a fully participating member. Merle, accepting a cup of tea from a sympathetic sister, said, "I'm surprised he wants her to see Karl in the state he's in. He's always so humiliated when his father is drunk. He hates anyone to know."

They drank tea, ate cake and discussed

generalities, testing the ground with trivia while those left with something to be said considered how best to say it if, indeed, it should be said at all.

Margaret mentioned having seen Albinia. Monica wished that she had not. She had kept her sister-in-law from the conversation deliberately, because Albinia knew something which was not in Margaret's best interest to find out and, by ignoring one, Monica hoped to stifle the other. She changed the subject.

"Victoria is seeing far too much of that young man," she said. "I can't think what she sees in him. His accent is appalling."

"He came to the house with Jill and Raoul, a few days before Raoul went back to London," Margaret told her. "He seemed all right to me. Quite handsome. The kind who would get on in the world, not easily put down."

Privately she wondered what such a forceful young man saw in Victoria. Shyness in her niece had the same effect upon Margaret as deafness in her housekeeper: she never could believe that either affliction was not an irritating affectation.

"He'll get on all right," Monica agreed, "one way or another."

"How do you mean?" Merle wanted to know, not conversant with the young man.

"He will either make money or marry it," Monica retorted significantly.

Margaret sat up. "Do you think he's after Victoria's money?" she asked. It made sense.

"Surely he doesn't know she has any," Merle protested. "I can't see Victoria telling him, not unless they were planning to get married. Only a fool would use a fortune to entice a man. Victoria has too much pride."

"There's the house," Margaret reminded her. "You couldn't be poor and live in that place."

Monica immediately said, "Well, I do and I'm poor enough."

They ignored her. Her poverty was a thing they had learnt to live with, too familiar to merit further discussion.

"At least he won't know Victoria is rich by looking at her," Margaret said.

"You can't tell that just by looking at anyone." Merle glanced at Margaret's fine woollen dress and beautiful patent leather shoes, the former set off by a thin gold chain of considerable length and matching ear-rings. She changed her opinion.

Margaret caught the glance. She was about to speak when the telephone rang. She froze for a moment, then leaned forward to stub out her cigarette in a thorough manner into the silver ash tray before her. She excused herself and left the room to answer it, unhurriedly, walking tall as was her manner.

"He's going to be late again," was Merle's enigmatic opinion.

"Albinia saw him at the airport on Monday, escorting Sadie Frobisher to a taxi," Monica told her. "I really don't know how Margaret remains in ignorance."

"Perhaps because she doesn't want to know."

Margaret returned. They watched her take her original place on the couch and light another cigarette. No one spoke. Monica poured more tea. Merle twisted her sapphire ring round and round. After a few minutes she helped herself to a piece of Mrs. Figgus' shortbread. Monica stirred her tea as if it was her intention to shorten the spoon. The silence lengthened intolerably.

Margaret spoke. Merle gulped. Monica carefully placed the spoon in her saucer.

"What miserable wretches we three are! Not one of us with a husband worth having."

That she should say that of Larry was indeed a revelation.

"Leonard was worth having," Monica protested in a shirty tone.

Margaret did not answer. She had her own opinion about Leonard Lacy.

Merle was going to protest also, out of habitual loyalty to Karl, then decided it was not worth it.

"My life is ruined," Margaret said dramatically. Her sisters regarded her with silent unease.

"I can see there is no need to tell you why," she continued with sarcasm. "As is usually the case, the wife is the last to know. I shall never forgive him, never!" She put her fine hands over her face, bending her head in an attitude of overwhelming grief.

Her audience looked at each other in consternation, unsure whether to admit knowledge or go on pleading ignorance. Merle plumped for the latter.

"What on earth has Larry done, darling? Forgotten your anniversary?" Larry having been the ideal husband for years, it was conceivable that Margaret, who loved to create an impression, might lament over something so monstrous, not realising that in many marriages it was a common occurrence.

Margaret's head came up, her hands dropped into her lap. Fixing Merle with a scornful glare she declared, "You know damned well we were married in May. Anyway, it would hardly ruin my life. How can you imagine such a thing?"

"I'm sorry," Merle apologised, starting to twist her ring again. "I didn't think."

"That's obvious," Margaret agreed, adding with reluctance, in a low voice rough with emotion, "Larry is having an affair with Sadie Frobisher. I have suspected something like this for some time now. I have just accused him of it and he has confessed. I wish I hadn't. It was much better not being sure. He needn't pretend to care about me any more. I preferred the pretence to his outright rejection. Now I have nothing, my future is a void." Tears ran down her face.

Her sisters looked away, pity in their hearts.

"What am I going to do?" Margaret asked in desperation, speaking rhetorically, for she knew that she would have to find her own answer.

"You could leave him," Monica suggested tentatively.

"You mean leave my home? Never!" Fresh tears spilled down her cheeks at the thought.

"If anyone leaves, he does," she said with spirit. She looked first at one sister and then the other. They shifted uncomfortably. Yes, she could read it in their faces, they had known, just as Jill had and God knows how many besides.

"I want this to go no further," she warned them. "It's humiliating enough to admit it to you. I intend to put a brave face on it. I want no one's pity. If it becomes common knowledge I shall retaliate by pretending I drove him into her arms by taking a lover myself. You would have to hint at the same thing. If anyone is going to have to accept pity, it will be Larry."

"But Margaret, you couldn't do that!" Merle gasped, indignant at the idea.

"Why not?" she wanted to know. "Is it so ludicrous? Don't think I haven't had the opportunity."

They believed her. There had been many times when the widow and the neglected wife had been envious of the admiration enjoyed by their more fortunate sister. Now they looked at her, wounded to the core, surrounded by elegance and luxury, her dark eyes dimmed, but her chin raised in brave defiance and they forgot they had ever envied someone whose happiness had been so exclusively and firmly fixed on the ephemeral possession of the love of one other human being.

"Are you perhaps making too much of this, dear?" Monica ventured to suggest. "Many men have affairs, it does not always mean the end of their marriages."

"Who's talking about the end of my marriage?" Margaret cried, turning on her fiercely.

"I thought you were," Monica faltered.

"Well, I am not now. The end of me, certainly. I shall never be the same again. But I'll not let that woman get away with it. She doesn't know Larry as well as I do. He needs me more than he realises."

"What will you do?" Monica asked.

Margaret made a gesture of bewildered helplessness, pathetic to see from one usually so decisive. "I don't know," she replied wearily. "I can't think. Now the truth has hit me, I feel numb. Do you mind going home? I want to be on my own."

As soon as her sisters had departed, Margaret 'phoned Jill. When she had spoken to Larry, he had been calling from a 'phone box to tell her he would not be home until about eleven. Her long-held suspicions made certainties by a telephone call that morning from Gerald Frobisher, she had coldly accused Larry of intending to dine with his mistress. He had admitted it, telling her that they must discuss the situation when he returned. Now she spoke to Jill, who was unaware of the turn of events but not unprepared.

"I want to see you, Jill. Can you come

here straight from the office? Have dinner with us tonight."

"What do you want to see me about, Mum?" Jill enquired cautiously.

"It will wait until you get here. You will come, won't you?"

"Of course," Jill promised, her spirits sinking. Was there an uncharacteristic pleading note in her mother's voice? She was filled with foreboding.

She arrived at her parents' home just before six. Mrs. Figgus told her that her mother was upstairs changing for dinner.

"And my father?" she asked.

"Not coming home until much later."

"Oh, I see."

Sandra leaped downstairs two at a time to greet her, followed by Helen at a more stately pace, emulative of her mother. The three girls went into the drawing-room, the two youngest with plenty to say. Jill listened to them inattentively, her thoughts preoccupied with the coming interview with her mother, which she supposed would take place before dinner. In fact Margaret made her appearance as they took their places at the table. It was the first time she had seen any of her daughters that day. She greeted them with her customary, "Good evening, girls," and, turning to Jill on her right, thanked her for coming, an ominous sign not lost on the others.

The conversation, so vivacious before their mother's arrival, became subdued and intermittent as they tried unsuccessfully to gauge her mood. They had noticed the absence of their father's place setting immediately they entered the dining-room. It was too usual to call forth comment, but to be regretted as it affected the spirits of their mother and the enjoyment of the meal, no matter what culinary magic Mrs. Figgus had conjured up.

Sandra took the empty soup plates through to the kitchen and helped carry in the roast lamb. Jill smiled at Mrs. Figgus and said how lovely it was to be enjoying her cooking again.

Margaret reminded her sharply that she had chosen to go. She could have been eating Mrs. Figgus' excellent food every day, instead of having to cook for herself, which probably meant existing on rubbishy convenience foods.

Despite the excellence of the meal,

Margaret hardly tasted anything, pushing the food round her plate and occasionally carrying tiny morsels to her mouth in a mere pretence of eating. Helen, who desperately wanted to see her father to wheedle some extra cash out of him, knew better than to enquire when he was to be expected, instead she said, "I saw Vicky and David Strang at lunch time in Woolworth's. They seem to be seeing quite a lot of each other."

"Monica disapproves of him," Margaret said shortly.

"Really! Why?" Helen asked.

"She appears to think he is not good enough for Victoria."

"In what way, for heaven's sake? Aunty Monica has changed since she moved to Grande Maison. She's getting more like Miss Lacy every day, a typical old maid. You wouldn't think she'd ever had a husband. If I were Vicky I'd marry David Strang quickly and escape."

Margaret looked at her dispassionately.

"Yes, I'm sure you would," she said. "Let's hope that Victoria has more sense of duty than my daughters appear to possess." She pushed her plate away as if its contents disgusted her, poured a glass of water which she sipped fastidiously for a few seconds, then, setting down the glass, said, "Let me caution all of you against seeing marriage as a means of escape from what you obviously consider the tyranny of family life. Believe me, marriage is as much a tyranny. A woman gives her all and is repaid with ingratitude from her children and less than that from the person for whom she has sacrificed everything."

Jill kept silent, sure now of what was to come.

Helen boldly asked, "Are you saying we should not get married, Mum?"

"What else is there to do, other than support oneself forever in independence and loneliness?" Margaret uttered tragically.

"We could live in sin," chirped Sandra, instantly regretting it, as three pairs of eyes turned upon her, two in shocked amusement, the third just shocked. Then, to everyone's amazement, Margaret laughed.

"Yes, so we could," she said, savouring the idea. "We could live in sin." Her laughter died as suddenly as it had erupted. She wiped her mouth on her napkin and rose.

"You two help Mrs. Figgus. I want to speak to Jill in my room."

"We haven't had the pudding," Sandra cried.

"Shut up," Helen advised in a fierce whisper. "We'll eat it in the kitchen."

Jill followed her mother with apprehension. Even her back looks miserable, she thought, trailing upstairs in her wake.

As soon as Jill had shut the door behind her, Margaret asked, "How long have you known about Sadie Frobisher?"

"Not very long."

"You're lying! You have been covering up for your father ever since you went to work in the office. You probably knew before that, which would account for your reluctance to work for him."

"It's not true, Mum. I gradually found out, honestly."

"Then why didn't you tell me? Did you think you were doing me a favour, keeping me in ignorance? Don't you realise, I could probably have put a stop to it. Now it's too late. It's your fault, you stupid girl. You should have warned me."

"How long have you suspected?" Jill asked her and when Margaret did not reply, added gently,

"It's not easy, is it? First I hoped it wasn't true, then, when I knew it was, I hoped something would happen to bring him to his senses."

"Before I found out, you mean," Margaret said bitterly.

"Yes, I didn't want you hurt. I know how much you love him," Jill began to cry, stricken by the misery in her mother's face. "I love him too, we all do. It hurts me as well."

But Margaret was only concerned with her own bruising; her daughter's appeared trivial in contrast.

"What are you going to do," Jill asked, knowing her mother too well to suppose she would do nothing. "Have you spoken to Daddy about it?"

Margaret did not reply, instead she rushed to the open window which overlooked the drive.

Jill took a startled step towards her, horror-struck, thinking she was going to hurl herself out, but, after a quick glance out, Margaret turned to her.

"He's back," she said, distraught. "He's returned earlier than he said. Go downstairs quickly. Tell him I must speak to him now, in here. Hurry, for heaven's sake!" Then, pushing past Jill she ran out of the room, to stand stock still at the top of the stairs, watching her husband ascending them in haste.

Jill fled past them both to what had once been her own room, flinging herself upon the bed, to lie in trepidation, imagining the scene taking place across the landing.

Margaret turned on her heel, leading the way back into her room. They faced each other in silence, both searching for the right words to describe a depth of emotion beyond speech. For the first time since he had known her, Larry de Valois' wife looked upon him with dislike.

He said, simply and sincerely, "Darling, I'm sorry."

"For being found out?" she asked bitterly.

"For hurting you," he said.

"I'm not hurting, Larry. Nothing can

hurt me now. I'm dead inside. You have killed me."

He took a step towards her, from which she retreated, backing up to the bed.

"For God's sake, Margaret, don't be so melodramatic. I want to explain."

"I'm sure you do, it would make you feel better. I suppose Sadie Frobisher is doing the same thing, explaining to her husband and children. Well, I shall not give you the satisfaction. You can pack your things and go."

Instantly she regretted her words. Panic-stricken she waited for him to take his leave, words of pleading forming on her lips, but he was as surprised as she was. He had not expected instant dismissal. It was extremely inconvenient. Margaret was entertaining some important French clients of his at the weekend. They were invited to a dinner party tomorrow night at Alex Stuart's place. Alex had no idea that his affair with Sadie had reached such an alarming crisis. He teased Larry about her occasionally, playfully threatening to tell Margaret. God, things were getting out of hand.

The devil of it was that the affair was

coming to an end anyway. Sadie was getting cold feet. Her husband, usually so complacent, was growing difficult and she no longer enjoyed the freedom of movement she once had; added to that one of her boys was ill and would need an operation in the near future, on which would depend his ability to walk. Her maternal concern was swamping her romanticism. Guilt was replacing the excitement of illicit meetings. The days abroad, planned so carefully to coincide with her husband's business trips, had already ceased now that she had an invalid son home from boarding school. Sadie was beautiful and sexually satisfying, but Margaret was his luxurious, well-run home, his family, his ambition, his future of declining years. He needed her wisdom, her impeccable taste, her social expertise, more than he needed Sadie's warmth and loveliness. Somehow he had to convince Margaret that she needed him. In the meantime, he would refuse to go, play for time. He would gradually charm his way back into her favour, he knew he could, given half a chance.

Looking at her now, pale and rigid

before him, he acknowledged it was a formidable task, but he would learn from his children how to tread with caution about her every mood. The time had gone, he had forfeited it, when he alone was to be favoured with the sunny side of her disposition. No longer protected by her adoration, he would have to develop tactics of his own. Regretfully he mentally surrendered that part of his life that he had previously jealously preserved from her. He would let her participate more in his business affairs and take her whenever he went abroad. What more could he do?

Margaret saw no trace of this self-annihilation in his demeanour, just as he could not guess the pain she felt in the heart she had pronounced dead.

"I'll move into the guest room," he told her. "We have to discuss this further, Margaret. I am not so ready to lose you, as you are to get rid of me."

Without waiting for her angry retort, he left the room. He made his way to the kitchen for solace, from whence issued the voices of his youngest daughters in heated argument. He was welcomed with cries of delight and satisfaction. Sandra ran to him to show him her poem printed in the school magazine, Helen bided her time, waiting for the right moment to ask him for an advance on her allowance. Mrs. Figgus bustled about making him coffee. After a while, Jill joined them there. She met her father's smiling welcome with a look of deep reproach, smiting him with remorse.

20

THE short, bleak winter days crept on towards another Christmas. Raoul arrived home for a month's vacation, followed two days later by Stephen with his girl, Alison, who was to be summed up by the family as "a nice little thing", because her looks were nondescript and she had enough sense to keep her very decided opinions to herself.

Unlike Victoria, she was neither shocked nor intimidated by Karl's drinking. She watched him dispassionately as he helped himself to more whisky whenever Stephen and Merle were out of the room, and he did not feel the need to be constantly making facile excuses to her to cover up his craving. She did not approve, he did not suppose she would, but neither did she judge. To his surprise he found the extra glasses dwindling in number beneath the steady gaze of her pale blue eyes and, when she accepted a drink from him, which was not often, they sat in companionable silence, he nursing his glass, she nursing her thoughts.

She was angular and a little clumsy in her movements, but sitting still, as she liked to do, there was a controlled composure about her which Karl found pleasing. Merle had once possessed the same quality of calmness before anxieties had taken their toll of her disposition and worn her nerves to shreds. Not that Karl's whisky-dulled senses were able to make comparisons or draw conclusions. He just felt drawn towards this unemotional young lady of Stephen's and was more at ease in her presence than he had ever been in his eldest son's. Buoyed up by the novelty of the girl's presence and by anticipation of seeing Bob again in the near future, he kept his problem under control, and a visitor less observant than Miss Alison Jeaves might have believed that Stephen's embarrassed warning had been exaggerated. He had explained the situation to her, he thought it only fair, so that she could choose whether or not to come; but in fact, a young lady with no parental home and the prospect of spending Christmas with her brother and his three unruly children in a household mismanaged by a lazy wife, needed a deterrent greater than alcoholism in her host.

Her first week was spent in equanimity. Merle found her capable but not overwilling, indeed her services were usually offered by Stephen, but given with a good enough grace. The younger members of the family came to call, out of curiosity to see Stephen's girl. Helen and Sandra dropped in one morning for coffee and Victoria stopped by one afternoon on her way to town. Opinions were taken home and freely distributed, but Stephen did not take her to visit his aunts and they were too busy just then to keep the weekly rendezvous.

Bob arrived home three days before Christmas and brought the house back to life. His friends, among them his cousins, started to ring up asking for him, requesting his presence at parties and pubs. Previously, Stephen would have accompanied him on many of his forays; this time he preferred to stay at home with Alison, or take her out alone.

"It's typical of Bob," Merle complained to Alison. "He's never in. It was a relief to me when he decided to join the merchant navy. He needs a discipline greater than he gets at home."

Alison was intrigued.

"What does he get up to?"

"Goodness knows!" Merle answered. "If I knew, I might not worry so much. He's far too fond of going out drinking with his friends, that I do know."

So that was it. She was worried that he would become an alcoholic like his father. How different were the two brothers! It was apparent to Alison after just a couple of days in Bob's company. He was too easy-going for her. She had gravitated towards Stephen for his sober dependability. Her father had been something like Bob, sociable, well-liked, fond of a good time; only further acquaintance would tell if Bob resembled him in extravagance and fecklessness. She hoped not, for she liked him already, despite his gently teasing manner. She hated to be teased, yet Bob accomplished it without malice, in a way that made her feel accepted into the household.

On Christmas Eve, Margaret and Larry were having their customary party, with the difference that this year it was to include only family. Margaret was not quite so fond of entertaining their mutual friends as she once had been. Now there was always present an element of distrust between herself and her husband which was considerably lessened when he was not in the company of other women. It was common knowledge that Jill and Raoul were to announce their engagement in the New Year, so Fiona and Richard Bellinger were among the guests, as was Albinia Lacy. There would be only one stranger in their midst, Stephen's girl. She would be observing them as individuals and as part of each other and would be fascinated by the scene and the ensuing drama.

Stephen drove them there, with his father next to him and Bob sitting in the back with the two women. They were met at the door by a young woman whom Alison knew to be one of the family by her dark hair and eyes. She was of medium height with a well-proportioned slim figure and one of the loveliest smiles Alison had ever seen. It was Jill. She welcomed them warmly, introducing Raoul who was standing behind her and there followed kisses all round, much to Alison's dismay, for her family did not go in for that kind of thing. It was just the beginning of her ordeal. They were the last to arrive and, having been divested of coats, were soon in the drawing-room greeting the rest of the assembly. Alison was introduced to one after the other in rapid succession, but once the flurry of welcoming embraces was over, she was able to place herself at one side of the room, away from the door and a little behind Stephen, where she could sort out the names and faces at leisure. Her host and hostess she judged a remarkably fine couple. Margaret was not as pretty as her plumper sister, Merle, but she certainly had more presence, a certain style and grace that was distinctive. She did not look happy. Her husband did, as he listened attentively to something his youngest daughter was telling him in an excited, laughing manner, her hand on his sleeve, as if to prevent him from disappearing before she had finished. That was Sandra, dark again, while her sister standing near her, so like her mother in looks and bearing, had in fact her father's colouring, light brown hair and blue eyes.

Helen was looking at Alison, aware she was being scrutinised. She slowly turned her head away, unmindful, to speak to Fiona Bellinger who was sitting next to her.

"Where's Vicky?" Bob asked.

So there was someone missing. Of course, the other girl who had called soon after her arrival.

"She's taking a 'phone call," Monica told him. She did not seem pleased about it, Alison thought. This third sister was neither plump and pretty nor tall and elegant, but somewhere in between, with the same dark, eloquent eyes and almost black hair. There was an air of abstraction about her, as if she had something on her mind, but this vanished when her daughter entered a few minutes later, to be replaced by an air of watchfulness, as if Victoria was giving her some cause for anxiety. Alison wondered what that cause could be.

Three people noticed Victoria's entrance: her mother, Alison and Bob, but only one of them was aware of the effect it had. She immediately looked around the room until her eyes found Bob's. He smiled and moved to her side, saying something that made her flush with pleasure. In fact he had remarked that her hair had grown a bit and looked quite nice, but Alison could not hear that, only notice how captivated he seemed to be by the slight, very fair girl in the blue dress, who did not look as if she belonged there, she was so unlike the rest. The next moment he was bringing her over to be introduced, leading her by the hand, unaware that they had met already.

Victoria, whose preference had always been for observation rather than participation, was meeting, could she but have known it, a kindred spirit, although there the similarity ended. A look at their respective chins told much of the remainder of their characters. Victoria's was soft and round, almost childlike in form, Alison's was full and firm, hinting at definite opinions stubbornly held.

"It must be awful for you," Victoria commiserated, "meeting so many people all at once."

"Not really," Alison said. "I'm not shy and you all seem very friendly. Who is the formidable looking woman next to your mother? I can't remember her name."

Victoria followed her look. "Oh, that's my Aunt Binnie. Albinia Lacy, my father's sister."

"She doesn't look the party sort."

"No, I suppose not. She is not used to family get-togethers, poor thing. She came mainly to please my mother, but I think she would be just as happy at home on her own. Mother always assumes other people are happier in company."

Bob was amused by this.

"Vicky has spent her life trying to hide in corners and her mother has been just as busy prising her out of them. She is the only one of us who is shy and has had to suffer in consequence." He turned to her, "By the way, I hear you are not spending the holiday with us this year. It's our turn, but Mum said you are remaining at Grande Maison. I'm disappointed, it won't be the same without you."

Victoria admitted that she was disappointed also, but her mother did not think it would be fair on Aunt Binnie to leave her on her own for ten days.

"But we're coming with the others

tomorrow," she said, her large grey eyes regarding him earnestly, hoping her words had cheered him.

"Good. I'll be gone before New Year anyway. I have to be back by the 30th."

It was her turn to be disappointed,

"Oh, I didn't know."

"Do you miss me, Vicky?" he asked teasingly, but she did not answer, except with a look that he found impossible to interpret.

"I answer your letters, don't I?" he asked, defensively.

"It takes you long enough. I have a good mind not to write any more."

"Really?" he asked, watching her closely. She shook her head, smiling.

When Stephen had finished talking to Raoul and came back to her side, Alison said to him, "Bob and Victoria seem very fond of one another."

"Yes," he agreed. "They have always been close. More like brother and sister than cousins."

"Are you sure it's not more than that?" He glanced at her sharply.

"Of course not. Vicky's the kind of person who is over-sensitive, easily hurt, and Bob is tender-hearted. He's dried her tears for so long that he hasn't realised she's a big girl now and can do it for herself."

He turned away from her, as if to indicate the subject was closed. She had detected a note of resentment in his explanation; perhaps he felt it was none of her business. It made her feel even more of an outsider. She wished she had gone to her brother's home in Exeter instead. She looked across the room towards Miss Lacy with a certain amount of sympathy and was on the point of going to sit next to her, when a voice asked her if she was enjoying her stay on the island.

Richard Bellinger was at her elbow, smiling kindly, keen to engage her in conversation. She learned more about the family in the next quarter of an hour than she had learnt from Stephen in all the months she had known him. Raoul's father was not indiscreet, but he seemed to sense she was interested in the common history of the people in the room. From him she learned that he had known Albinia Lacy since she was a child, because their fathers had been good friends in their youth; that

Victoria's father had died when she was only two years old; that he himself was the family solicitor; that Raoul had been Stephen's friend since infant school and, just when he could think of no more to tell her, his wife joined them, beginning the conversation all over again. However, Fiona talked in a manner which called for constant participation from her listener, something which did not suit Alison at all. She found herself giving away personal information, which was uncharacteristic. She would have been surprised had she heard Fiona's comment to her husband as they drove home that night.

"What a reticent girl that Alison is. I found it quite difficult to talk to her."

Richard smiled. He would never have believed it!

In fact it was a relief to many of those present when the party came to an end. Merle spent the entire evening surreptitiously watching Karl re-filling his glass, trying to establish the exact moment when his bumbling affability was about to change into vacuous incoherence and trigger off their hurried leave-taking.

Albinia, dressed for the occasion in a

silk dress of hideous green, her hair out of the uncompromising bun and twisted about her head in thick plaits, entered into the spirit of the evening with forced enthusiasm, telling anyone who cared to listen just how much she was enjoying herself, approving of everyone and everything, including the food when it arrived, with patronising gusto. The cousins, well-bred to a nicety, plied her with delicacies, re-filled her cup with coffee, engaged her in conversation when she was left alone—a difficult task this, for, apart from Victoria, they knew so little of her—and listened politely as she valiantly produced the small talk she felt appropriate to the occasion. Small talk was something Albinia despised, but she thought it was the least she could do in return for hospitality she could well have done without. Her opinion of the family into which Leonard had married had never been very great. It had not improved much on acquaintance. None of them were happily married. Margaret, too fond of gadding about and spending money on expensive knick-knacks, seemed determined to keep that unfaithful husband of hers. Albinia could see him now, talking to that silly, affected woman, Fiona Bellinger, who was hanging on his every word, giggling like a schoolgirl. What a frivolous dress she was wearing for a woman of her age! Then there was Merle, saddled with a drink-sodden weakling. There was something about these Le Feuvres that drove their husbands to excesses. It would probably have been the same for Leonard had he lived, although to what particular excess Monica would have driven him it was hard to say. Poor, dear Leonard! How gentle and reserved he had been, so much like Victoria. Albinia's eyes sought her niece, but she was not in the room. Surely it must be nearly time to leave.

Monica was not enjoying herself as much as she usually did on these occasions. David Strang had phoned Victoria almost as soon as they arrived. She wondered why, but her enquiry had been rebuffed with the remark that it had not been important, just a desire on his part to wish Victoria a happy Christmas. Monica was not satisfied. She would not rest until she had discovered what it was about. They must be planning a meeting in the next day or so. Really, he was becoming a thorough nuisance! Monica was regretting having declined to spend the holiday with Merle. When she was in the company of her sisters she was not fond of Albinia. It was only when they were together at Grande Maison that she felt an affinity, an enveloping of a subtle influence that she could not define, as if she were inhabiting a different world from the rest of the family and had to ingratiate herself with the aliens to ensure the survival of her offspring. She watched Albinia now, responding heartily to something Stephen had said. Oh God, must she try so hard to enjoy herself?

Stephen was not even trying. Frankly, he thought his father should have been left at home. He had said as much to his mother yesterday, but she would not hear of it, declaring that Karl had never made an exhibition of himself in company and, until he did, she was not ashamed to take him to family gatherings where everyone was aware of his problem and sympathetic. Stephen did not want their sympathy for his father or for himself. He hated to see people patronising Karl. They certainly did not talk to him for the benefit of his stimulating conversation. He spoke in cliches now and it was difficult for anyone who attempted to converse with him to sustain it. Usually it ended up in fatuous smiles on both sides, followed by embarrassed tactical withdrawals from those kind enough to have made the effort.

In the kitchen, helping Sandra and Victoria to load the washing-up machine with the first lot of used dishes, Helen confided that she was pig-sick of family parties.

"They are so boring," she wailed. "I asked Mum if we could invite some of our friends for a change, but no way! Prissy and Roy have gone to the Nightwatchman to a disco. I asked if I could go with them and she nearly had a fit. She could have at least let me invite Roy; after all, I am going out with him."

"Does mother know that?" Sandra asked.

Helen frowned and slammed the door of the machine.

"Well, I've told her, but I don't suppose she bothered to listen. One day I'll do something to make her take notice. It would have to be pretty drastic. Dad's only got to cut himself shaving and she practically has hysterics."

"Not any more," Sandra observed. "She's beginning to ignore him as well now. That is, if she does notice him it's to find fault, no matter how hard he tries to please her. I feel sorry for him, poor Daddy."

"Are you letting your hair grow again, Vicky?" Helen asked her, ignoring Sandra.

Victoria nodded.

"Why? I thought you preferred it short. You shouldn't be so influenced by your mother."

"It's not that," Victoria said, but they remained unconvinced.

"Why don't you buy a car?" Helen asked. She would have loved one herself, but her parents would not allow her to have one until she was working. It was different for Victoria, she had a fortune to spend. She could run one easily.

"I've thought about it," Victoria confessed. "I'm starting driving lessons next month. David has promised to let me practise in his car."

"And what does Aunty Monica think about that?"

"I haven't told her yet."

"Well, you're over eighteen," Sandra pointed out, "so you can please yourself."

"Theoretically," Helen added, who had yet to see her cousin please herself about anything of importance.

"What are you girls doing?"

Margaret was standing in the doorway, viewing the chaos in the kitchen with disfavour. Why did Annie Figgus have to choose tonight to visit her late husband's sister?

"Not a lot by the look of it. Slice that gateau, Helen. Be sure Merle gets a piece, it's her favourite. I think she will be departing soon from the look of your uncle, unless they intend carrying him to the car."

"Poor Uncle Karl," said soft-hearted Sandra. She was beginning to wonder if anyone was ever really happy. I could be happy, she thought, if everyone else was. Even if you had no problems of your own, other people inflicted theirs on you.

Half-an-hour later, Stephen decided he had endured enough.

"I think we should be going, Mum."

Merle immediately cast an anxious look towards her husband, who was harmlessly minding his own business in a corner, nursing the eternal glass and, which was more important, standing up.

"A little longer, dear," she murmured.

Stephen shook his head decidedly.

"If he tries to move, he'll fall over," was his opinion.

"Oh, no," his mother assured him, but she could tell that there was no point in arguing. She knew from experience that Karl had another hour left in him of cautious sipping, she also knew that Larry was not letting him pour his own drinks and was heavily diluting the ones he handed to him. The fact that Karl was meekly accepting dilution meant he was still able to make an effort on his own behalf, but another look at Stephen's face as he waited for her to make a move was enough to bring her to her feet. A glance passed between her and Margaret; all was understood, the leave-taking began.

Albinia decided this was her opportunity. Monica was easily persuaded to go, but not Victoria, who enjoyed so little of her cousins' company now that she intended to make the most of it.

"Let her stay, Aunty," Bob pleaded for her. "I'll bring her home."

They were all surprised when Alison turned to Stephen and asked, "Must we go now? I should like to stay a little longer. If Bob drives your parents home, he can bring the car back for the rest of us."

Stephen readily agreed. As long as he got rid of the humiliating presence of his father, he was quite happy to remain. The Bellingers decided that they would stay as well; after all, they did not want to drag Raoul away from his friends. They were aware that Jill could have driven Raoul home in her mini, but Fiona wanted the opportunity of a quiet chat with her parents. She had heard rumours about Larry's goings-on with another woman. She wanted them to know that she was not in favour of this early engagement and would appreciate it if Margaret would have a talk with Jill on the subject of the importance of Raoul completing his degree in medicine unencumbered by marital responsibilities. Jill was wilful. Fiona hoped her mother could temper this with a few words of council; she also hoped that Larry's philandering nature had not been passed on to his eldest daughter. Once Jill had what she wanted, namely Fiona's only child, would she begin to lose interest, fixing her sights on some other prize?

When Bob returned, having taken rather a long time despite the short journey, because he had helped to make his father comfortable for the night in the smallest bedroom which was his exclusively out of the holiday season, he found his cousins letting their hair down in the dining-room, dancing to their favourite records on the parquet flooring with the furniture and rolled-up rugs pushed to the walls. His aunt and uncle were closeted in the library with Fiona and Richard Bellinger, enjoying a quiet talk and drink. He presumed they were enjoying it, but in fact Margaret and Fiona were fencing dangerously with words, the latter's guard of soft femininity slipping a little to reveal the tougher fibre underneath, no surprise to astute Margaret who had suspected it during years of only slight acquaintance. Jill had never under-estimated Fiona either.

When it was time to bring the party to an end, that is when the two sets of parents entered the dining-room demanding a cessation of the cacophony in favour of the soothing strains of the last waltz, Victoria felt Bob's arms close round her with a sigh of contentment. She had imagined being in them so often, whenever David had held her close. They had been a refuge for her mind, to bring uneasy submission to her body, as she accepted David's kisses and light caresses. Bob's embrace caused no fears. He held her as a cousin, in easy companionship, safe and uncomplicated. She lifted her face to his with a sleepy smile of happiness.

"What are you thinking?" she whispered, wondering at his serious expression, but he just held her closer, rubbing his cheek against her soft hair.

Alison caught his eyes over Victoria's head as she waltzed past in Stephen's arms. They exchanged a look of complete understanding.

21

THREE weeks later, Helen got her wish and became the focus of her mother's attention; also the rest of the family's, but she hardly noticed that.

It was six-fifteen on a Friday evening of driving sleet, visible in slanting white clouds beneath the street lights. Helen descended from the damp warmth of the bus into the biting cold of the ill-lit country road and set off determinedly into the wind and wet, well wrapped up against it in padded, hooded school coat and lamb-skin mittens. Her face was frozen in seconds; the pit of her stomach became colder as she neared home. She approached the house from the side, where the kitchen windows gave forth a welcoming glow of yellow light. She hurried towards this as to a refuge.

Inside the kitchen, Mrs. Figgus and Sandra were standing side by side at the hob, deep in conversation. Mrs. Figgus, wrapped, as always when cooking, in a white overall resembling a laboratory coat, was stirring a pan of soup with a wooden spoon. Sandra was watching a pan of milk, ready to lift it swiftly from the boil. She turned at the sound of her sister's entrance.

"You look frozen," she said, immediately transferring her attention back to the milk.

Mrs. Figgus smiled over her shoulder, stirring rhythmically.

Helen slowly took off her coat. As the hood fell from her head, Mrs. Figgus shrieked.

Startled, Sandra looked to see what was the matter. The milk boiled over and burned on unattended.

"Bloody hell!" said Sandra.

When she could find her voice, Mrs. Figgus gasped, awestruck, "What will your mother say?"

"I don't care!" Helen said, defiantly. She sat down in the nearest chair, the cold in her stomach suddenly melting into nausea.

The other two stared transfixed at Helen's hair, which was short and spiky and, horror of horrors, bright orange!

"You've gone punk," Sandra squealed, scandalised. "They won't let you go to school looking like that. Miss Farley will never allow it."

Miss Farley was their headmistress, a woman after their mother's heart, not sympathetic to youthful whims and fancies, having never succumbed to them herself.

The door opened. Margaret entered.

"What's that terrible smell?" she cried. "Sandra, what are you doing? You've let the milk boil over." She rushed over to the hob, which Sandra and Mrs. Figgus began desperately mopping up.

"How could you be so careless!" Margaret scolded. "Imagine having people to dinner with such an obnoxious smell in the house."

Stink would have been a better word for it, Sandra thought, but her mother would never use it. As she held the pan under the cold tap, she came to the opinion that people should not be frightened of soiling their lips with highly descriptive words. She liked language to be colourful. Her mother could have said stench, if she objected to stink. Just then another screech rent the air, from her mother this time. Sandra dropped the pan into the sink with a clatter. She and Mrs. Figgus turned simultaneously, rather guiltily for some obscure reason, to face the object of horror.

"My God!" Margaret cried, "I don't believe it! Get out of my sight, you stupid child. I don't want to see you again until you have returned to normal," and as poor Helen stood up, trembling, hesitating, gathering together her forces of defiance which had mysteriously dispersed since helping her commit the dastardly deed, her mother shouted—actually raised her voice and shouted:

"Go, do you hear me! Go!"

Helen fled, passing her father in the hall, who was hastening to discover what had caused his wife to screech. He anticipated that it was something too dreadful to contemplate—after all, his infidelity had not raised a shout. He watched in amazement as the apparition that was his middle daughter rushed up the stairs and, it must be admitted, he smiled. She looked adorably ridiculous with that orange hedgehog hair style, perched like a mop on her slender stick of a neck. Poor child, he sighed, she never could get it right. He was beginning to know the feeling. He braced himself and walked into the kitchen, which was reeking of burnt milk and resounding with angry words. Margaret was threatening to sue the hairdresser for doing something so appalling to someone who was only sixteen, without her parents' consent.

Helen went straight to her mother's bedroom and 'phoned Victoria.

"Can I come and stay for the weekend, Vicky?"

"Of course," Victoria said, delighted.

"Don't tell Aunty Monica or anyone."

"Why not, for goodness sake? I shall have to, they'll see you at meal-times."

"You can smuggle me up some food," and as Victoria started to protest, she added hurriedly, "please Vicky. I'll explain when I arrive. Let me in at the side door, when no one's about. Please!"

The pleading note in her voice touched Victoria's heart.

"All right. Have you done something awful? Are you running away?"

"I'll tell you when I arrive. Bye!"

Helen rushed to her own room, stuffed a few things in her sports bag, grabbed her briefcase and ran downstairs, desperate to get out the house before her mother forgot she did not want to set eyes on her again.

At Grande Maison, Victoria waited for fifteen minutes before going into the passage that led to the side door. It was ill-lit and very cold. She went back into the house to fetch an anorak, then she paced backwards and forwards to keep warm, her hands stuffed in her pockets. She gave up wondering about Helen, a riddle that would soon be solved, transferring her thoughts back to Bob, to whom she had been writing when the telephone rang. He was somewhere in mid-Atlantic, having flown out to New York to join his ship, which was now heading for the Middle East. This next year would be spent at sea, on voyages lasting between three and four months. The following year would be devoted to study and practical courses at college in the north of England, then back to sea again as an officer cadet. In about three and a half years he would become an officer. He had promised to send her postcards from the exotic places he would be visiting.

There was the sound of feet on gravel, followed by a light knock on the door. Victoria ran to open it. Helen fell in on a flurry of sleet.

"You haven't told anyone, I hope," were her first words.

Victoria reassured her.

"Are you going out?" she asked anxiously, noticing the anorak.

"No. It's freezing out here. Why have you come? Why is it a secret?"

"You'll know soon enough," Helen assured her, following her to the door that led into the hall at the side of the kitchen.

"Wait here," Victoria whispered. "I'll make sure that no one is about."

She went into the house. The kitchen was in darkness. Mrs. Grey was in her own room watching television. Her mother and aunt were doing the same thing in Monica's sitting-room. Something had gone radically wrong with Monica's strategy. Albinia, who would not have a television herself and would object to its presence in the living-rooms downstairs, had no reservations about watching it upstairs. The haven Monica had made for herself and her daughter to escape from Albinia and Mrs. Grey's pervasive presence, was now shared with the former most evenings in companionable intimacy. When she put the kettle on at nine-thirty for their cocoa, Monica smiled wryly to herself at the peculiar twist events had taken. She had suggested a few weeks ago that they carry the set downstairs, but Albinia would not hear of it. "It's more cosy up here," she had declared. One evening a week Albinia spent at her literary club, where, after listening to a visiting speaker, she dined and talked with her few friends, usually about anything but literature. In her absence, Monica indulged herself by watching the kind of programmes which her sister-in-law reviled as trash, usually falling asleep over them. Albinia, on the other hand, never took naps. She had spent many hours of boredom while her feeble old father dozed in his chair. It was a sign of old age which she intended resisting vigorously. Only she knew how hard she struggled to resist and only Victoria suspected that she sometimes struggled in vain. On the occasional evening she spent alone downstairs reading, or embroidering and listening to the radio, Victoria brought her cocoa when she and her mother had theirs. Only once had she enquired gently, "Were you sleeping, Aunt?" The indignant denial had been enough to make her more tactful in future.

Victoria hurried back to the chilly passage. Helen quietly followed her through the darkness of the ground floor, up the wide staircase, lit only by the window on the curving half-landing, which was sleetily opalescent in the light from the street, along the main landing where the television was clearly audible, to the second, narrower staircase leading up to Victoria's studio. Once there, Victoria switched on the light and the gas-fire before turning to Helen for an explanation. From beneath the hood, orange wisps of hair stuck out frenziedly.

"What have you done!" Victoria said, rhetorically.

Her tall cousin slowly took off the thick coat, a rueful grin on her face.

Victoria started to laugh.

"Aren't you shocked?" Helen asked,

surprised by her conservative cousin's reaction.

"You should see the sights amongst my fellow art students," Victoria told her. "They wouldn't give you a second glance at college."

Helen was deflated. She shook the wet from her coat as if she had something utterly objectionable by the scruff of the neck.

"Hang it on the back of the door," Victoria said. "Does Aunty Margaret know you're here?"

"No-one knows, except you. Let them worry. After the way mother screamed at me, it would serve her right if I drowned myself. Have you got something to eat? I didn't get any dinner."

"I'll get you something, also I'll 'phone your mother. You can't let her worry about you."

"She won't be worrying. She is having people to dinner. They will all be talking and smiling and stuffing themselves. They're having steak."

"Well, you're not," Victoria told her heartlessly. "Mrs. Grey would be mad if she found anything like that missing."

Helen caught her arm. "Don't 'phone Mum yet, Vicky. Wait for a couple of hours. I expect she thinks I've gone to Jill."

Victoria agreed. As Helen said, the dinner party would be in full swing. Aunty Margaret would be acting the part of the consummate hostess. When her guests were gone she would revert to the role of outraged parent.

Later, while Helen ate soup and sandwiches, sitting in Victoria's one and only comfortable chair as near to the gas fire as possible without singeing, Victoria, squatting on a floor cushion with a bold Union Jack design, tried to get out of her why she had taken such a drastic step.

"Why did you have your hair chopped short?" Helen countered, her mouth full of ham sandwich, spoon poised over her bowl.

"I wanted to change my image, I was sick of myself," Victoria confessed.

"I didn't want to change anything," Helen said. "This isn't a new image, it's me. Now you see me as I am, not as people think I am. If they don't like me, it's too bad!"

"Your mother seems to object," Victoria pointed out.

Helen sighed, "Yes, it's as I suspected. She doesn't really like me. She only tolerated me while I conformed and she could ignore me most of the time. If she doesn't intend seeing me until I'm back to normal, as she put it, then she's got a long wait."

Victoria relieved her of the empty bowl and handed her a large slice of fruit cake.

"You can't stay up here in the attic forever. This isn't Thornfield Hall. When I join Mum and Aunt Binnie later, you are coming as well. Now I'm going to tell Aunty Margaret that you're here."

"I'm not going home," Helen warned her.

"You can stay here as long as you like."

It was Sandra who answered the telephone. She was surprised to learn that Helen was at Grande Maison. Everyone there assumed she was in her room.

"I was just going to take her up some dinner. One of the guests turned out to be a vegetarian and there's heaps left over, because he won't even eat prawns and things. Mum said he should have let her know. Mrs. Figgus had to make an omelette and cheese salad and do things with the vegetables. When is Helen coming home? Has she got her homework with her? She can take ages to do it, because they won't have her back at school looking like that."

Eventually she promised to tell her mother at the first opportunity where Helen was. Victoria went back upstairs to report the conversation. Helen was not amused to hear they had not even missed her.

At nine-thirty Victoria went to her mother's sitting-room. Monica and Albinia were sitting in arm-chairs before the television, both knitting.

"Cocoa?" she asked brightly. They assented without turning. Victoria took the kettle along to the bathroom to fill it. When she returned, she said to her mother, "Helen's arrived. She's upset Aunty Margaret and would like to stay for a few days. Is that all right?"

"What has she done to upset her mother?" Monica wanted to know, putting down her knitting.

"She has had her hair cut and changed its colour."

"Changed its colour?" Both women gaped at her in astonishment.

"Yes. It looks quite nice really, once you get used to it. Very modern. Helen likes to be fashionable."

Victoria stirred cocoa and cold milk with vigour, watching the kettle. The door opened. Helen had grown tired of waiting to be summoned.

"Gracious heavens!" Albinia cried, dropping a few stitches.

Monica said drily, "I can see why your mother is upset, Helen." She remembered the fuss she had kicked up when Victoria had had her hair cropped and was a little remorseful. At least it was tidy. Helen's resembled a scruffy lambswool duster, crimped and teased. To say it looked out of place above the conservative navy school uniform she was still wearing, was to understate the matter.

"I like it," Helen told them defensively. "You should see Prissy's."

"Has she had hers done as well?" Victoria asked, trying not to laugh.

"Yes, but she chose green and copper. I don't think it suits her."

"Green and copper," Monica and Albinia

repeated simultaneously, exchanging horrified glances.

"She has also had her ears pierced three times," Helen informed them, so that they could appreciate how moderate she was in comparison. She took a mug of cocoa from Victoria, crossing the room to hand it to her aunt. Monica uttered the kind of thank you we give in return for small mercies.

"I might be here some time," her niece warned, "if that's all right, of course."

About ten o'clock the following morning, a Saturday, Jill and Sandra arrived at Grande Maison. Helen watched their approach from Victoria's bedroom window. She was cold. The house was difficult to heat. The rooms were large and the ceilings high; the partial central heating was inadequate even in the few main rooms it served. A hotch-potch of gas and electric fires were used to remedy the insufficiency, which proved extremely uneconomical. Albinia kept saying something would have to be done about it. In fact the house could have done with complete modernisation, but the thought of the upheaval involved was unpleasant. She and Monica made do with extra cardigans and thicker stockings. Only the young were too vain to dress sensibly and preferred to suffer.

Helen's first stay there in winter had dispelled any romantic notions she cherished about the place. Formerly she had envied Victoria, now she felt sorry for her. It was not as if the house would soon be hers and she could sell it. Albinia Lacy at fifty-three looked as if she would live forever.

Helen heard the door bell ring. There was a pause while Mrs. Grey made her unhurried way from the rear of the house to answer it. A few minutes later her sisters joined her upstairs, followed by Victoria, who had been talking to her mother across the landing.

Helen and Jill stood looking at each other, watched expectantly by Sandra with a "Well, did I exaggerate?" look on her face.

Jill told Helen that she had come to take her home, that she should never have left in the first place. It was no good slapping her mother in the face, so to speak, and then running as soon as she retaliated. If you challenge someone, you must fight the duel. It was no defence to say that she had been ordered out of sight. She should have braved it out. Sooner or later Helen would have to face her mother. Running away made it more difficult. Jill's advice was for Helen to go home and act normally, which had always meant seeing very little of their mother. Meal times would be the most gruelling. Margaret's tongue could not be escaped at the table.

Sandra chipped in to say that the more her mother saw Helen's hair, the sooner she would get used to it. The shock soon wears off, she assured her sister.

At first Helen resisted, but when Sandra told her that her father had spoken in her defence and had seemed more amused than offended by the controversial hair style, she reconsidered, ignoring Victoria who had hoped she would stay a little longer, dwelling instead on the discomforts of this house compared with her own home and the thought of lunch, with Miss Lacy and Mrs. Grey begrudging her every mouthful.

She collected her things together. When she said goodbye to her aunt, Monica felt sorry for the foolish child, whose cheeky impudence was for once subdued. She seemed truly sorry for her impulsive act and Monica thought it penance enough that she had to go round looking such a freak, until nature could re-assert itself.

Helen kept up the act of quiet acceptance in the face of doom right up to bedtime. She did not see her mother. She had strict orders to eat her meals alone in her room, but in fact she ate them in the kitchen, fussed over by Mrs. Figgus and leaping into the utility room every time her mother's arrival was imminent.

She spent the early part of the evening listening to her records and doing homework at the same time, a feat of concentration which her generation find no problem, but which would have left their elders deaf and ignorant. She was comforting herself with a long soak in a hot bath, up to her ears in Margaret's luxury foam, when Sandra pounded on the door to tell her she was wanted on the telephone. Wrapping herself in a pink bath towel, she padded along to the extension in her mother's room. It was Prissy. Listening to the sad chronicle of her friend's experience and recounting her own, unaccountably brightened up her countenance. It was comforting not to be alone in misfortune. Prissy, in the middle of a recital of her father's terrifying threats of punishment, one of which was that she should be shaved bald and wear a wig to school, was offended to hear hysterical laughter.

"I can't help it," Helen sobbed. "I have just caught sight of myself in the dressing table mirror. My hair clashes horribly with this pink towel I'm wearing. I must ask mother for some green ones, or I'll offend her sight even more. She likes things to be aesthetically pleasing, don't you know!"

Prissy's sense of humour made a miraculous recovery.

"They always used to threaten me with a convent education," she said. "Now they say the nuns wouldn't have me. I must go, someone's coming and I'm supposed to be in bed asking God's forgiveness, not for the way I look, but for upsetting my family. Roy sends his love. He's getting one of his ears pierced on Monday. Bye!"

The receiver was slammed down.

"One of his ears pierced," Helen thought disparagingly.

On Sunday morning, Sandra was sent to tell Helen she was forbidden to go to church.

"Mother won't be seen with you."

"Very Christian, I must say," Helen retorted. She took off her dressing-gown and got back into bed.

"I shall just have to endure a lie-in," she said, grinning at her sister. "Say a prayer for me."

"Say one for yourself," Sandra told her with envy.

Mrs. Figgus also went to church on Sundays, to the earlier service. She cooked lunch on her return and ate it with the family, getting up from the table to disappear about her own affairs for the rest of the day, appearing miraculously on Monday morning to begin another week. Ever since they were old enough to manage it, the girls had cleared and washed-up after Sunday lunch. At four-thirty they ate a simple tea of sandwiches and cakes and had a light supper of cold meat during the evening, all of which was set out by Margaret and cleared away by her daughters. This Sunday, with Helen confined to her room, Sandra felt some cause for grievance. A few months ago there had been three pairs of hands to do the Sunday chores, today they were reduced to one.

"It's not fair," Sandra told her sister, when she carried up her lunch tray. "Why should you laze around up here, while I do all the work? Room service doesn't seem much of a punishment to me."

"It's jolly boring," Helen confessed.

"But you often stay in your room all day."

"Banishment and escapism are two very different things," Helen informed her. "How long is mother going to keep this up?"

Sandra went downstairs to join the others at the dining-room table. After lunch, as soon as Mrs. Figgus had left the room, she aired her grievance. Her father, who had already put in a plea for Helen's pardon, in vain, promptly and cheerfully offered his help.

"I can't think what you're complaining about," Margaret said. "After all, we have a washing up machine."

"It doesn't do everything," Sandra reminded her. "It doesn't do the pots and pans, or put things away and wipe the surfaces."

"Stop making such a fuss," she was admonished by her mother, who was making her way to the library and the Sunday papers.

After supper that evening Margaret went to Helen's room.

Helen was sitting at her bureau, copying out a favourite poem, which seemed to match her mood of impotent rebellion. Her mother regarded her steadily for a few moments with a look of distaste, then she gave a slight shudder and averted her eyes, looking at a picture on the wall to Helen's left.

"I shall be accompanying you to school tomorrow," she said, her eyes on the picture.

Helen did not answer.

"I shall 'phone Miss Farley first, of course."

Unstudied alliteration, Helen thought.

"I shall not tell her the reason. Just to expect us. I don't want her to come to any hasty decision over the telephone. You will wear your school hat with your hair stuffed inside it. You may begin to circulate freely around the house again, on condition that you hide your hair under a scarf. You will get no pocket money, which means an end to your social life for the time being. You were obviously getting too much, if you could afford to do something so foolish with it. I dread to think how Miss Farley will react tomorrow."

"I hope she expels me," Helen said. "I'm sick of school."

"I'm sick of a lot of things, including your behaviour." Margaret turned abruptly and left the room.

Helen sighed. She hated her school hat, she had not worn it for years, except at special functions, like Speech Day, when it was obligatory, but she resigned herself to cramming it on her head in the morning.

"But I won't wear a headscarf all the time," she told the closed door mutinously. Then she had an idea, which brought a smile to her eyes.

The next morning she appeared at breakfast with a brown paper bag over her head, in which she had cut two eye holes.

It caused amusement to everyone except her mother, who pretended it did not exist.

22

VICTORIA watched Helen depart in Jill's little car, feeling forlorn. What had started as an eventful weekend was ending all too soon as just another quiet one. She went back to her room and occupied herself with college work until lunch-time, finishing her letter to Bob in the last ten minutes, telling him about Helen's hair. She also promised to visit his parents on Sunday.

Helen's hair was the main topic of conversation between her mother and aunt at the lunch table. Now that the shock had worn off, they were both inclined to see the funny side of it. Victoria did not have a lot to say, which brought forth the usual enquiries about her health; did she have a headache, perhaps? When it became obvious that only her spirits were affected, both women exerted themselves to cheer her up, something which, if they only knew, depressed her further. As she was leaving the table her aunt had a brain-wave.

"Why don't you decorate your studio, Victoria? You may have *carte-blanche* as to colour and materials."

Victoria loved the idea.

"Well, work out what you want. We shall need to have some idea of cost."

"May I have a studio couch and a new chair?"

"Yes, whatever you need. The size of the room limits you enough, I think."

Saturday had brightened up considerably. On her way upstairs the telephone rang. She answered it to find it was Jill, asking her to go to the cinema that evening. There was a film she very much wanted to see, but she did not like going alone. Helen was *incommunicado*, so to speak, and too young, being under eighteen. Would Victoria go?

She would indeed. The few intervening hours before Jill called for her were spent partly doing homework and partly devising great schemes to transform her utilitarian studio into something both exciting and functional.

After church on Sunday morning, Victoria walked part of the way home with Monica and Albinia. When they reached the park gates she left them to continue their way up the hill, herself cutting through the park towards Merle's house.

It was a beautiful clear, crisp day, with frost still lying in strips and patches in the shade beneath walls and trees. Too early for even the promise of spring, winter still clutched with strong twiglike fingers at the heart of matter, resisting the bright sunshine that valiantly spelled its eventual enfeeblement.

Victoria walked the familiar path between shrubs and brown flowerbeds, lost in thought. Her trip to the cinema with Jill had included more than entertainment: it had left her uneasy, faced with questions to which she had to find answers.

Jill was moving into an unfurnished flat in a week or so. She had discussed her ideas for furnishing and decorating it. Margaret was taking an interest in Jill's new home in proportion to her lack of interest in the present one. Jill could have the bedroom furniture from her old room, for a start. The project was a much larger and grander one that Victoria's for her studio, and her enthusiasm was dampened down a little as she listened. It never entered her head that she was in a position, financially, to emulate her cousin and have a home of her own. Even if it had, there were other considerations, such as deserting her mother and leaving the large house even less inhabited, which seemed wrong when there were so many people sharing cramped accommodation for want of somewhere else to go.

Victoria had been perturbed to learn that Larry de Valois was still meeting his mistress occasionally. She thought, along with the rest of the family, that the affair had finished when his wife found out. She knew her mother assumed this, because she had heard the matter under discussion between her and Merle. They had been saying how thankful they were that the sordid business had been kept from Helen and Sandra. Merle had said, "Can you imagine deliberately spreading rumours about Margaret's non-existent lover, to save her face. I'm glad it never came to that." The sisters had chuckled comfortably at the ludicrous idea.

Jill, whose sympathy had been with her mother while she remained in suspicious ignorance, was now switching sides. Margaret rarely let her husband out of her sight, and she was interfering more and more in his business affairs, something Jill heartily resented, as did Alex Stuart, who had never been fond of Margaret at the best of times. What was worse, he apparently approved of Mrs. Frobisher; but then, being a man, Jill supposed that also was inevitable, given that the woman was blonde, curvaceous and comfortable, in the sense that she appeared to give much and demand little in return—so different from the woman she was wronging. The fault lay with Mr. Frobisher, who was away too much, which meant his wife had too much time on her hands. It was a pity he did not take her with him, silly man!

Then Jill had changed the subject yet again to ask Victoria about David Strang. Jill had a friend who said she knew him as well. This friend seemed surprised to hear he had a regular girl. Was Vicky aware that he sometimes worked behind the bar in the hotel?

Victoria was aware of nothing, but did not say so to Jill. She had never been sure what he did at work and was too reticent to ask. She had given him many opportunities to tell her, which he had cleverly declined. The Regency was a large hotel in the town centre, of past grandeur and present mediocrity, attracting a seedy middle-aged clientele to its bars and dining-room during the winter months. In the summer this colourless substrata was inundated with a flow of fun-seeking visitors from the mainland on package holidays, bringing a spurious vitality to its habitual air of shabby senility. If Jill was trying to tell her that David had other girls, Victoria was not surprised. She had suspected as much ever since his return to the island—indeed Raoul had hinted that David had been living with a girl in London. David had never spoken of her. His conversation was varied and amusing, but not self-communicative. She knew next to nothing about his private life. Friends assumed she had a tiger on a string; her experience so far suggested he was a mere lamb. It was mortifying to be ready to repel advances which never came. Initially Raoul had seemed amused by his friend's infatuation with Jill's dull little cousin, presumably not expecting it to last. Now that it showed no sign of ending, his concern was being transmitted though his letters to his love.

"Are you serious about David, Vicky?" Jill had asked as she stopped the car outside Grande Maison.

"Is there any reason why I shouldn't be?" Victoria wanted to know.

"Raoul seems to think he likes a good time, but perhaps he is ready to settle down now."

As she neared her aunt's home, leaving the park to cross the road adjacent to it, Victoria considered the implication of Jill's words. Did they mean that she was destined for the settled David, when he had finished sowing his wild oats? Was he practising his good behaviour on her? Worst of all, had she attracted him because she was shy and never likely to be anything but dully respectable? Perhaps he thought marriage meant the end of pleasure and she would make the ideal wife. If he thought that, the wonder was that he should want to get married at all. It could be that her mother was right when she insinuated that he was after her money. Victoria was beginning to be as intrigued as Raoul about her role in David's scheme of things. There was another explanation, of course, one that hardly bore contemplating: that he felt sorry for her and asked her out as a weekly charitable exercise.

Merle greeted her arrival with pleasure. There had always existed a chord of sympathy between the quiet girl and her kindly aunt. Of the three sisters, Merle was the gentlest, the most understanding, the only one who could be relied upon to listen before giving advice. She looked tired this morning. There were lines on her face that Victoria had not noticed before, in the days of contentment when her aunt had been fuller-faced, before her husband noticeably took to drink and her sons to independence. She had not been at church, which was why Victoria was calling now, rather than in the afternoon. Either her aunt was unwell or something else had kept her from her customary place in the family pew.

"I've brought you a little present," Victoria said, handing over a flat, brown-paper parcel.

Inside Merle found a pastel portrait of her younger son.

"I'm afraid I did it from a photograph," Victoria said apologetically.

Merle was delighted with it. She had been the recipient of Victoria's works of art since she had been at infant school. She had cared enough to put the immature drawings and paintings on her kitchen walls, rubbishy things which Monica had greeted with, "Very nice, dear," and placed ready for the dustbin. Consequently, it was Merle who was reaping the harvest. Monica thought it enough that Victoria was allowed to display her art on her own bedroom and studio walls; whilst Margaret jealously refused to admit that there was anything worth displaying. She had encouraged her three daughters to be artistic—alas, encouragement had not been enough where talent was lacking.

As Merle was standing, gazing happily at the likeness of Bob, wondering just where his ship was at that moment, Victoria heard her uncle approaching across the tiled hallway. She watched the door with apprehension, but when he came in he was relatively sober. She could relax. Had he been over-genial she would have remained embarrassed and tongue-tied beneath his barrage of alcoholic bonhomie; had he been shuffling and truculent she would have made her excuses and fled.

Merle showed him Victoria's present. He was pleased with it, complimenting her on the quality of her work, eagerly going on to discuss her subject and his whereabouts. He had a huge map of the world on which he intended to plot each of Bob's voyages, in this way sharing in them.

For the first time, Victoria realised that her aunt was not alone in missing her sons. She had stopped thinking of her uncle in any way but his relation to whisky and its effect upon his family. She felt ashamed. If everyone did their best to avoid him, as she did, then this very isolation must aggravate his problem. She smiled at him warmly, thanking him for his compliments.

Merle urged her to stay for lunch. She started to refuse, with the excuse that her mother and aunt were expecting her, then changed her mind. They would not miss her for once. They did not depend entirely upon her presence for conversation, whereas one got the feeling that Merle and Karl were past talking for the sake of it and would welcome a third person to animate their small-talk. Not that Victoria was much of a conversationalist, but other people always made an effort on her behalf and were rewarded with close attention and interest in whatever interested them. She rang home to inform them of her intention.

The contrast between this and the last time Victoria had stayed for lunch could not have been greater. Now just three of them sat at the breakfast room table. The rest of the house reposed in cool winter emptiness and orderliness. She recalled the last occasion with a pang of nostalgia. It had been a Saturday in August, when she had come along to help Doreen with the bedrooms. There had been six of them around this table then, exchanging light-hearted repartee. The house had been tidy, but not restfully so. It had been chivvied into tidiness by Merle, Doreen and herself, in a state of panic and good-humoured hard work. While they ate, it had enjoyed a respite in the fragrant summer warmth drifting in through the large open windows, before accepting another influx of noisy strangers with their clutter of impedimenta.

Now Victoria watched her uncle forcing himself to eat a little and her aunt pretending not to notice his lack of success. She accepted a second helping to show her appreciation of the excellent cooking, not because she needed it. When they had eaten, Karl excused himself and went upstairs, refusing the offer of a cup of tea. Merle sighed. She and Victoria cleared the table and washed up. Merle was glad of the girl's company; she knew she would not see Karl again until the evening. Victoria was wondering just how soon she could leave without being ungracious.

"Why don't you walk back to Grande Maison with me?" she suggested. "Uncle Karl wouldn't miss you for a couple of hours, would he?"

"Oh, no! He wouldn't know I had gone and by the time he found out he would be past caring, but I won't come, dear. I am nervous about leaving him alone. It would be so easy to turn my back on him, when nothing that I can do is any help, yet I must go on making the effort. Both of us can't give up, can we?"

They spent half-an-hour drinking tea and looking at the latest photograph album. There was a photograph of Bob in his midshipman's uniform, which Victoria had not seen before. Merle had another, which she let her have, handing it to her with a small smile and asking gently,

"Are you still going out with that young man who works at the Regency Hotel?"

Victoria was surprised. Suddenly, everyone was interested in David Strang.

"Yes. Why?"

Merle shrugged, as if it were of little consequence, yet she looked embarrassed, as if she would like to ask more. Eventually she said, "Serious about him, are you?"

"I don't know," Victoria answered with truth. She would not know until her emotions were put to the test by David.

She wanted to say, "What if I were?" but found it almost impossible to be rude, especially to someone as kind as her aunt. Instead she asked, "Has Mum been talking about him?"

Merle shook her head. Victoria knew she had, but took her aunt's denial in the spirit it was meant, that her mother's dislike had nothing to do with it. Poor David.

"Mum and Aunt Binnie don't like him very much," she confessed.

Merle commiserated with her.

"Probably they are jealous. They do try to monopolise you, between them. You are all they have to love. It will take them a long time to reconcile themselves to losing you to a husband."

"Heavens, I haven't thought about marriage yet," Victoria said, blushing a little at the lie, for as a means of escape it had entered her mind quite frequently of late—but not, it must be confessed, to David.

There is my question answered, Merle thought complacently. She can't be serious about him. Merle was old-fashioned enough to see love and marriage as cause and effect. She could answer Bob's letter now, stating the case as she saw it. He was another one who was not anxious for Victoria to see too much of David Strang. Really, that young man appeared to have an unfortunate effect upon people. Merle wondered why. He appeared attractive enough to her on their short acquaintance; she could have fancied him herself in her young days. The kind who would not easily take no for an answer. Hardly Victoria's type!

As Victoria was leaving, Merle told her of her intention to take guests throughout the year, instead of just at Easter and the summer. She did not know how successful she would be during the winter months, but it made sense to try, now that the boys were away so much. Karl's deteriorating health was threatening his work. The time was fast approaching when the patience of his superiors would run out and he would be asked to leave. Merle wanted to be in a stronger financial position when that happened. Doreen had found full-time employment, so someone else would have to be found to help out when the need arose. Merle had mentioned this to

Stephen and, to her astonishment, received a prompt reply to her letter, offering Alison's services.

Merle explained to Victoria that Alison would arrive at the same time as the first lot of guests, in two weeks, at the beginning of March.

The change goes on remorselessly, Victoria thought on her way home. Now there will always be visitors at Aunty Merle's and no Doreen cheerfully undertaking the extra work and poking irreverent fun at their idiosyncracies. I wonder if I shall enjoy helping Alison as much on Saturday mornings?

On her arrival at Grande Maison, she was greeted by her mother.

"That young man 'phoned an hour ago." As if she did not know his name.

"David? What did he want?"

"I have no idea. I told him you were at Merle's. He said he would 'phone back later."

Twenty minutes later, Monica complained of having a fearful headache and feeling faint. Victoria accompanied her upstairs.

Monica lay on her bed looking wan.

Victoria fetched water and aspirin in a flutter of anxious concern. Before they had moved, her mother was rarely ill, only suffering from the occasional cold or influenza attack. Over the past few months she had often complained of feeling unwell, with vague symptoms which usually included a headache. Victoria constantly urged her to see the doctor, but she would not.

When David 'phoned to say he had the evening off unexpectedly and would she meet him, she regretfully declined, too concerned about her mother's health to contemplate leaving her. He sounded disappointed, which made her feel sorry.

His free evening had suddenly lost its appeal. He would have been willing to spend it quietly in Victoria's company at her home, but the invitation was not extended.

By tea-time, her mother had rallied enough to eat and drink a little from the tray her daughter brought her. In the evening they watched television together. Albinia went to church, returning to read and listen to the radio in solitude.

23

BOB returned from a four-month voyage at the end of April. His ship docked at Miami, and the following day he flew to London and then to the island. He was met at the airport by Stephen, bearing bad news. Their father was dead.

He heard the story from his brother in the car going home and again when he arrived, less coherently, from his tearful mother. It was the middle of the afternoon. A white-faced, composed Alison was in the kitchen valiantly taking over the task of preparing dinner for nine guests, four of whom were children.

Merle was sitting on the end of her bed in the attic room, crying gently, her worst fears realised. Bob sat beside her, one arm around her shoulders, listening in stunned disbelief.

Karl had returned very late the night before last from his club. Why he had decided to return and not stay there over-night was a mystery, as was how he had got home, probably by taxi. He had been very drunk. Merle heard the door slam at the bottom of the attic steps and the sounds of his lumbering ascent. He appeared to be having some difficulty with the door into the attic. She was climbing sleepily and none too cheerfully out of bed to aid him, when she heard him fall. There were the heavy sounds of his body on the wooden staircase and the final dull thud as he hit the door at the bottom. She had rushed down to help him, but his body was wedged between the door and the bottom step. While she struggled, helped by Alison who had followed her down, the door had been opened from the landing by two guests, who had managed to drag him clear. It was immediately obvious that he was dead. He had broken his neck.

Stephen had been sent for first thing in the morning and Bob's imminent arrival awaited with anxious anticipation.

"I have always hated this attic," Merle sobbed. "Now I know why."

A conclusion which Bob did not find illogical.

So it was that Richard Bellinger, with his wife Fiona, found himself once more facing the three Le Feuvre sisters across a yawning grave. While those who love, grieve, those who observe, speculate. Richard speculated.

It could have been a re-enactment of old Mr. Lacy's funeral, with a few extras in the cast. Merle stood between her sisters. Next to Margaret was Larry, with Sandra holding tightly to his hand for comfort. Around Monica were the rest of the children, with Stephen and Bob nearest to their mother. Alison and Albinia Lacy were a little apart, then came relations of Karl's—a brother and sister from the mainland—and friends of the family, among whom Richard recognised drinking partners of the deceased, sober and sombre, no doubt considering the likelihood of their own demise in similar sodden circumstances. Karl's employer was there, relieved of any painful decision he had been contemplating in the future, accompanied by a colleague of Karl's who no longer need move to gain the promotion he so keenly desired. Death not only creates problems, it solves quite a few.

As her solicitor, Richard knew that, apart from the house, Merle was left with a few thousand pounds' capital and just enough income to live on. She would need to continue with her paying guests to provide money for necessary extras like house maintenance; unless she intended dipping into her small capital every time she had a large bill to pay. It was a good thing that she had Stephen's young lady living with her now. A calm, sensible girl, who would be a support and comfort to her over the coming months. Richard understood that Bob was to be home for four weeks, which was a blessing. He glanced over to where Bob stood, pale and rigid in his uniform, his cousin Victoria next to him. As usual, he was struck by the contrast she made with her dark-haired cousins. Helen was not as dark, of course, but her brown hair was hidden beneath a hideous mauve and black woollen scarf, inappropriate for one so young; he wondered that her mother had allowed it. Her head was held high, as if defying anyone to criticise her. Definitely her mother's daughter in temper, if not in taste. She saw him regarding her; as her eyebrows rose slightly he hastily averted his gaze.

The handfuls of chill earth fell with small sounds of desolation upon the wooden coffin. Richard wondered who would be the next amongst those present to quit the world. His hand closed possessively about his wife's to lead her from the grave. Many things had happened since Theodore Lacy's funeral. Even the death of a harmless old recluse wrought change in some measure. Change was what the living anticipated, in either thankfulness or dread.

As he stood in mute contemplation of the family wreaths, with Fiona whispering the inscriptions to him, an emotional catch in her voice, Jill came to his side, placing a hand upon his arm. His spirits immediately rose above gloomy thoughts of eternity. It was impossible not to feel life surging with all its promise when one contemplated someone as youthful and beautiful as Jill. Unlike his wife, he had no reservations about her engagement to his son, nor did he set time limits which, as a young man in Raoul's position, he himself would have found difficult to keep.

When they felt ready to marry, let them, with his blessing. He knew his Fiona would give in gracefully. Raoul could do no wrong in her eyes and she would see it was unfair to blame Jill for an eagerness his son must surely share.

When the occasion was appropriate, Richard indulged in a little mild flirtation with his prospective daughter-in-law, but he had learnt to do it when Fiona was not watching. She had shown unbecoming signs of jealousy, and certainly it was unbecoming in him to give her cause, however absurd the reason.

Now he turned to Jill with a warm smile which she readily returned, reprimanding her in a teasing manner for neglecting them of late.

He was so like Raoul that Jill could not help being fond of him. She was not yet fond of Fiona, but she understood her. Jill knew that beneath the light, fluttery manner of incompetence lay a scheming, clever mind. Once Fiona accepted the fact that she no longer held the premier place in Raoul's life, she and Jill could build a close, affectionate relationship. Until then they must treat each other with polite caution; the mother enthusiastically discussing every communication with her son; the fiancée concealing the extent of her own for fear of provoking jealous dislike.

Margaret had made a magnificent gesture and lent Mrs. Figgus to Merle for the day. So it was that the mourners returned to a light lunch attractive enough to tempt the most jaded palate and generous enough to satisfy the biggest appetite. It consisted of soup, to warm away the chills of the grave-side, followed by an excellent cold buffet, set out attractively in Annie Figgus' inimitable manner, approved of by her employer, whose first action on entering her sister's home after the funeral was an inspection of the dining-room. It received a small nod of satisfaction, then Margaret went to take off her hat and coat.

There were paying guests in the house who would expect an evening meal, funeral or no funeral. Mrs. Figgus had that under control as well. She had made a list of all the food she would need and Margaret had sent her three daughters shopping for it the day before. Merle was to be relieved of all household anxieties for the day. It was a measure of the disorientation brought about by her grief that Merle never questioned the arrangements, nor gave the kitchen and its occupants a thought. Had Sandra been in charge out there and served them all bread and jam, she would still have sat immobile, in abject misery, uncaring amongst her solicitous family and friends. How she would have felt afterwards, when feeling returned to animate her numbed self-respect, is another matter. Fortunately, she had a sister whose pride extended to everything remotely connected with her. It was difficult to envisage a calamity great enough to make Margaret oblivious of events in the kitchen, or the prospect of bread and jam emanating from it at a wake.

The atmosphere was one of damped-down liveliness, so often present at gatherings after funerals amongst those whose lives will not be drastically affected by the event. Sometimes it can even be detected in those nearest and dearest to the deceased, who have watched a slow, inevitable decline, grieving inwardly, attending the burial service over and over again in lurid imagination. The relief at the cessation of dread gives way, once the burial has become reality, to a short-lived, hysterical lift of spirits, recalled a few weeks later with uncomprehending guilt.

It was not so with Merle and her sons. The shock of Karl's sudden death had left them sad and bewildered. Not for them the long nights looking into long days without him, projected into a loss still to be realised. True, Merle had prophesied he was drinking himself to death, but there had always been hope that he would stop at some time during the years ahead which she had comfortably considered he would have before he reached that conclusion. If she had not hoped for an end to his drinking, she could have hoped for nothing.

Stephen grieved for his mother's loss, not his own. He would have been hypocritical had it been otherwise. He had despised his father and been ashamed of him, those feelings effectively blotting out the fact that Karl had been a kindly, generous man who loved his family. As Stephen grew to years of discernment, he had perceived only his father's faults and the consequence of them upon his mother and himself. Even his death had been dishonourable, an accident brought about by inebriation, the last in a long series of humiliating incidents now buried in Stephen's memory as deep as the corpse was buried in the earth.

He stood by his mother's chair, tall and stern, inwardly impatient to get on with the business of life under new, more advantagous circumstances.

Bob, very much a part of the gathering rather than an observer of it, shared his mother's grief and, like her, was grateful to those whose presence helped mitigate it. He readily received warmly expressed sentiments of condolence. His father had been well-liked, an affable, good-natured fellow with more tolerance for the weaknesses of his fellow men than he had for his own. Few of those present had seen him very much the worse for drink. Those who had, apart from his closest family, were not in a position to criticise. In fact one of them was already forgetting his penitence at the graveside under the soothing influence of Merle's best sherry.

In the kitchen, Mrs. Figgus had marshalled her forces. It was a novelty to work in different surroundings, made easier by having familiar aides. She and the four girls had worked together at many family functions, from the time the eldest could be trusted to carry a plate of biscuits without dropping or tipping it. She knew her work force and its limitations. Victoria preferred to remain behind the scenes, doing anything, no matter how menial, rather than mingling with strangers: consequently she did a lot of washing up. Sandra, who became clumsy through over-eagerness to please, was never entrusted with anything delicate or intricate, in fact she was usually persuaded to help Victoria. Helen liked to be amongst the company, showing off. She was given the roll of temptress, especially when appetites began to flag. She sallied forth with delicacies and came back empty-handed, a triumphant seductress.

Her initial entrance into the dining-room on this occasion, bearing a bowl of steaming hot minestrone, caused quite a sensation. Minus the drab head-covering, her hair flared out like a shock wave above the severe high neck of her dark grey dress. The uninformed were bereft of speech. Horrified glances were exchanged, softening almost at once to unconcern hiding inner amusement. Beneath defiant blue eyes above a hovering soup ladle, generous helpings of minestrone were meekly accepted.

"That child is wearing too much eye make-up," Albinia muttered in scandalised tones to Monica and wondered what had caused Richard Bellinger to splutter over his soup.

Jill, always very much mistress of herself and any situation, was the trusted second in command, sent for in a crisis, deployed in an emergency, as charming and tactful as her father in the drawing-room, as efficient as Mrs. Figgus herself in the kitchen. Now she had a rival for efficiency, if not for charm. Alison quietly and competently worked at Mrs. Figgus' side, keeping just a step ahead of any request, earning the older woman's respect and approval. Annie Figgus suspected that Alison would have coped quite well without her, had the troops not mutinied under her command, which seemed more than likely from the signs of jealousy which were evident in Sandra and Helen and even in Victoria.

By three-thirty only the family was left. Margaret went into the kitchen to applaud the results of her magnaminity. Alison bridled a little at the patronising congratulations, but Mrs. Figgus accepted them equably, calmly wiping over the work surfaces ready for the onslaught of dinner in a few hours' time.

"Shall I leave the girls here?" Margaret offered.

"There's no need. Alison and I will manage between us."

"Very well," Margaret agreed, not too pleased. "Stephen will bring you back this evening, Mrs. Figgus." She returned to the drawing-room to find her sister in tears —Monica, surprisingly enough, not Merle. Victoria was kneeling by her mother's side, holding her hands and pleading to know what was the matter.

"Too much sherry," was the opinion of teetotal Albinia, drawing upon herself a swift look of reproach from her distressed niece.

"What is it, Mum?" Victoria murmured.

Monica shook her head, unable to say.

Merle, supposing that the tears were for her, comforted her with brave assurances of managing and being all right, which were backed up by her elder son who said, of course she would, in a confident manner that she found slightly irritating.

Bob came to Victoria's rescue by offering to drive them home immediately. Monica accepted with pathetic haste, wiping her eyes dry before she said farewell.

"I have a headache," she told the room in general, as she departed on her sister-in-law's arm.

Her sallow skin looking yellow in its paleness, Monica was silent and withdrawn on the drive back to Grande Maison. She went to lie down in her bedroom as soon as they arrived. Bob left at once, anxious to return to his mother, but he promised Victoria he would call in a day or so to see her refurbished studio, about which she had been so enthusiastic in her letters.

Victoria went upstairs to make sure her mother was comfortable. Monica was in tears again, sitting on the side of her bed, her black hat in her lap, her hair still flattened by its weight, her head bowed.

"Is your headache very bad, Mum? I'll get some aspirin."

"I've had some."

"Then lie down. I'll take your shoes off."

Monica permitted her daughter to remove her shoes and her hat. She lay down on the bed and shut her eyes, the tears trickling beneath the lids.

"What is it?" Victoria beseeched her.

Her mother gave the age-old reply, "Nothing," because the matter was too complex to be explained. In fact she hardly understood it herself. She was depressed, that was the easy explanation, but it did not do justice to the feeling of misery and dread she had felt an hour ago at the prospect of returning to this house. Standing with her sisters beside Karl's open grave, she, like Richard Bellinger, had recalled Theodore Lacy's funeral. She particularly remembered the awesome emotion that had rooted her to the spot as she vividly heard again his death-bed words, apparently spoken to her from his coffin. Since then she had been morbidly haunted by his injunction that she should look after Victoria, because, she presumed, she would answer to him, ultimately, for her happiness. It seemed to her dismal fancy that his supernatural interference had influenced her actions continuously since then; it was the only way she could account for living in this awful place, every day becoming more and more estranged from her sisters with whom she had always been so intimate, and growing closer and closer to her sister-in-law from whom she had always desired to remain estranged.

When she and Victoria had lived together in her parents' house, their lives had felt safe and secure, and she had endeavoured to make them so. They had been happy with each other's company. Now she was losing Victoria; just living at Grande Maison was accomplishing that. They could be in the same room and be far enough apart to put a strain on familiar conversation and make the sharing of a secret amusement an impossibility. Half the time she did not know for certain if Victoria was in the house or not, she had to track her down to be sure. Now she was in danger of losing her altogether to that dreadful, pushy young man. Victoria persisted in seeing him, even though she knew her mother disliked him. It was difficult to prevent a daughter of nineteen from going out with whom she chose. It was not fair of Leonard's father to expect her to do the impossible. She wanted Victoria's happiness as much as he had ever done, but how was she to achieve it, if Victoria would not co-operate? Victoria was not a happy child! Robbed of a husband when he was twenty-seven, was she to be robbed of a daughter at an even younger age? Appalled at the idea of growing old with only Albinia and Mrs. Grey for company, of wandering around the emptiness of that forbidding house wrapped in layers of woolly cardigans, worrying about Victoria unhappily married, dreading the recriminations she was to receive throughout eternity for not guarding her daughter's happiness more zealously, Monica moaned inwardly at her wretchedness.

"Are you worried about Aunty Merle, Mum?"

Instantly she felt remorse. She had

managed to forget that this was the day to be devoted to her sister's grief. It helped to stifle her self-pity and, for a short while, put her own nebulous anxieties into the background.

Meanwhile, at Merle's, Stephen was saying to Alison, quietly, so that his mother and Bob could not overhear,

"I think Aunty Monica is going peculiar. She seemed to think it was old Mr. Lacy being buried again. Did you hear her muttering at the graveside something like 'I'm doing my best, but it's none of your business, father'? Unless she meant her own father, of course. Another thing, she hardly ever takes her eyes off Vicky. It's as if she expects her to disappear any minute in a puff of smoke. I don't know how Vicky can put up with her continual fussing. She never used to be so bad."

Alison admitted she had noticed all these things, but being a newcomer she had not realised they were abnormal.

24

STEPHEN remained at home for a week. Before he left, he informed his mother that he and Alison would be getting married in September, just before the start of his final year at university. Meanwhile Alison would remain on the island with Merle, to continue to support and help her with the paying guests. Still in the early stages of her bereavement, drifting like an automaton through each day as it arrived, looking neither forward nor backward, too bemused with the insensible present, Merle thanked him for his concern and forethought, glad to have someone planning on her behalf.

Bob, seeing how firmly Stephen was implanting himself and his intended wife into his mother's future, felt shut out and lonely. He missed his father dreadfully. Now that the house was to be a permanent hotel, it was no longer home as he had known it. He planned to remove as many of his personal belongings as he could manage when he returned to the Marine and Technical College in three weeks' time. While he had been away, he had lost interest in all his former girlfriends, or they had lost interest in him—it amounted to the same thing. He was too miserable to exert himself to seek out his former friends, who were growing used to filling their leisure time without him. He turned instinctively to the one person he had always been able to rely upon, the one whose letters arrived regularly, who had always been grateful for any love he could spare. To his dismay, he was to discover that his need now seemed greater than hers.

Victoria was preoccupied with her mother's health, her college work and David Strang, in that order, or rather, she was trying to keep them in that order, despite David's growing efforts to head the list.

Bob knew nothing of this when he arrived on Saturday morning to give his opinion on Victoria's new studio. Mrs. Grey let him in, informing him that Victoria was in the garden and he could go through the dining-room if he liked. As he stepped through the french windows, he heard her laughing. A few moments later she came into view around the shrubbery carrying a kitten, closely followed by David. Neither of them was aware of his presence. He stood watching them, his mind considering possibilities that were unwelcome. He had not seen them together since Jill's party, when he had been annoyed with Victoria for having her hair cut short and she had retaliated by ignoring him all evening. He knew she had been seeing David occasionally since then, his mother had told him as much in her letters, but Victoria mentioned him very seldom in hers and then only as incidental to an anecdote. He had no idea that their relationship had grown into anything special. He had supposed it never would, simply because Aunty Monica did not approve of him, neither did Miss Lacy. Victoria disliked causing anyone distress, especially her mother, which seemed reason enough for her to keep David on a casual footing. What Bob had not reckoned with was that Victoria liked him too well to want to distress him, either. He frowned as he considered this, stepping forward involuntarily, which broke their illusion of being on their own.

Victoria was pleased to see him, David was not. He drew comfort on both counts.

"Look, Bob, isn't it sweet," she called, holding the kitten up for his inspection. "Sandra brought it over yesterday. Aunty Margaret said she had to get rid of it."

"Are you to be allowed to keep it?" he asked.

She smiled archly. "Of course. Mrs. Grey isn't too keen, but Aunt Binnie talked her round. Have you come to see my studio? So has David. I'll take you both up. Come on."

They followed her into the house. Stepping from the sunlight on that clear April morning, with a stiff breeze moving the white cloud masses briskly across blue infinity, into the static cavern of the crimson-carpeted dining-room, was like stepping back in time, everything was so old-fashioned. Mr. Lacy must have left the place exactly as he had inherited it from his father. Victoria, in yellow bat-wing sweater and old jeans, with crimson leg warmers above leather pumps, looked distinctly out of place. She had been painting, Bob surmised, for there were streaks of green on her ear lobe and neck. How on earth did she manage to get it there? Actually she had put the paint brush behind her ear in mistake for a pencil.

As they crossed the first floor landing, Monica came out of her sitting-room.

"Bob and David have come to see my studio, Mum. I'll be making some coffee in a few minutes, would you like some?" Victoria spoke quickly in a nervous, defensive manner.

"No, thank you," Monica said stiffly. She ignored David and, turning to Bob, said, "How is your mother?"

"Bearing up quite well. She would like to see you. Aunty Margaret has been."

"We're coming tomorrow afternoon," Monica told him.

"I can't come, Mum. I've promised to go out with David," Victoria said apologetically.

Monica looked annoyed, but she merely said, "Very well, I'll go alone."

David, who saw little enough of Victoria, was not prepared to sacrifice the pleasure of her company. He had some friends he particularly wanted her to meet and tomorrow was the ideal opportunity. Victoria was looking at him, waiting for him to release her from the engagement, but he chose to ignore her.

She turned from him to Bob, who could usually be relied upon to come to her rescue, only to find him stern and silent.

"Perhaps we could go in the morning, after church?" she suggested to her mother.

"No. It's quite all right. I don't mind going on my own," Monica said, adding as she turned to go downstairs, "I'm getting used to it."

David said he would have to go soon.

"Can we see this fantastic studio now?" he asked, attracting Victoria's anxious attention from her mother to himself.

"Yes, of course," she answered, leading the way towards the second staircase.

Both young men were astonished at the sight of the room. Bob, because he had known it before its transformation, in all its stark simplicity, and David, because he had not expected such a violent contrast to the rest of the house, nor had he expected it to be so large, hardly his idea of a garret.

His bedroom at home in London had not been half the size.

Three aspects of Victoria's complex character had been given full rein. Her love of colour, which was lavishly and daringly exploited in fabrics and wall-coverings; her orderliness—not for her the litter of paints, brushes, canvasses and other paraphernalia associated with many artists; and, lastly, something which even Bob had not suspected and which he saw now with consternation, a taste for opulence. She had mentioned her scheme to Helen in Margaret's presence, telling her that Albinia had said she could spend as much as she needed, to which Margaret had replied that surely Victoria was at liberty to spend her own money without sanction from her aunt. This had set Victoria thinking. Brought up to watch every penny, it was difficult to grasp that she was wealthy, especially as money was never discussed at Grande Maison, to do so being considered bad taste. Apparently it is only when you have none that you may continually talk about it. Her mother, now with very few living expenses to meet, was carefully saving every spare pound towards the inevitable rainy day, when, childless and homeless, due to Victoria's marriage and Albinia's demise, she would have to find a home of her own or go into an institution. Consequently, she lived amidst the ageing grandeur of Grande Maison in the same frugal way she had lived in her modest terraced home, scrupulously avoiding even the smallest extravagance.

Victoria had not actually forgotten that she was rich. Every month when she received her allowance, agreed upon by her mother and aunt, she was reminded of it. Money of her own, to do with as she wished! In fact, it was not as much as Helen received from her father, but Victoria thought it was, unaware that since they had last discussed their pocket money, Helen had put in two successive bids to cover inflation and been awarded both.

Reminded by her aunt that she was a young lady of independent fortune, Victoria dropped in on Richard Bellinger at his office in the town, as he had continually encouraged her to do since her grandfather's death. He had listened with interest to her project, serious-faced, but inwardly amused that she should be asking him tentatively for a few hundred to do up one room, when she could reasonably have asked for as many thousands to do up the whole house. Sooner or later someone would have to spend a lot of money on the place, instead of just what was absolutely necessary to keep it in good repair.

Richard had asked her exactly what she intended to accomplish, then mentioned the sum of money he supposed she would need to do it. It was much larger than she had estimated, but having no idea of the relative cost of furnishings and materials, she had accepted his figure, thinking she would not dare spend so much, her mother would have a fit if she knew. As it happened, she spent a little more.

"What do you think?" she asked the two young men at her side, setting the kitten down gently on the deep pile of the carpet.

"Hardly my idea of a studio," Bob told her drily. "A trifle sybaritic, don't you think?"

"I'm sick of austerity," she said lightly.

David looked surprised. He wondered

what she had ever known of austerity, or was she referring to her mother's general attitude of frugality and its inevitable effect upon her? She was watching him now, waiting for his reaction.

"It's great!" he said. "I had no idea you possessed such a flair for interior design."

"Neither had I," Bob admitted. "Presumably you will put newspaper down before you paint."

She laughed. "I've moved my easel next door. This is strictly for non-messy work, like drawing and reading. I got carried away, I'm afraid. It's become a glorious bolt-hole, filled with all my own things. Sit down and I'll make some coffee."

They dutifully sat down, side by side on the commodious, deeply cushioned couch, which opened up into a double bed. A curious thing for her to have bought, with so many bedrooms in the house, and one she had found great difficulty in justifying to her indignant mother, already horrified at the expense. The truth was that she needed somewhere to work or day-dream as the fancy took her, where she could feel tranquilly at home, whether in happiness or misery; but she could not explain this to Monica without wounding her deeply. Her bedroom was filled with furniture that she thought ugly and she found it unsympathetic to her moods, a place to escape from rather than to, in which her few prettily feminine possessions looked as out of place as she felt.

Victoria went to her mother's sitting-room to make the coffee. When she returned, Bob and David were standing in front of the gas fire discussing the screen she had painted to block up the original fire-place.

"You ought to have a power point put in up here, Victoria," David said.

"I will when the house gets re-wired. Apparently it needs to be done quite soon. It's all rather ancient, I'm afraid, but that's part of its charm."

An opinion which her companions did not share, but they refrained from saying so.

"I've got the L plates," David told her.

"Oh, good," Victoria answered, hoping she did not sound as dismayed as she felt.

"I'll give you your first lesson tomorrow afternoon."

Bob said, "I didn't know you were keen

to drive, Vicky. I could have given you a go in Dad's car. He wouldn't mind—that is, have minded," he corrected himself quickly.

She was about to say that "keen" was hardly the right word, but was forestalled by David, who said,

"She's going to buy herself a car to learn in."

Bob looked impressed.

"Good for you," he told her warmly.

"I haven't made up my mind yet," she said. A car of her own was David's idea, backed up with encouragement from Jill. She had not mentioned it to Monica, because she expected opposition on the grounds of the risk of an accident and more extravagance. A lifetime of being encouraged to save fares with pedal-power made her sensitive to the last argument. She glanced across the room at the gorgeous rich fabric she had chosen for the curtains and ottoman cover and was assailed by pangs of guilt. Only Aunty Margaret would guess accurately how much a metre it had cost and remain unscandalised.

Victoria became aware, as they drank

coffee and ate chocolate biscuits, that there was a tension, a coolness between the two young men which betrayed itself in their stilted conversation. It made them less than natural towards her. David annoyed her by behaving more lover-like than he ever did when they were alone, taking every opportunity to put his arm around her, to speak for her as if he knew her mind better than she did herself and talk about a future which was exclusively theirs. Bob, on the other hand, for the first time, reminded her of his brother Stephen, cold and un-communicative, listening gravely and replying disapprovingly. Having always enjoyed the privilege of a favourite, she began by excusing him because of his grief for his father, but gradually became convinced that she had seriously displeased him.

Lunch time drew near and her two difficult guests showed no sign of taking their leave. David insisted on looking through her portfolios, watched morosely by Bob, who criticised everything that David praised in a manner that showed little respect for her feelings, of which previously he had always been so protective. She cast him one or two hurt looks which were totally disregarded. David's immoderate praise began to get on her nerves, especially as she felt it was based on goodwill rather than knowledge. She ended by snatching a sheaf of sketches from his hand and telling them, not very politely, that it was time to go. David looked at his watch and agreed. He had to be back at the hotel for lunch. Bob was seen off the premises at the same time.

"Didn't you ask Bob to stay for lunch?" Monica asked.

"No," was the short reply.

Monica did not go to church on Sunday morning. She felt unwell, but insisted that Victoria accompanied Albinia. When they returned it was to find Monica too ill to come down for lunch.

"What do you think is the matter with her?" Victoria asked her aunt, as they sat over the traditional fare of roast beef and Yorkshire pudding.

Albinia placed her knife and fork carefully on either side of her plate, dabbed her mouth delicately with a worn damask napkin and replied thoughtfully that she really had no idea. Ill-health was something she associated almost exclusively with incipient old age in her father; it came upon one as a consequence of too much introspection, resulting in morbidity of mind. The one exception had been her brother, Leonard. Marriage had mysteriously done for him; it had aggravated his weak heart.

"She used to be so well," Victoria said, refraining from adding, "before we moved here."

"If only she would see Dr. Raines again for a check-up."

"He couldn't find anything wrong the last time," Albinia reminded her. "If you ask me, she's showing all the signs of hypochondria, something your grandfather suffered from all his life. I believe many women are prone to it with the onset of middle-age." She picked up her cutlery and began to attack her roast beef with vigour. Not given to fancies herself, she could hardly be expected to have patience with other people who indulged in them.

After the meal, Victoria went upstairs to see her mother. She was fully clothed, lying propped up with cushions on the settee in her sitting-room, looking wan.

"Ring Merle for me, dear, and tell her I'm not well. I'll go tomorrow if I feel better. Perhaps you'd like to go along instead."

"I can't, Mum. I'm going out with David."

"Is it so important?" Monica asked, plaintively.

"Well, I did promise. He won't be off work again for a week."

To her consternation, her mother began to moan softly, putting a hand to her forehead as if she were suffering considerable pain. Victoria crossed to her and placed a hand on her shoulder, which was irritably shaken off.

"I feel so wretched," Monica complained.

"Is your headache worse?"

"It's not only that. I'm so depressed. No one ever visits me here, neither Merle nor Margaret, yet they expect me to visit them."

"They are both so busy," Victoria reminded her.

"Yes, of course! I'm the only one with

nothing to do, leading a useless existence. Nobody needs me. I could die tomorrow and no one would care, not even you."

"How can you say that?" Victoria cried, cut to the quick. "You know it isn't true!"

"You have your own life to lead now. Even Albinia has a life of her own. I'm the one stuck in this wretched house all day, going crazy."

"You could get a job," Victoria suggested.

Monica sniffed disparagingly at the idea. "What could I do?"

"You could try. There must be something."

Monica could not be persuaded that she was good for anything.

"Sooner or later you'll be getting married and leaving me. Then what shall I do?"

This was a familiar theme now. Victoria denied any such intention, but Monica was not mollified; somehow her daughter's denial lacked conviction. It was the kind of conversation that could go on forever, with one person offering comfort which the other was determined not to accept. Victoria surreptitiously glanced at her watch. David was calling for her at two o'clock. Her mother caught the fleeting action.

"Don't let me keep you. Go and enjoy yourself. I'm getting used to spending long hours on my own. It's no wonder I get depressed."

Victoria suggested that Albinia might be asked to keep her company.

"Heaven forbid!" Monica exclaimed unkindly. "She would only make my headache worse."

Victoria left her in order to 'phone Merle. Afterwards she 'phoned David to say she could not go out with him after all. He was extremely annoyed, virtually accusing her mother of being ill on purpose to keep them apart. Victoria denied this indignantly, but suspected that there might be an element of truth in it. She went into the kitchen to make a pot of tea, miserably reconciled to an afternoon in the company of her gentle gaoler.

An hour later Bob arrived. Victoria answered the door. Her face lit up at the sight of him and he was almost dragged inside.

"I'm so glad you've come," she told him, smiling with delight. "I was just about to cut my throat."

"You prefer an audience, do you?"

She laughed, realised she was still holding tightly to his hand, dropped it and blushed. He could not remember ever having caused her embarrassment by his proximity before and was intrigued by it.

"Come up to my studio," she invited, leading the way.

"Actually, I've called to see how Aunty Monica is. Mum sent me. She's rather concerned about her."

"She's a little better now. She's watching television with Aunt Binnie. I was so bored with it, I was getting desperate. The door bell was like a heavenly summons."

As they passed the sitting-room, Victoria put her head round the door to tell them it was only Bob.

When they reached her own room, he said, "I thought you were going out with David."

"I was, but I changed my mind."

He was curious to know why and a little

disappointed when he discovered that her mother had effectively changed it for her.

"David was awfully cross. I doubt whether he'll bother to ask me out again."

"Do you mind?"

"Of course," she said, with more conviction than she felt.

"Well, I wish you didn't. I've been hearing some unsavoury tales about him."

"Such as?" she demanded, instantly on the defensive.

"I'd rather not say."

She was furious.

"That's typical! You're as bad as the rest. Jill keeps hinting, but won't actually say anything, Mum doesn't care for him, but won't give a good reason. Raoul, who's supposed to be his friend, is painfully surprised that I'm still going out with him. Why? That's what I'd like to know."

"He goes out with other girls, you know."

"So what? We're not engaged."

He stood looking down at her with a worried frown. She glared back, waiting for him to say more. He could not. He could not bring himself to tell her that David was sexually promiscuous. He did

IOG26

not know how to say such a thing to Victoria, but he knew he had to prevent her from becoming another of David's victims. At last, he asked gently, "Just how far has this affair gone, Vicky?"

It was her turn to be at a loss for words. She was not stupid. She guessed that Jill, Raoul and now Bob were trying to safeguard her chastity. If only they knew how little she needed their concern. The wolf was still wearing sheep's clothing and, while it was exciting to smile and flirt with him a little while he wore that guise, the minute he showed his true predatory self, she knew she would run in alarm. Suddenly, her displeasure was no more. Her grey eyes looked into his serious brown ones and her expression changed from outraged innocence to a tender smile. She was amused at the thought that she could only tolerate David's innocuous embraces by imagining they were being administered by the person who now stood before her.

Bob interpreted the secretive smile quite wrongly as one of triumph and, supposing the affair to have progressed beyond the bounds of discretion, was wounded beyond caution.

"I thought you were different from other girls," he said bitterly, "but obviously my protection isn't needed any longer."

"Of course I'm not different from other girls, what a stupid thing to suppose. As for your protection, you're right, it's a bit late for that now. If you and my mother have taught me anything, it's that I have to look after myself."

"What do you mean by that?" he asked, white-faced.

Wanting to wound him, she answered,

"Do you remember that evening on the dunes, just before my grandfather died? Someone tried to rape me that evening, Bob. I was looking for you. When I found you, it was all over."

He held out his arms, but she stepped back quickly, pushing him away, telling him to go, that what she did was none of his business anyway, then she threw herself face down on the couch, burying her face in a cushion.

He watched her for a few minutes, horrified by her revelation, although not entirely surprised by it. Eventually she looked up, saw him still standing there and yelled at him to go. He went, perceiving no comforting significance in the fact that she behaved more atrociously in his presence than in anyone else's.

Left alone, Victoria wept. What a ghastly day it had turned out to be. I might just as well forget about ever getting married and be an old maid like Aunt Binnie, then everyone will be satisfied, she thought, and I shall never be put to the test.

A week later Bob left to go to sea for another three months, unhappily convinced that David was Victoria's lover. He sent her a post-card from each port of call, bearing a few words of greeting and best wishes. She wrote one letter, stilted and brief, but waited in vain for an answer.

25

THE distressful process of growing out of a sheltered childhood, which had been set in slow motion by the death of an old man and accelerated by an act of violence, was now running out of control. It would have been difficult to speculate which way Victoria would have jumped to save herself, had not an incident happened that effectively applied the brakes.

It was the last week in May. Bob had been back at sea for three weeks and Victoria was preparing for examinations and busy putting the final touches to some work which was to go in an end-of-term exhibition. David had 'phoned a few times to ask her out, but she had been unable to spare the time. He had never felt sure of her, in fact it was an elusive quality about her that he had always found so attractive, but now he sensed she was inexorably slipping away. He was used to being constantly sought after by his other women and it was the novelty of having to pay assiduous court to her that made Victoria a conquest worth having—that and her money, of course. He was determined not to lose either her or her fortune. They were to be a combined prize in reward for persistence and he was not going to relinquish that prize without a struggle. He liked her, of course he did, he was attracted by her delicacy. He had not sunk so low as to value her only for her money; after all, he told himself, dialling her number yet again and praying he would not get the toffee-nosed aunt, when first he met Victoria he had not known she had any money. This time his call paid off. Victoria, feeling in need of a break from her work and from her mother, consented to go out for a meal with him the next evening.

He called for her at Grande Maison. She was ready, watching for his car at the landing window. The second he turned into the drive, she ran downstairs and out of the front door. He took her eagerness to meet him as an encouraging sign, when in fact it was her way of keeping him from the other members of the household, who had shown disapproval, even dismay, when she had told them with whom she was spending the evening.

"I didn't think you were seeing him any more," her mother had said on a note of complaint. "I thought perhaps you had quarrelled."

Now, settling herself beside David in the car, Victoria's feeling of joyful release gradually subsided, leaving her unaccountably depressed. David, not over-sensitive to other people's moods, nevertheless soon became aware that, despite every effort on his part to charm and joke his way into her favour, he was not succeeding. As they ate their pub meal, he grew increasingly alarmed and gradually his alarm gave way to annoyance. He had other girls who would have jumped at the chance of a night out with him, girls who would have felt obliged to him for the privilege. By the time they left the pub he had come to a decision. He was fed up with being strung along half-heartedly by this introspective young woman. He had pussyfooted around her long enough. Perhaps what she needed after all was a more robust approach. His other women approved of it, why shouldn't she?

Instead of driving her straight home, he turned along a country road which led to a wild, deserted strip of coast.

Immediately she asked in a worried voice, "Where are we going?"

"I want to talk to you, Vicky."

When, after a few minutes silence, she realised that whatever he wanted to say was to wait until they reached their destination, she said, "But we can talk now, can't we?"

He felt the tension building up within her. "No!" he answered roughly, "I'm at a disadvantage when I'm driving."

So she sat beside him uneasily, while they completed the short journey to a deserted car park above a long beach, swept desolate by a stiff off-shore breeze and a strong ebb tide. Massive clouds sailed across the sky in ponderous flight towards the horizon. Victoria gazed up at them with eyes as grey and unfathomable as the late evening sky, yearning for the same unfettered motion. Beautiful vaporous clouds, freer than the sea birds that emulated them, for ultimately the birds were tied to their nests.

David wrenched at the hand-brake. She turned towards him, reluctant for his first words, but, instead of saying anything, he pulled her into his arms. No matter how hard she tried, Victoria could not persuade herself that she was safely in her cousin's embrace. Her eyes flew open in sudden disgust that she should even be attempting the pretence. Pushing David away, she shakily asked to be taken home and when he tried to coax her back she reacted angrily, opening the door and springing out with every intention of walking home.

David leaned across, one hand against the door to prevent her shutting it, absolutely baffled by her behaviour. "What on earth is the matter with you? Please get back in the car," he pleaded—actually pleaded to a woman! "What have I done? I was only kissing you," and after a short silence, during which she made no move, "of course I'll drive you home," he said, utterly exasperated. "For God's sake, get in!"

She complied slowly. As he started to drive away she said, staring straight ahead,

"David, I never want to go out with you again."

"Why? What the hell have I done?" he asked again in disbelief.

"You haven't done anything," she answered.

"I'm glad we are agreed about that," he muttered sarcastically.

She tried to explain. "I've been deceiving myself into believing that I like you more than I do."

"You're not the only one who has been deceived," he retorted with bitterness.

"Yes, I realise that and I am sorry, but don't pretend that you are heartbroken," and she smiled a little shakily at his frowning profile. "After all, I'm not the only girl in your life."

"You could be," he told her quickly.

"No!" she answered with firmness, and the rest of the journey was completed in an unhappy silence. When they reached Grande Maison, she could not get out of the car quickly enough. Her last words before she shut the door upon him were, "I'm sorry, David."

Humiliated, he drove away at speed, anxious to put as much distance between them as possible. Victoria watched him go. As the rear lights of the mini disappeared around the curve of the drive, she heaved a deep sigh of relief and, turning towards the house, thought, Mum and Aunt Binnie will see this as their victory, but it isn't, it's mine. But for their opposition I might have stopped seeing David even sooner. I know he's not for me, but I had to find out for myself. Sometimes the more you are cautioned about someone, the more you feel you have to defend them to justify your perversity. Surely when they were my age their judgement of people was not infallible.

David Strang was married in July. His mind had been made up for him by the young lady and her father. The pressure they brought to bear was additionally weighted by the fact that the family owned two public houses and was not short of money. He left the Regency hotel to participate in the family business, fired with ambition and dreams of expansion, which in one sense were soon to be fulfilled.

The day after Bob returned in late

August, he met Jill in the town. She was doing some shopping in her lunch hour and invited him to join her for some sandwiches and coffee in a nearby café.

"You do look handsome with that gorgeous tan, Bob. If you weren't my cousin, I could fancy you."

"Can't cousins fancy each other?" he asked her.

She regarded him seriously for a few moments, sipping her drink, then, carefully placing the cup onto the saucer, answered, "You mean Victoria?"

"Perhaps."

"What do you mean, perhaps?"

"I mean, I don't know," he told her. "I've grown up with a sense of responsibility for her. When we were young and encouraged to take care of her, what was that phrase? 'Take her out of herself', I was the only one who took it seriously, until it became a habit. You could say that Victoria is a habit I cannot kick."

"Sounds like love to me," Jill said lightly. "That's exactly how I would describe that grand emotion."

"If you're right, then I have problems."

"Such as?"

"David Strang, for a start."

She chuckled at this. "No problem. He's married. Didn't Vicky tell you?"

Bob was astounded.

"Poor Vicky!" he said.

Jill gulped on a bite of sandwich.

"What a peculiar reaction. I thought you'd be pleased."

"Isn't she upset, then?"

"Why should she be? As far as I know, she hasn't been going out with him for months. Not that I see much of her. Helen and Sandra drop in at Grande Maison occasionally and keep us in touch. I don't think Victoria has much of a life with Aunty Monica and Miss Lacy. It's a pity she hasn't any brothers and sisters to take the pressure off her. When we were kids she used to have the rest of us, but now she's really on her own—except for you, of course." Jill waited, curious for his reply.

He looked guilty, but said nothing.

"I always suspected that David was after Victoria's money," she said, instantly regretting it.

"Yes, whoever marries her will be suspected of that," Bob agreed.

"It's my opinion it should be kept in the

family." Jill laughed, but getting a stony response, added, "You're right, it is 'Poor Vicky.' She's going to have to suffer all her life from two afflictions, being an only child with an over-possessive mother and being too rich to marry the man who loves her." Jill drank the last of her coffee and stood up. "I must go, or I'll be late back and Dad is expecting a client. Come and see me soon and bring Victoria."

She left him abruptly. Two young men sitting nearby gave up envying him and felt sorry for him instead, their eyes following Jill as she made her way between the tables and chairs to the door. She turned to give Bob a quick wave before disappearing into the crowded shopping arcade.

Bob stirred his lukewarm coffee, deep in thought.

As Jill wended her hurried way through strolling crowds of aimless people, some extremely pretty china in a shop window caught her eye. She paused for a few seconds to admire it and price it, then, as she turned to hurry on, she saw Sadie Frobisher, accompanied by the young son who had recently undergone an operation on his legs. He was walking slowly and with some difficulty, holding on tightly to his mother's arm, his face raised to hers as he spoke to her animatedly. She was listening to him with a small smile of amusement, tinged with maternal pride. She did not see Jill, who crossed the road quickly to avoid them.

She's the antithesis of mother, Jill thought, in looks and in nature. Blonde and attractive in a soft curvy way, as against dark and severely elegant; also she's able to pay rapt attention when her children speak, amused rather than irritated by them. Jill felt a quick surge of affection for her mother, which swamped her disloyal thoughts. Her father should make a deliberate choice between his mistress and his home. Jill was not naïve enough to suppose that it was any longer between his mistress and his wife, yet it never dawned on her that his mistress might exercise a similar choice.

The client whom Larry was expecting was a nondescript woman in her late thirties. Jill showed her into his office and stayed just long enough to watch her inevitable response to him as he smilingly rose to greet her, hand outstretched. She closed the door, mentally warning the foolish female that Mr. Larry de Valois was a charming, adorable, ambitious, spineless rat, whose formidable wife was due in about ten minutes on one of her frequent visits, called "dropping in while . . ." This afternoon it was while on her way to a Lifeboat committee meeting. Although Jill knew he was still meeting Sadie Frobisher, she was baffled how he managed it, with Margaret monitoring his every move. Sadly she tried to recall how long it was since her mother had responded vivaciously to the challenge of her husband's undivided attention. Mother and I have become immune, she concluded, feeding paper into her typewriter.

The first thing Bob did when he returned home was to 'phone Grande Maison. There was no reply. He mentioned this to Merle as she was crossing the hall on her way to the kitchen.

"They're all away, dear. Monica, Victoria and Miss Lacy have gone to the

Lake District for two weeks and Mrs. Grey is visiting some relations in Southampton."

"When will they be back?" he asked, disappointed.

"Let me see, how long have they been gone? Victoria was here a few days before they left. That must have been about a week ago, so they must be returning in about ten days' time. She wasn't keen to go, she wanted to go camping in Wales with some college friends, but Monica prevented her."

"How?" he wanted to know.

"She didn't say no, but she put up all kinds of objections and took all pleasure out of the holiday for the poor child. As Victoria said, it was pointless to go and feel guilty all the time."

"I don't know how Vicky can stand it," Bob said.

"She hasn't much choice, has she? If she retaliated by being uncaring and unkind, she wouldn't be Vicky." Merle smiled gently at her son, walking past him towards the kitchen, where Alison was waiting to start the preparations for dinner.

IOG27

Bob went up to the attic bedroom he was once again sharing with Stephen, passing the closed bedroom doors of perfect strangers. He never mounted the flight of wooden stairs, with the landing door slamming shut behind him, without thinking of his father and lamenting his death. He could understand now how Victoria had felt after the death of her grandfather, when she complained that nothing would ever be the same again. Life rolled on smoothly for years over small vicissitudes, then something cataclysmic happened to change its course and, instead of swimming, one was floundering, frantically searching for a haven of smooth water.

On his narrow bed lay a picture postcard of Buttermere. He turned it over. The message was short. "It is beautiful here. Hope you have arrived home safely. Love from Victoria."

He placed it in the drawer beside the carved bone elephant he had brought back for her from Singapore.

That evening Jill and Raoul had a pub meal and returned to her flat about ten o'clock for coffee, sitting close together before the television to drink it.

This flat, although not large, was a complete contrast with her previous one. It was modern and furnished with her own possessions, many of them gifts from her mother who could be generous when circumstances met with her approval. After about ten minutes, Raoul got up and switched off the television, although the programme they had been watching was not yet finished. He remained standing in front of her as he said, "Mum wants us to go on holiday with her and Dad."

"When?"

"The middle of September. Switzerland."

"I can't Raoul. I've had all my holiday, except for a couple of days. Dad would probably let me have more if I asked him, but it wouldn't be fair. I don't like to take advantage of the fact that I'm the boss's daughter. I know Alex Stuart wouldn't approve. Why don't you go without me?"

He declared he would not. In his opinion they were apart far too much already. Jill tried to persuade him and they were in the middle of an argument that was showing signs of becoming heated, when the door bell rang.

Raoul went to answer it. It was Sandra. She rushed straight past him without a word, to throw herself into her sister's arms.

"I've come to stay," she said, tearfully. "They're having the most awful row at home and I can't stand it."

Raoul excused himself and left hastily, glad to get away before he capitulated beneath the relentless logic of his beloved.

As soon as he was gone, Sandra poured out her story. As she listened, Jill's spirits sank lower and lower.

Apparently, according to Sandra, things had been "grotty" at home for over a week. Mrs. Figgus had broken her wrist and was combining convalescence with a much-needed holiday. Helen was also away, "doing Paris" with Prissy Bideau. Sandra had been very much left to her own devices most of the time, except on the few occasions during the day when she and her mother had been home at the same time, when she was at the latter's beck and call.

"It's awful being in the house with just

mother, especially when she's mad with Daddy," Sandra complained.

"Why is she mad with him?" Jill asked with dread.

"That's the worst thing. Dad doesn't love Mum any more. He likes someone else better. I think he's going to leave us, Jill."

Jill's heart went out to her. She recalled her own feelings when she had first known. "What makes you think that?" she asked.

"They thought I was in bed. Well, I was, but I had left my book downstairs, so I got up and went to fetch it for the morning. As I passed the dining-room I heard Mum almost shouting at Daddy, something like, 'That woman is obviously more important to you than I am'. I thought he would deny it, but he didn't. He said everything was over between him and Sadie—that's her name, Sadie. It must be Mrs. Frobisher, do you remember her?—because she would not leave her children, and Mum could divorce him if that was what she wanted, even though it might ruin his career. Why would it ruin his career, Jill?" she asked, wide-eyed and puzzled.

Jill shook her head to signify that she did not know, but she suspected it was a ploy of her father's to make Margaret think twice about her answer. The last thing either of them would want in any circumstance was something that would jeopardise his successfully expanding career. "What did Mum say?"

"She said that she would rather die than let anyone know her marriage was less than perfect and Dad said that was her trouble, everything and everyone had to be perfect. It was too much to expect of human beings and he for one could take no more." Sandra paused for breath.

"What happened then?" Jill prompted gently.

"Mum said in a low voice so that I could hardly hear, 'You were perfect to me once, Larry. I never wanted anyone else in my life. Now I have only pretence left. If you take that away from me, I shall die.'"

"Oh, heavens," Jill groaned. "What did Dad say?"

"He said that she was being over-dramatic as usual and started to move towards the door. Thinking he was coming out, I fled upstairs. When I crept down later to come here, I could hear them still arguing. Can I stay with you?"

"You can stay until Helen gets back," Jill promised. "I'll take you home first thing in the morning, before work, so that you can collect a few clothes and tell mother."

"She won't miss me," Sandra said. A statement that Jill did not think it worthwhile to refute.

Jill drove to her parents' home next morning with some misgiving. Approaching her mother was never easy. Knowing of the scene that had taken place the night before made her even more apprehensive. Sandra sat beside her, still and quiet, experiencing similar feelings as they drove along the narrow country road, flanked by high hedges. They turned sharply left onto a steeply winding lane that led to the cliff top and, suddenly, there was the house high on a solitary promontory, surrounded by strategically placed groups of flowering shrubs and trees, set against a vast sky which, this morning, was hazy blue with the promise of heat. A lump rose in Jill's throat at the sight. The house had been her father's gift of love to his bride, an exquisite shell around which she had devised a natural setting in harmony with its elevated position and into which she had lavishly poured an aura of luxury without ostentation. It was a pleasant experience, for family and friends alike, to be inside that home. Margaret had reached an artistic fulfilment in its creation, to be shared with her husband. Her munificence extended to all who visited them.

This morning, however, this generous all-pervading spirit was not in evidence. Jill had never realised before how much the welcome extended by the opulent house had emanated from the being who was its mistress. Today, Margaret was not in a mood to be sociable and neither was her home. The beauty was evident in both of them, but even in the warmth of the early morning sunshine they remained cool and aloof.

The girls entered by the kitchen. In the absence of Mrs. Figgus, even that room was unfriendly. Apparently no one had eaten breakfast; there was no delicious aroma of bacon and fresh coffee. Everything sparkled in unused cleanliness.

They found their mother in the conservatory, watering her lush pot plants. She was pale, with dark rings beneath her lustreless eyes as if she had shed tears, yet her manner was so composed that it was difficult to believe she had. She raised her eyebrows at her daughters' entrance, her only sign of surprise at seeing them together so early in the morning when she could have supposed Sandra to be still in her bed upstairs and Jill on her way to the office.

"Is it all right if Sandra comes to stay with me for a few days, Mum?" Jill asked, not mentioning the fact that Sandra had already made the move. They both expected opposition. It was Margaret's way to demand her daughters' company, even though she ignored it when it was made available. She felt aggrieved when she was left alone by them, but never supposed them to feel the same way about her frequent absences. However, all she said was, "Yes, if she wants to, although I can't think why she should."

"She's going to help me do some decorating in the kitchen," Jill said on the spur of the moment.

"Good heavens, is she really? I think she'll make a frightful mess."

Margaret continued to water her plants, picking away the occasional dead leaf and flower.

"Do you intend going to work today?" she asked Jill, without looking at her.

"Yes, of course. I don't want to be late, so we'll just pack a few things for Sandra and be off."

"Old things, if she's going to decorate," her mother advised, drily.

"Are you sure you'll be all right, Mum?" Sandra asked, suddenly feeling like a deserter.

"Why shouldn't I be? If you're as much help to Jill as you've been to me this last week, then I don't envy her. Thank goodness Mrs. Figgus will be back soon." A cry that came straight from her heart.

"If you need help with the cooking, Mum, I'll come any evening," Jill offered.

Margaret said, "I have no plans for entertaining at the moment." Adding after a short pause, as if to herself, "God knows if I ever will again." She sighed, stopping in her task to gaze abstractedly into the garden.

"Why?" Jill could not refrain from asking.

Margaret came instantly to life, resuming the watering.

"I haven't the inclination," she said, then realising that the small can was empty, she walked the length of the conservatory to fill it from the rain butt.

Jill and Sandra exchanged knowing looks of dismay and went to pack.

When Jill eventually arrived at work, fifteen minutes late, her father was impatiently waiting to speak to her. He called her into his office at once. She expected to be reprimanded for her tardiness, but in fact it was to tell her that he would be out of the office most of the day and ask her to cancel two appointments. She waited for an explanation, but as one was not forthcoming, asked what reason she should give the clients if they asked, to which he replied tartly that it was none of their damned business. Jill put this unusual irritability down to the row with his wife and supposed miserably that he was going to seek comfort from his mistress.

No one was sure when Helen was due back; her holiday plans had been vague, involving over-night stays in youth hostels.

Consequently, it was a surprise to Jill when she turned up in her office on Tuesday afternoon.

"Where's Dad?" were her first words.

"Talking to Alex Stuart."

"Which office?"

"Alex's, why?"

Helen cast a quick look around the room, as if she suspected that someone was lurking behind the filing cabinets, then, leaning over the desk, she whispered,

"Did you know he has left home?"

"Nonsense," Jill whispered back.

Helen straightened up and reverted to her normal voice; it could sound more indignant than a whisper.

"He has. Mother is wafting round the house like a lost soul. It's terrible. Where's Sandra? I didn't like to ask Mum too many questions. As a matter of fact, she was so distant and peculiar, I couldn't leave fast enough."

"Sandra is staying with me. Look, are

you sure about Dad? He hasn't said anything to me, but then I haven't seen much of him since Wednesday, when he and mother had a row and Sandra came to the flat. He seems normal enough when I do speak to him, a bit irritable perhaps."

However, when he came in a few minutes later, he almost walked past Helen without seeing her, and when she greeted him, he stood looking at her for a second or so before recognition dawned.

"Hello, darling. Had a nice holiday?" he asked, but he did not wait for her answer.

"Yes," she told the office door, as it shut behind him. "Lovely, thank you. I jumped off the Eiffel Tower and landed on my head!" Then, turning to Jill, she added bitterly, "If I had known things were like this at home, I might have been tempted. Where do you suppose he's staying?"

Jill shrugged, not wishing to discuss the matter any further at present. She told her that she had a lot of work to do and suggested she went to the flat, where she could help Sandra prepare the dinner for the three of them, unless her mother was expecting her.

"Mother is not expecting anything. I felt

like an intruder in the house. When will Mrs. Figgus be back? Sandra will have to come home with me this evening. I'm not staying there on my own."

Jill agreed. It was her opinion that Margaret should have someone with her constantly for the time being, keeping a surreptitious eye on her.

She went into her father's office just before five o'clock with everything that needed his signature. He handed the papers back to her when he had finished with them, saying, "Shut the door, Jill. I want to speak to you."

He told her to sit down, which she did, feeling an apprehensive wave of nausea well up inside her, dreading what was coming. There was a pause before he spoke again and, when he did, it was in an apologetic, hesitant manner, at variance with his usual cheerful, half-teasing tone. She listened, but afterwards could not remember the words he spoke, only the gist of what he had said. He was going to open a branch of the practice in Paris. He had been working to that end for some time, or rather, Alex Stuart had on his behalf, as he had not wanted anyone, including Jill, to know until it was all settled. He was leaving the next day. Alex would be moving into his office and Jill would continue as before, only she would be collecting a different signature, of course. (Here he smiled sadly at her, making her want to cry.) He asked that his three lovely daughters should be especially kind to their mother, who would need their support until she grew accustomed to the new arrangement, and he ended by saying that he hoped they would forgive his tactical withdrawal from the scene of his dismal failure enough to visit him in Paris as often as possible.

When he stopped speaking, all Jill could think of saying, was "What will become of mother?"

He showed his complete lack of understanding and sympathy when he answered, "She'll be all right."

"She'll have nothing left," Jill said, appalled at the thought.

"I am taking nothing away from her but myself," he pointed out.

"But you are everything to her, no one else counts, nothing matters but you."

He sighed deeply, wiping a hand across his brow and eyes.

"Jill, don't you see, that is what I can't stand. Your mother's love is a burden which I am not strong enough to bear."

"You were strong enough once," she said accusingly, getting to her feet.

His eyes looked into hers, as he answered, "Yes."

She waited for him to start excusing himself, but all he said, in a dismissive manner, was, "Say goodbye to your sisters for me. I shall miss you all. Don't think I shall have no regrets. This isn't easy, Jill."

"No, not for any of us," she cried bitterly as she rushed from the room.

So he had made his choice at last! That woman in place of his family.

"Coward!" she muttered, folding the letters and stuffing them into envelopes. "Bloody coward! He's not even going to see Helen and Sandra before he goes. They are the ones who are going to have to endure mother's suffering. How will she ever get accustomed to the idea, for God's sake? How?"

Blinded by tears, she grabbed the post and her handbag and left, almost running in her eagerness to depart. When she reached her flat, the post was still clutched in her hand, although she had passed two pillar boxes.

26

WHEN the taxi from the airport drew up in front of the house, the returning travellers were somewhat surprised to see Sandra sitting on the steps outside the front door.

"Does this mean that Mrs. Grey hasn't returned?" Albinia said, crossly.

Sandra leaped up at the sight of them and ran down the steps. Victoria hurried to her side, knowing instinctively that something was wrong. Sandra explained that Mrs. Grey had asked her inside to wait, but as they were expected back any minute, she had preferred to wait out here.

"I've been for a walk round the garden," she explained.

She helped Victoria to carry her bags upstairs. As soon as they were alone in the bedroom she burst out with her explanation.

"I thought you were returning this morning. Something awful happened while you were away, Vicky. Daddy has left us and gone to live in France. He went on Wednesday and since then we've hardly seen Mum."

"This is very sudden, isn't it?" Victoria asked, sinking onto the edge of the bed.

"That's how it seems to me, but Jill says it's been brewing up for ages. Did you know about Mrs. Frobisher?"

Victoria nodded sadly, wishing she could deny it.

"I know her son, Ben," Sandra said forlornly. "I met him at the Bideaus'. I bet Mrs. Bideau knows all about it. I've gone right off Prissy. I can't think how Helen stands her. Jill has come home to stay with us until Mrs. Figgus gets back tomorrow. She says we have to keep Mum company, show her that we love her, but actually I loved Daddy best and now he's gone I don't know what to do." She sat beside Victoria and burst into tears. Victoria put her arm around her, filled with pity.

We're all fatherless now, she thought, and our mothers, once so close, have drifted apart, drawing us with them. It's as if the whole family started off on the same iceberg in a vast, unfriendly ocean, then, one by one, some fell off. First my father, so far back in the dim and distant past that I never even noticed, then Grandpa Lacy followed by Uncle Karl and now Uncle Larry, assuming he is as irretrievably lost. Gradually the iceberg started to disintegrate beneath those of us who were left, great chunks sailing off on diverging currents until now only we children are close enough on our floes to be able to leap from one to the other to keep in touch and, as time goes by, this feat becomes increasingly difficult. Stephen has given up the attempt. The rest of us struggle with varying degrees of success, but soon we shall all give up, all drift off into utter isolation—it's terrifying.

There was a perfunctory knock on the door and Monica entered.

"What on earth is the matter?" she asked, noticing the two dreary faces with consternation.

Sandra poured out her tale again.

"Your poor mother," Monica said. "How is she?"

Then Sandra remembered, too late, that the only thing her mother had said to her since her husband's departure had been a warning not to discuss the affair with anyone. She wanted no one's pity, no one's jealous triumph. Having been brought up in a family that disseminated its troubles and emotions freely amongst its members, Sandra had not supposed the warning to include her mother's sisters; now, seeing Monica's excited sympathy and imagining her mother's reception of it, she had second thoughts.

"Mum won't talk to anyone," she warned. "She's pretending to all her friends that nothing has happened."

"I thought you said that you had hardly seen her since your father left?"

Sandra admitted that was true, but explained that her mother was carrying out her social engagements as normal—those that did not include her father, of course—which meant mainly day-time activities.

"I don't suppose she'll ever go out at night again," Sandra said, dismayed at the thought. "Who's going to invite her without Daddy?"

The implications of this on Margaret's life-style sank into all three.

"I shall have to go," Sandra said, blowing her nose to clear the aftermath of her tears. "Jill said we have to be in for every meal, in case Mum decides to join us, but so far she has stayed in her room. Helen and I are doing the cooking until Mrs. Figgus gets back. Mum is getting up at six every morning to do the housework. I expect it's because she can't sleep."

As soon as Sandra had left, Monica 'phoned Merle. The crisis was bringing two of the sisters together again, if only for the duration of the seven-day wonder.

That evening, Victoria dragged her bicycle out from behind the skirts of numerous raincoats in the passage. She pumped up the tyres, deflated from neglect, much the same way as she felt, and cycled slowly away from the house along the drive pretending she did not know where she was going.

Fifteen minutes later she walked into Merle's deserted kitchen. With all the signs of dinner cleared tidily away, it reposed in the tranquillity of the evening sunlight, clean and fresh, waiting for the renewed activity of breakfast.

As she walked through the breakfast room into the hall, she called her aunt's name and was answered from the sitting-room, where Merle was watching television with three small children who were too young to accompany their parents to the theatre.

"I'm baby-sitting," she explained unnecessarily, when Victoria joined them. "Is Bob with you?" and when Victoria answered that he was not, she said he must have missed her, because he had left a short while ago for Grande Maison.

"I'll go home, then," Victoria said.

"Oh, won't you stay until he gets back?" Merle suggested, disappointed as she saw her so rarely. "The children will be going to bed soon and we can have a chat. You could tell me about your holiday."

Victoria wrinkled her nose slightly at this suggestion and Merle laughed. "Well, another time then, dear," she said regretfully, watching her leave.

"Can we change the channel now?" a small voice piped. "We don't like this programme."

"Yes, of course," Merle said and there was a scramble for the television knobs. With no interest in the programme that the children wanted to watch, she rested her head on the back of the chair and sank into a melancholy reverie. How sad it is, she thought, that the three of us are without husbands now. Larry is only in Paris, of course, it's conceivable that he might return to Margaret one day. She would have him back, I'm sure of it, if only for the sake of appearances and her unbearable pride, but my God she would make him suffer! The girls must miss him dreadfully. Already Helen has expressed a wish to join him there—that would cramp his style! He's too attractive to remain without a woman for long; for all we know there is already someone else. How I miss Karl!

Now that he was no longer with her, Merle discounted the misery and anxiety of their last few years together and dwelt upon the happier times, when the family had been close and mutually supportive. Karl had been kind and considerate, quick to excuse other people's faults, very different from Stephen. Had Stephen's criticism of his father been too harsh? Merle was beginning to suspect that it might have been, because recently she was finding herself the victim of that same unbending judgement. Her elder son did not think she was exerting herself enough to make the guest house business a success. He and Alison were constantly pressurising her to do things differently: extend the house so that it would accommodate more guests; extend the menu, which was unexciting; redecorate the ground floor, which was shabby and old-fashioned; put a small swimming pool in the back garden. Merle had taken Alison's advice about the food, but was resisting the other plans. How long could she continue to resist against such a determined couple? Would it not be better to take a back seat and let them have their way? Or was she already in the back seat without realising it? She dreaded the day when Bob went back to sea. It was ironic, for the similarity to his father which had once so tormented her now made her feel closer to him. She saw no signs of the weakness she had feared and often recalled his words when he had accused Stephen of being contributory to his father's lack of self-esteem. At last she understood what he had meant, because she was feeling her own worth diminishing beneath Stephen's well-meant criticism and advice. Once she had been too busy and preoccupied to notice. One day her fine and upright son might discover a weakness in himself, or had he already done so? Was he mastering it at the expense of his compassion?

As Victoria was retrieving her bicycle from the side wall of the house, a car drew up, driven by Stephen with Alison at his side. Bob got out of the back seat. Stephen shouted, "Had a nice holiday?" Alison smiled and waved to her and the car drove off again.

Bob strode towards her.

"Hello," he said, not smiling.

"I was looking for you," she admitted, at which his expression lightened considerably.

"I'll get my bike," he said, "as you haven't bought a car yet."

"I'm having lessons," she answered with spirit.

They cycled some way in a constrained silence, both reliving the trauma of their last meeting and wondering how much had been altered by the events of the intervening three months. Victoria, pensively preoccupied, never thought to ask where they were going, and it was not until she found herself riding along the bleak dune road, so familiar to her in nightmares, that she nervously queried their destination.

"You said you were looking for me this evening, Vicky. Well, this time you have found me. I remember a time when you were not so fortunate. It has left us both with a legacy. Yours is of fear, mine is regret. We are going to dispose of those legacies." He stopped and she followed suit, her worried eyes fixed upon his face, wondering what he intended to do.

"It was about here you left your bike that evening, wasn't it?"

Reluctantly she transferred her gaze to examine the pattern of the dunes against the clear evening sky, swallowing a rising sickness in her throat. She nodded.

Bob dropped his own bike onto the grass verge and wrenching hers from stiff fingers, dropped it alongside. Then, taking her hand firmly in his, he said quietly, "Come on, we'll go together this time."

They took the winding path that led away from the road towards the grass-topped outcrop of rock. As they walked, she explained in a low voice how she had sat there, looking across the deserted beach out to sea and how, gradually, she had become aware that she was being watched. Every now and then she cast a swift look round, but this evening only the breeze disturbed the landscape.

She did not intend to climb to the summit, but Bob insisted, going up first and pulling her after him. When they reached the top he took her by the shoulders, feeling her rigid beneath his hands and remorselessly turned her round to face the way they had come. No still figure stood there, only for a fleet second in her vivid imagination.

Without a word they descended and when she turned, involuntarily, to take the path away from that secret, horrid place, he insisted she went by freeing his hand from hers and putting an arm firmly around her waist. He gently urged her forward towards the spot where she had been jolted from childhood and shocked into seeing the world as it really is. When they reached the small dell, she took a step backwards to stand close against him, saying in a stifled voice, which he could hardly hear, "This is where he dragged me." Then, turning quickly, she hid her face in Bob's thick jumper, clinging to him and trembling with the memory, not only of the event but also of the horror of constantly reliving it, first in imagination and then, when she had conquered that, in dreams.

Bob held her tightly until she grew calmer, gazing over the top of her head, seeing the wild expanse of undulating, coarse grassland. It was the same now, as it had been then, wild and beautiful, yet with a lurking ugliness beneath its peace. Nothing is as it seems; even nature has two faces.

"Have you found me too late, Vicky?" he whispered in her ear.

She lifted her eyes to his and as her only answer was to cling closer, he kissed her, erasing the ugliness from the scene for them both.

27

VICTORIA had been back at college a week, at the start of the second and final year of her art and design course, when, on returning home from an early evening lecture, she was informed by her mother that Margaret had 'phoned and wanted to speak to her. She turned towards the telephone, only to be told that Margaret wanted to see her at home, the sooner the better.

"What can it be about?"

Monica said she had no idea and offered to go with her, but Victoria declined her offer as tactfully as possible, saying she would cycle over as soon as she had eaten something.

When she arrived there it was to find not only her aunt, but also her three cousins waiting for her. Margaret looked strangely triumphant, the girls rather bemused, as if they were in the process of assimilating some peculiar phenomenon.

"I have decided to make a new life for myself, Victoria," Margaret said exultantly.

The light of battle was back in her eyes, the drama that was her life was about to open again in a new production.

"I have been discussing my plans with my daughters. They approve, I think." She looked at them. They readily murmured their approval. She addressed her niece again.

"I have seen the room you have furnished and decorated at Grande Maison. I like it. It's not to my taste, I prefer simplicity. You obviously adore being clever with colours and use design where I should prefer texture, but that is all the better. It wouldn't do if we both liked exactly the same things."

Completely at a loss, Victoria glanced appealingly at her cousins, only to receive blank looks from Jill and Sandra and the hint of a wink from Helen.

Margaret continued. "Your mother let me see all your artwork. I was impressed. I hadn't realised how talented you are."

Sandra chipped in to the effect that she had often told her mother about Victoria's talent, but was ignored as usual.

"I'm going to set up in business as an interior designer and I wondered if you would like to join me in the venture."

"I'm still at college," Victoria reminded her, hardly able to believe her ears.

"Well, I know that," Margaret said impatiently. "It will take me some while to get started. You could begin by helping me on a part-time basis until next summer. What do you think? You might just as well invest some of your money in a business, rather than wait to hand it over to a husband to fritter away for you."

Victoria and Jill caught each other's eyes and Victoria felt an hysterical desire to laugh. Here was her Aunty Margaret, who had always despised her as a rubbishy little thing with no backbone, asking her to join her in a business venture—it was incredible!

"It sounds exciting," she faltered, because she was expected to say something and could think of nothing constructive.

"Yes, well, think it over. There will be a job for you anyway, whether you decide to join me as a partner or not. Jill is going to do the secretarial work for me. Helen and Sandra can be the main sources of advertisement for the time being; they will be unsurpassed at that, judging by past performances."

These two exchanged guilty looks, but knew better than to protest.

"Your best advertisement must surely be your own home," Victoria said warmly, inadvertently erasing forever the remnants of her aunt's poor opinion of her.

Before she returned home, Victoria was invited to accompany Jill on a stroll round the garden. There was much Jill did not wish to say in front of her sisters, who were despatched to the kitchen to make supper.

Once outside, in the scented and salt-tangy air of the gathering dusk, Jill talked about her mother.

"She's amazing. I have always admired her and now more than ever. After Dad left, she braved it out magnificently amongst her friends, pretending nothing unusual had happened. If anyone mentioned that Dad was away, she explained he was very busy setting up the Paris office and meeting clients over there. At home it was a very different story. She kept apart most of the time and hardly spoke when she was with us. I thought at one stage that she was contemplating suicide. Now I realise she was thinking things out and coming to grips with the situation, not losing control at all. When she reached a decision about her future, everything changed. She became her usual dynamic, sarcastic self, but only on the surface, you understand. Underneath she is desolate. Desolate but indomitable, that's my mother. I'm supposed to do any secretarial work she needs in my father's time. It's her way of paying him back. Actually, I shall be glad to leave the office. It's awkward working for Alex Stuart. He's always aware that I was foisted on the firm by mother and he detests her."

She stopped talking and walking at the same time. Turning to Victoria, she asked, "What about you? Anything new at Grande Maison?"

"Mum is a lot better," Victoria said. "Now that David has disappeared from the scene she seems happier, that and the fact that Aunt Binnie has somehow persuaded Mrs. Grey to retire and go and live with her sister in Southampton. Mum and Aunty Merle are seeing a lot of one another again; they are even talking of going on holiday together when the season is over."

Jill smiled. "I suppose Aunty Monica doesn't feel she will be losing you now."

Victoria blushed and admitted this was true. Bob was a favourite at Grande Maison, not afraid to poke gentle fun at the two older women and make them laugh at their own idiosyncracies. "Guess what?" she said, laughing, "we actually have the television downstairs now."

As they walked back to the house, Jill said, "Next year I intend going to live in London with Raoul. I'm afraid I am like my father and need to escape." She turned her head to look at the younger girl walking beside her, so fair and gentle, a tender victim for other people's emotional battles. "Think twice before you let mother dominate your future, Vicky."

"She won't," Victoria said, smiling with a confidence born of the comforting knowledge that she and Bob now shared the same ice floe. When it melted, as she knew it must, they would drown together.

This book is published under the
auspices of the
ULVERSCROFT FOUNDATION,
a registered charity, whose primary object is to assist those who experience difficulty in reading print of normal size.

In response to approaches from the medical world, the Foundation is also helping to purchase the latest, most sophisticated medical equipment desperately needed by major eye hospitals for the diagnosis and treatment of eye diseases.

If you would like to know more about the
ULVERSCROFT FOUNDATION,
and how you can help to further its work,
please write for details to:

THE ULVERSCROFT FOUNDATION
The Green, Bradgate Road
Anstey
Leicestershire
England

GUIDE
TO THE COLOUR CODING
OF
ULVERSCROFT BOOKS

Many of our readers have written to us expressing their appreciation for the way in which our colour coding has assisted them in selecting the Ulverscroft books of their choice.

To remind everyone of our colour coding—this is as follows:

BLACK COVERS
Mysteries
★
BLUE COVERS
Romances
★
RED COVERS
Adventure Suspense and General Fiction
★
ORANGE COVERS
Westerns
★
GREEN COVERS
Non-Fiction

FICTION TITLES
in the
Ulverscroft Large Print Series

The Onedin Line: The High Seas *Cyril Abraham*
The Onedin Line: The Iron Ships *Cyril Abraham*
The Onedin Line: The Shipmaster *Cyril Abraham*
The Onedin Line: The Trade Winds *Cyril Abraham*
The Enemy *Desmond Bagley*
Flyaway *Desmond Bagley*
The Master Idol *Anthony Burton*
The Navigators *Anthony Burton*
A Place to Stand *Anthony Burton*
The Doomsday Carrier *Victor Canning*
The Cinder Path *Catherine Cookson*
The Girl *Catherine Cookson*
The Invisible Cord *Catherine Cookson*
Life and Mary Ann *Catherine Cookson*
Maggie Rowan *Catherine Cookson*
Marriage and Mary Ann *Catherine Cookson*
Mary Ann's Angels *Catherine Cookson*
All Over the Town *R. F. Delderfield*
Jamaica Inn *Daphne du Maurier*
My Cousin Rachel *Daphne du Maurier*

Enquiry *Dick Francis*
Flying Finish *Dick Francis*
Forfeit *Dick Francis*
High Stakes *Dick Francis*
In The Frame *Dick Francis*
Knock Down *Dick Francis*
Risk *Dick Francis*
Band of Brothers *Ernest K. Gann*
Twilight For The Gods *Ernest K. Gann*
Army of Shadows *John Harris*
The Claws of Mercy *John Harris*
Getaway *John Harris*
Winter Quarry *Paul Henissart*
East of Desolation *Jack Higgins*
In the Hour Before Midnight *Jack Higgins*
Night Judgement at Sinos *Jack Higgins*
Wrath of the Lion *Jack Higgins*
Air Bridge *Hammond Innes*
A Cleft of Stars *Geoffrey Jenkins*
A Grue of Ice *Geoffrey Jenkins*
Beloved Exiles *Agnes Newton Keith*
Passport to Peril *James Leasor*
Goodbye California *Alistair MacLean*
South By Java Head *Alistair MacLean*
All Other Perils *Robert MacLeod*
Dragonship *Robert MacLeod*
A Killing in Malta *Robert MacLeod*
A Property in Cyprus *Robert MacLeod*

By Command of the Viceroy *Duncan MacNeil*
The Deceivers *John Masters*
Nightrunners of Bengal *John Masters*
Emily of New Moon *L. M. Montgomery*
The '44 Vintage *Anthony Price*
High Water *Douglas Reeman*
Rendezvous-South Atlantic *Douglas Reeman*
Summer Lightning *Judith Richards*
Louise *Sarah Shears*
Louise's Daughters *Sarah Shears*
Louise's Inheritance *Sarah Shears*
Beyond the Black Stump *Nevil Shute*
The Healer *Frank G. Slaughter*
Sword and Scalpel *Frank G. Slaughter*
Tomorrow's Miracle *Frank G. Slaughter*
The Burden *Mary Westmacott*
A Daughter's a Daughter *Mary Westmacott*
Giant's Bread *Mary Westmacott*
The Rose and the Yew Tree *Mary Westmacott*
Every Man a King *Anne Worboys*
The Serpent and the Staff *Frank Yerby*

MYSTERY TITLES
in the
Ulverscroft Large Print Series

Henrietta Who? — *Catherine Aird*
Slight Mourning — *Catherine Aird*
The China Governess — *Margery Allingham*
Coroner's Pidgin — *Margery Allingham*
Crime at Black Dudley — *Margery Allingham*
Look to the Lady — *Margery Allingham*
More Work for the Undertaker — *Margery Allingham*
Death in the Channel — *J. R. L. Anderson*
Death in the City — *J. R. L. Anderson*
Death on the Rocks — *J. R. L. Anderson*
A Sprig of Sea Lavender — *J. R. L. Anderson*
Death of a Poison-Tongue — *Josephine Bell*
Murder Adrift — *George Bellairs*
Strangers Among the Dead — *George Bellairs*
The Case of the Abominable Snowman — *Nicholas Blake*
The Widow's Cruise — *Nicholas Blake*
The Brides of Friedberg — *Gwendoline Butler*
Murder By Proxy — *Harry Carmichael*
Post Mortem — *Harry Carmichael*
Suicide Clause — *Harry Carmichael*
After the Funeral — *Agatha Christie*
The Body in the Library — *Agatha Christie*

A Caribbean Mystery	*Agatha Christie*
Curtain	*Agatha Christie*
The Hound of Death	*Agatha Christie*
The Labours of Hercules	*Agatha Christie*
Murder on the Orient Express	*Agatha Christie*
The Mystery of the Blue Train	*Agatha Christie*
Parker Pyne Investigates	*Agatha Christie*
Peril at End House	*Agatha Christie*
Sleeping Murder	*Agatha Christie*
Sparkling Cyanide	*Agatha Christie*
They Came to Baghdad	*Agatha Christie*
Third Girl	*Agatha Christie*
The Thirteen Problems	*Agatha Christie*
The Black Spiders	*John Creasey*
Death in the Trees	*John Creasey*
The Mark of the Crescent	*John Creasey*
Quarrel with Murder	*John Creasey*
Two for Inspector West	*John Creasey*
His Last Bow	*Sir Arthur Conan Doyle*
The Valley of Fear	*Sir Arthur Conan Doyle*
Dead to the World	*Francis Durbridge*
My Wife Melissa	*Francis Durbridge*
Alive and Dead	*Elizabeth Ferrars*
Breath of Suspicion	*Elizabeth Ferrars*
Drowned Rat	*Elizabeth Ferrars*
Foot in the Grave	*Elizabeth Ferrars*

Murders Anonymous	*Elizabeth Ferrars*
Don't Whistle 'Macbeth'	*David Fletcher*
A Calculated Risk	*Rae Foley*
The Slippery Step	*Rae Foley*
This Woman Wanted	*Rae Foley*
Home to Roost	*Andrew Garve*
The Forgotten Story	*Winston Graham*
Take My Life	*Winston Graham*
At High Risk	*Palma Harcourt*
Dance for Diplomats	*Palma Harcourt*
Count-Down	*Hartley Howard*
The Appleby File	*Michael Innes*
A Connoisseur's Case	*Michael Innes*
Deadline for a Dream	*Bill Knox*
Death Department	*Bill Knox*
Hellspout	*Bill Knox*
The Taste of Proof	*Bill Knox*
The Affacombe Affair	*Elizabeth Lemarchand*
Let or Hindrance	*Elizabeth Lemarchand*
Unhappy Returns	*Elizabeth Lemarchand*
Waxwork	*Peter Lovesey*
Gideon's Drive	*J. J. Marric*
Gideon's Force	*J. J. Marric*
Gideon's Press	*J. J. Marric*
City of Gold and Shadows	*Ellis Peters*
Death to the Landlords!	*Ellis Peters*
Find a Crooked Sixpence	*Estelle Thompson*
A Mischief Past	*Estelle Thompson*

Three Women in the House *Estelle Thompson*
Bushranger of the Skies *Arthur Upfield*
Cake in the Hat Box *Arthur Upfield*
Madman's Bend *Arthur Upfield*
Tallant for Disaster *Andrew York*
Tallant for Trouble *Andrew York*
Cast for Death *Margaret Yorke*

ROMANCE TITLES
in the
Ulverscroft Large Print Series

The Smile of the Stranger	*Joan Aiken*
Busman's Holiday	*Lucilla Andrews*
Flowers From the Doctor	*Lucilla Andrews*
Nurse Errant	*Lucilla Andrews*
Silent Song	*Lucilla Andrews*
Merlin's Keep	*Madeleine Brent*
Tregaron's Daughter	*Madeleine Brent*
The Bend in the River	*Iris Bromige*
A Haunted Landscape	*Iris Bromige*
Laurian Vale	*Iris Bromige*
A Magic Place	*Iris Bromige*
The Quiet Hills	*Iris Bromige*
Rosevean	*Iris Bromige*
The Young Romantic	*Iris Bromige*
Lament for a Lost Lover	*Philippa Carr*
The Lion Triumphant	*Philippa Carr*
The Miracle at St. Bruno's	*Philippa Carr*
The Witch From the Sea	*Philippa Carr*
Isle of Pomegranates	*Iris Danbury*
For I Have Lived Today	*Alice Dwyer-Joyce*
The Gingerbread House	*Alice Dwyer-Joyce*
The Strolling Players	*Alice Dwyer-Joyce*
Afternoon for Lizards	*Dorothy Eden*
The Marriage Chest	*Dorothy Eden*

Samantha	*Dorothy Eden*
Waiting for Willa	*Dorothy Eden*
Winterwood	*Dorothy Eden*
Countess	*Josephine Edgar*
The Emerald Peacock	*Katharine Gordon*
Jane of Gowlands	*Anne Hepple*
Rebel Heiress	*Jane Aiken Hodge*
On The Night of the Seventh Moon	*Victoria Holt*
Wind on the Heath	*Naomi Jacob*
It Was The Lark	*Catherine MacArthur*
The Empty House	*Rosamunde Pilcher*
Sleeping Tiger	*Rosamunde Pilcher*
Under Gemini	*Rosamunde Pilcher*
Wychwood	*Nicole St. John*
The Reluctant Orphan	*Sara Seale*
To Catch a Unicorn	*Sara Seale*
The Truant Bride	*Sara Seale*
The Blue Sapphire	*D. E. Stevenson*
Five Windows	*D. E. Stevenson*
Kate Hardy	*D. E. Stevenson*
Sarah Morris Remembers	*D. E. Stevenson*
Sarah's Cottage	*D. E. Stevenson*
Summerhills	*D. E. Stevenson*
Adair of Starlight Peaks	*Essie Summers*
The Forbidden Valley	*Essie Summers*
Moon Over the Alps	*Essie Summers*
Not by Appointment	*Essie Summers*

South Island Stowaway	*Essie Summers*
The Painted Caves	*Kate Thompson*
Richard's Way	*Kate Thompson*
The Silver Nightingale	*Sylvia Thorpe*
A Visit to Marchmont	*Frances Turk*
The Hospital in Buwambo	*Anne Vinton*
The Gone-Away Man	*Lucy Walker*
Heaven is Here	*Lucy Walker*
Home at Sundown	*Lucy Walker*
More Than All	*Marjorie Warby*
The Singing of the Nightingale	*Marjorie Warby*
All I Ask	*Anne Weale*
Hope For Tomorrow	*Anne Weale*
The Sea Waif	*Anne Weale*
Sullivan's Reef	*Anne Weale*
Seven Tears For Apollo	*Phyllis A. Whitney*
Silverhill	*Phyllis A. Whitney*
The Trembling Hills	*Phyllis A. Whitney*

Ulverscroft Large Print Books Ltd.
The Green, Bradgate Road
Anstey
Leicestershire
England